COVET

The truth does not care who it offends,
what it offends, or why it offends,
but, that it offend those who do not seek it

-Anita L Nottuh

SOURCES/
ABBREVIATIONS

BLD   *Black's Law Dictionary*

BRIT   *Britannica.com*

CBD   *Concise Bible Dictionary*

PBD   *Parsons Bible Dictionary, 1999*

EWED   *Encarta ® World English Dictionary, 1998-2005*

HBD   *Holman Bible Dictionary for Windows, 1.0g, 1994*

HIST   *History.com*

ISBE   *International Standard Bible Encyclopedia, 1998*

JVL   *Jewishvirtuallibrary.org*

KJV   *King James Version Bible, 1611*

NIV   *New International Version for Windows, 1.0g, 1994*

WEUD   *Webster's Encyclopedic Unabridged Dictionary, 1993*

WNWD   *Webster's New World Compact School and Office Dictionary, 1995*

WIKI   *Wikipedia, The Free Encyclopedia, 2019*

WBE   *Wycliffe Bible Encyclopedia, 1975*

All scriptures were based on the *KJV* Bible, except where noted.

Contents

CHAPTER

    1   Introduction

PART 1: LUST

SAME-SEX RELATIONS

    2   Jonathan and David
    3   The Covenant

RAPE

    4   The Laws
    5   Sodom and Gomorrah
    6   The Concubine
    7   Why the Destruction?

FORNICATION

    8   Jude
    9   Strange Flesh
    10   The Church

COVETOUS BEHAVIOR

    11   About Paul
    12   Thorn in the Flesh

THE TRUTH

    13   The True Standard Bearer
    14   Follow and Obey

Contents

PART 2: PROPERTY AND LAND

 15 The Comparison (A Tale of Two Rapes)
 16 Women and Girls
 17 The Children of Israel
 18 The Lord's Army
 19 Race, Religion, and Pure Greed
 20 The Truth about Abraham

PART 3: THE PLAYBOOKS

 21 Segregation
 22 Slavery
 23 About Jesus
 24 About Japheth

PART 4: RELIGION AND POLITICS

 25 Makings Sense of History
 26 The Holy Bible

APPENDIX

 NT Books (Current Order)
 NT Books (Chronological Order)
 NT Books (By Authors)

1

Introduction

What is the Bible really about? Many believe that the Holy Bible is God's word or plan for the entire world; if so, why does it not mention Britain, France, Italy, China, Japan, Spain, Argentina, Brazil, Korea, Australia, Russia, and many other countries by name as it does Israel, Egypt, Jordon, Syria, Persia (Iran), Ethiopia, and Libya, all from the Middle East? Some believe that the Bible only portray King James' version of how he sees God, the church, and his own role in the world as a British monarch. Yet, others see the Bible as a man-made religion designed to control and indoctrinate the masses.

> **Bible:** 5. essential book: a book that is considered
> an authority on a particular subject
> *–EWED*

Therefore, in this introduction, it is important to know where the Bible came from. Why it is named after an English King? What is the true purpose for the Bible? More importantly, who owns the King James Bible (KJV) and many others today?

The Old - NT

The KJV Bible is said to be written in 1611; however, history tells us that parts of the NT Bible had been around prior to the seventeenth century and was the cause of the Protestant Reformation.

John Wycliffe (1329 – 1384), a theologian, was said to have translated the NT from the Vulgate: the Latin Bible (used only by the Roman Catholic Church), into English, by hand, in the fourteenth century.

William Tyndale (1494 – 1536), a Roman Catholic priest, was declared a heretic and publically strangled and his body was burned at the stakes, for printing an English language version of the NT.

Martin Luther (1483 – 1546), a Roman Catholic monk and scholar, believed to have translated the NT from the Vulgate, into German. Many believe that his protest against the Roman Catholic Church led to the Reformation and the birth of the Protestant (*Protest*-ant) Church.

Many priest, monks, theologians, and scholars, during this early era, challenged the Roman Catholic Church and the power it held over the masses on issues such as: forgiving the sins of men; and more importantly, the sale of indulgences (which some believed, involved taking money from the poor under false pretense). The Roman Catholic Church contended that the purchase of indulgences limited loved ones (or anyone who the indulgence was purchased for) from spending time in purgatory: an intermediary place of suffering, to pay for all their sins prior to going to heaven.

The one common theme among Wycliffe, Luther, and Tyndale was the Roman Catholic's NT Bible being taught in Latin to non-Latin speaking people. It is believed that they wanted everyone to read and study the NT Bible in their own native language, which the papacy vigorously fought against.

Papacy: 3. the system of government in the Roman
Catholic Church with the pope as the head.
–*EWED*

Men like Wycliffe, Luther, Tyndale, and including John Hus who challenged or criticized the church practices and authority were excommunicated: thrown out of the Church. There Bibles were confiscated and anyone found producing or just in possession of a Bible were declared a heretic, and publically burned to death. It would appear that the reason the Roman Catholic Church made their deaths a public spectacle for challenging their authority and printing the Bible into other languages was to intimate like followers and cause fear among the masses. Nonetheless, it is believed that the NT Bible survived to this very day.

The Birth of the Protestant
Church and Bible

The Roman Catholic Church is and has always been a theocracy. The Church was more powerful than the monarchs of England, until Henry VIII ascended to the throne in 1491 and ushered in the Protestant Reformation, by establishing the Church of England, in protest of the papacy, for not allowing him to divorce his first wife.

Theocracy: 1. government by a god or by priests
2. A community governed by a god or priests
–*EWED*

A king is an autocracy, in establishing the Church of England, identical in many aspects to that of the Roman Catholic Church, King Henry VIII took control over the Protestant Church and the State, and brought the Roman Catholic Church to its knees, in England.

Autocracy: 1. rule by one person: a government in which somebody holds unlimited power 3. place ruled by one person: a country governed by a single ruler who has unlimited power
–EWED

Now the question is: Did King James, a Protestant, commission the Bible, as it is today, to be written? According to *Britannica.com*, previous versions of the Protestant Bible "were corrupt and not answerable to the truth of the original." It included the following:

- The Great Bible – Authorized by King Henry VIII (1530)
- The Bishop Bible – Not Authorized by Queen Elizabeth I (1568)
- The Geneva Bible – Not Authorized by Queen Elizabeth I (1576)

Given the perceived need for a new authorized translation… By June 30, 1604, James had approved a list of 54 revisers, although extant records show that 47 scholar actually participated. They were organized into six companies, two each working separately at Westminster, Oxford, and Cambridge on sections of the Bible assigned to them…. The new Bible was published in 1611.
–BRIT

In 1611, King James reigned as the Supreme Head over the Protestant Church, during this same time, Pope Paul V (born Camillo Borghese) was the head over the Roman Catholic Church, from May 16, 1605 until his death in 1621. Is it a coincidence that the main character in the Roman Catholic's NT Bible is named Paul? In Acts 13:9, Saul, a notable character, name was changed to Paul without explanation having authority and power, and later referred to as an apostle. Taking on a new name such as, Paul, Peter, or John is a common practice among Popes to this very day; and Paul is believed to be the predominant writer of the NT Bible, writing a minimum of 14 out of the 27 letters/books. It is Paul's private letter's, that opens the door to understanding the Roman Catholic Church today and his letter to Rome (Romans) is the key.

Therefore, it would appear that in 1611 under King James' authority the Protestant's OT Bible and what is believed to be the Roman Catholic's NT Bible were both modified to create a new translation, now known as King James' Authorized Version of the Holy Bible. Now the question is: Who is King James?

About King James

James was born on June 19, 1566, in Scotland. He acceded to the throne at the age of 1, on July 24, 1567, as King James VI of Scotland. He married Queen Elizabeth I (born: September 7, 1533), of England, who is said to have already begun coveting land throughout the world.

- 1583 Newfoundland
- 1585 Roanoke Island
- 1600 into India

Upon the Queen's death on March 24, 1603, King James of Scotland ascended to the throne of England as King James I. He continued the English legacy of colonization in all three territories, and extended it even further sending British settlers into Bermuda and Jamestown. As King over Scotland, England, and many other territories and land, James ruled with absolute power and he alone was responsible for the citizenry in two countries; in addition, to his company of armies spread throughout the world.

Autocracy: 1. rule by one person: a government in which somebody holds unlimited power 2. the unlimited political power of a single ruler
–EWED

In 1607, under the authority of King James, British settlers coveted the land of the Algonquian Indians, and called it Jamestown (named after King James), in Virginia: the first of the *13 colonies* which later became a part of the United States. The British settlers dispossessed the native Indians from their own land and in doing so they killed men, women, and children. The settlers then set their eyes on Massachusetts.

By 1619, black slaves from the continent of Africa were brought into Jamestown. Some may dispute who brought them or on what ship they came, but, the truth is: slavery in the United States begin in Virginia under the authority of King James VI and I of Scotland and England.

The British Empire grew expeditiously throughout the world by coveting other territories, kingdoms, and nations from 1607 through the 1900's, which included: large portions of what is now known as the United States; parts of Europe; Canada; Australia; parts of the Middle East including Africa; Asia; and much more. The British monarchs were not alone in their endeavors for world domination; the French, Dutch, and the Spaniards, were all coveting other territories and people; however, it would appear that King James memorialized it in writing and called it the Holy Bible. Also known as the Word of God.

Train up a child in the way he should go:
and when he is old, he will not depart from it.
Proverbs 22:6

What is Christianity?

Christianity today appears to be a banner that encompasses both the Protestant and Roman Catholic Church (often referred to as the Religious Right). Although they differ in style of worship and beliefs, they share a common ideology, where Jesus Christ, the anointed one, is their standard-bearer.

Ideology: 1. system of social beliefs: a closely organized system
of beliefs, values, and ideas forming the basis of a social, economic,
or political philosophy or program
–*EWED*

Each religious sect has its own unique followers, true believers who share the same views and beliefs concerning worship, personal beliefs, values, and much more. They are called Christians. A Christian, by definition, is a follower of Jesus Christ which is based out of the NT, even though; Christians were given the whole Bible. It is the NT books and/or letters believed to be written by eight men that will more than likely determine for many their overall perception of who they believe God to be.

Christian: The Greek *Christianos* originally applied to the slaves
belonging to a great household. It came to denote the adherents of an
individual or party. A Christian is an adherent of Christ; one committed
to Christ; a follower of Christ.
–*HBD*

Now, why is it that after 400 plus years, that many still use and believe in King James' Holy Bible which supports both segregation and slavery for the masses? Are only Kings and Queen allowed to change or commission Bibles, or speak for God? Or, could it be that the Bible, as it is today, was named after King James because of his stance on segregation and slavery, the keys he used to maintaining his kingdom?

Segregation

In Paul's private letter to the church at Corinth, he openly expressed his views on segregation, based on religious beliefs in the NT scriptures.

2 Corinthians 6:14 – 18

> Be not unequally yoked together with unbelievers: for what fellowship has righteousness with unrighteousness? What communion has light with darkness? What peaceful coexistence has Christ with Belial? What part has a believer with an infidel? What agreement has the temple of God with idols? For you are the temple of the living God; as God has said, I will live and walk among them; and I will be their God, and they shall be my people.
>
> Therefore come out from among them, and be separate, said the Lord, and touch not the unclean thing; and I will receive you; and I will be a Father to you, and you shall be my sons and daughters, said the Lord Almighty.

Slavery

Paul's view on slavery is very clear and direct in his first letter to Timothy. He is instructing Timothy, what he is to teach to the masses: that it is righteous in God's eyes, to be content with being a slave, especially, if the owner of the slave(s) identifies as a Christian.

1 Timothy 6:1 – 6

> Let as many servants that are under the yoke [of slavery] consider their own masters worthy of all honor, that the name of God and his doctrine be not blasphemed. They that have believing masters [Christian master], do not despise them, because they are your brothers; but rather do them service, because they are faithful and beloved, partakers of the benefit [of slave labor]. These things teach and exhort. If any man teach otherwise, and consent not to wholesome words, even the words of our Lord Jesus Christ, and to the doctrine which is according to godliness; He is proud, knowing nothing and the result is envy, strife, evil conjecture, disputes

among men of corrupt minds who are destitute of the truth, supposing that gain is godliness: from such do not participate. But, godliness with contentment is great gain.

Paul went even further in his instruction for the masses, justifying why it is profitable to be a slave:

1 Timothy 6:7 – 12

> For we brought nothing into this world, and it is certain we can carry nothing out. Being provided with food and clothing, let us be content.
>
> But they that will be rich will fall into temptation and a snare, and into many foolish and hurtful desires, which will bring men to ruin and danger. For the love of money is the root of all evil: although some coveted it, they have erred from the faith, and pierced themselves through with many sorrows.
>
> But you, a man of God, flee these things; and follow after righteousness, godliness, faith, love, patience, and meekness. Fight the good fight of faith, lay hold on eternal life, where you were called, and have professed a good occupation [of slavery] before many witnesses.

Many think of dictators as someone or something other than a Church (which is a business); or a minister (who runs a business). A Church as a whole is a dictatorship. Ministers are dictators: they are next or second to God, in the lives of many.

Dictator: 3. somebody whose opinions on a
subject are listened to and followed by society at large
–EWED

It is the minister's job to dictate to the masses, using the Bible, that they are sinners in need of salvation through Jesus Christ; and most ministers, if not all, will regurgitate biblical scriptures as though every word came directly from God or a higher power without questioning it, mainly, because it is profitable for them to do so. Now, think about it, who wants to be a slave!

Slave: 1. somebody forced to work for another: somebody who is forced to work for somebody else for no payment and is regarded as the property of that person
–EWED

The NT Bible is used to indoctrinate and control the masses, by focusing on 'sin.' Not sin, as it relates in the narrow sense to the last five of the Ten Commandments to not murder, steal, lie, commit adultery or covet (because most people may never intentionally break any of those commandments), but, something much broader that relates to human nature, such as, sexual attraction, desire, and activity which is as common as a batted eye and could affect everyone.

Masses: ordinary people: ordinary people in society, as distinct from people who are rich or powerful
–EWED

Human Nature: character of human beings: the typical character that all human beings share, often seen as being imperfect
–EWED

This one simple word 'sin' is used to alienate many individuals from their own natural sexual desires by causing them to believe that everything they feel or do is wrong, in another word, sinful; thereby, creating the mindset that is in constant need of forgiveness and a Savior.

Matthew 1:21

You shall call his name JESUS: for he shall save his people from their sins.

Jesus is the standard-bearer for two reasons: first, to indoctrinate the masses, by establishing sin; secondly, to push back against the Protestant Church's OT views on social issues, such as adultery and divorce. For example, the following:

Adultery

In the OT, the law of adultery, in essence, says that a man should not have sexual relations with a married woman and if he does, both of them 'shall' be put to death.

Leviticus 20:10
> The man that commits adultery with another man's wife, even he that commits adultery with his neighbor's wife, the adulterer and the adulteress shall surely be put to death.

In the NT, Jesus responded:

Matthew 5:27 – 30
> **You have heard that it was said by them of old time, you shall not commit adultery: But I say to you, that whoever looked upon a woman to lust after her has committed adultery with her already in his heart. If your right eye offend you, pluck it out, and cast it from you: for it is profitable for you that one of your members should perish, and not the whole body be cast into hell. If your right hand offend you, cut it off, and cast it from you: for it is profitable for you that one of your members should perish, and not the whole body be cast into hell.**

Breaking the commandment, You Shall Not Commit Adultery, is a sin; and the OT law which pertains to adultery, puts both sinners (man and woman) to death for the act itself; therefore, for them there is no need for forgiveness or a savior.

What Jesus said concerning the sin of adultery, changed the OT law from a physical sexual act to sexual thoughts of the imagination or heart to make adultery much broader to affect more people, because most men may never intentionally have sex with a married woman. Now the question is: How does a man lust after a woman in his imagination or heart? It is more than likely that Jesus was referring to pornography and masturbation, when he used the right eye and hand as offenders. Therefore, Jesus is simply saying that it is a sin for a man to have sexual thoughts. Although, the punishment would no longer be physical death for the masses today, but, a guilty conscious, always in need of forgiveness and a savior to help ease the shame and the constant threat of doom and everlasting hell fire.

Divorce

When you look at the issue of divorce, the tension between the Old and the NT is palpable.

The OT states that it is a man's right to divorce his wife for any reason, as it was when King Henry VIII first established the Church of England, because the Roman Catholic Church refused to give him a divorce from his first wife.

Deuteronomy 24:1
> When a man has taken a wife, and she no longer pleases him, because he has found some uncleanness in her: then let him write her a bill of divorcement, and put it in her hand, and send her out of his house.

In the NT, Jesus responded:

Matthew 5:31- 32
> **It has been said, whosoever shall put away his wife, let him give her a writing of divorcement: But I say to you, that whosoever shall put away his wife, saving for the cause of fornication, causes her to commit adultery: and whosoever shall marry her that is divorced commits adultery.**

Now notice, the OTs stance on divorce, did not involve sin. Jesus on the other hand, made divorce a sin for the woman, by tying it to adultery, in essence saying, she is still married to her first husband all the days of her life. In the old days, labeling a woman as an adulterer was to shame her; therefore, making life harder for women who may choose to leave an abusive and/or unloving husband or simply find someone else more suited to their own liking. In addition, to make it even broader Jesus made it a sin for men to love and/or marry a divorced woman.

When anyone is told who they can love, marry or leave; and that their every imagination can be a threat to their own salvation, is to make them into the image of a slave. Many have become slaves to a religion or ideology, knowingly or unknowingly, that defines who they should be and not accept them for who they are.

Some have never questioned where the Bible came from, they just accept it, as the Word of God and/or inspired by God. Others believe that the Bible came from the Dead Sea Scrolls, which were dated around the time of Jesus, and more recently found in caves, around the time the State of Israel, became a nation.

Dead Sea Scrolls

Manuscripts containing biblical texts: a collection of ancient manuscripts, discovered in caves near the Dead Sea, that provide important evidence for biblical scholars and historians. They were discovered between 1947 and 1956, and are generally held to have been written between 100 bc and ad 68.
–EWED

Many believe and say that the OT Bible was originally written in Hebrew, by Jews, and the NT Bible was written in Greek, by Greeks, because that is what they were taught. By saying this, is in essence blaming the Jews and the Greeks for the Bible, as it is today. Selling Bibles or the 'Word of God' to the masses is a multi-billion dollar business. Where does all God's money go? Is it to the Hebrews or the Greeks?

There are many Bibles being sold today, the two longest American Bibles in circulation are the *Thompson Chain-Reference Bible* (1908) and the *Scofield Reference Bible* (1909); however, the most popular Bible sold today is the New International Version (NIV). Overall, the majority of the Bibles being sold are owned by a small number of people and companies, such as the Oxford University Press, Inc. and B.B. Kirkbride Bible Co., Inc., and a few others; however, by far a variety of the majority of Bibles sold today, such as: NIV, Amplified Bible, King James Bible, and the New King James Bible, are owned by Rupert Murdock, the owner of News Corp, which includes Fox News, Sports, and Business TV networks, countless Newspapers; Magazines; Biblical/Spiritual Books; and many publishers such as, HarperCollins, which includes Zondervan and Nelson's Bible publishers. Therefore, this conglomerate of mass media can more effectively indoctrinate and control the masses worldwide, all at once, more so than any Church, Minister, or TV Evangelist alone into accepting the Bible as the Word of God, even if it enslaves them.

It is not clear how much, if any, of the OT originated under the authority of King Henry VIII or how many times the Old and NTs were modified to fit into what is 'now known' as the authorized KJV Bible; but, one thing is clear, anyone can date their Bible and/or book any time period they want, that does not mean that's when it was written. The KJV Bible is more than likely dated 1611 (17th Century), for two reasons: The first is, to make it appear prophetic to the masses today, for events that may have already happened; and for what is predicted in the scripture to happen in the future. The second is, for deniability, by taking the responsibility away from the actual writer(s) and owner(s), because the Bible, primarily, the Protestant's OT, is anti-women and girls, anti-men, anti-Semitic, anti-freedom, anti-education; and supports segregation, slavery, and covetous behavior, just to name a few.

Semitic: languages spoken by Semites: a group of
Languages belonging to the Afro-Asiatic family and

spoken in North Africa and Southwest Asia, including
Hebrew, Arabic, Aramaic, Maltese, and Amharic
–EWED

The following is a brief outline of Parts 1 – 4.

Part: 1 – Lust: Demonstrates through the stories of the Bible how social issues, such as same-sex relationships, fornication, multiple marriages, divorce, rape, etc., are accepted behavior by men, especially men of authority in the OT, whereas, many of the same issues such as: same-sex relationships, fornication, and adultery, in the NT are used against the masses to control and indoctrinate them.

Part: 2 – Property/Land: Demonstrates two separate themes using stories from the Bible: the first, details how women and girl are seen as property and diminished throughout the Old and NTs. The second, details how a world view of colonialism comes to light. It also details a variety of topics such as: lying; slavery; the sanctioning of murder, even against children; racism; torture; and covetous behavior. Topics include the land of Israel, Jerusalem, Palestine, Egypt, Ethiopia, Syria, and others.

Part: 3 – The Playbooks: Outlines how and why to segregate allied nations; and how to enslave a nation by manufacturing a crisis. Also, it demonstrates how the NT is the same 'playbook' as the OT in many aspects, with different titles, characters and staging. Topics include Israel, Russia, Egypt, Iran, Ethiopia, Libya, Saudi Arabia, and others.

Part: 4 – Religion and Politics: Demonstrates how history and the Bible are intertwined.

PART: 1

LUST

SAME-SEX RELATIONS

Jonathan and David

When the topic is same-sex relations, many cite scriptures from the NT demonizing it, such as Paul's letter to Rome saying:

Romans 1:26 – 27, 32
> God gave them up to vile affections: for even the women did change the natural use into that which is against nature: likewise the men, leaving the natural use of the woman, burned in their lust one toward another.... knowing the judgment of God, that they which commit such things are worthy of death, not only do the same, but have pleasure in them that do them.

The one thing that is not taught or explained in the OT is the covenant of love between two men, Jonathan, the son of a king, and David, the great warrior who would later become king. Their love story is powerful. It has all the trapping of a great love story today. It has intrigue, jealousy, deceit, plots of murder, and suspense thinly spread and *intertwined* between two books, First and Second Samuel in the OT. Their love story begins with Jonathan and David making a covenant because Jonathan was in love with David.

In order to establish whether 'God' gave up on men and women in or desiring a same-sex relationship (as Paul described in Romans 1:26–27) is to determine biblically how God felt about David in the Old and NTs.

The Covenant of Love

1 Samuel 17:57 – 18:4

As David returned from the slaughter of the Philistine, he was brought before King Saul [of Israel] with the head of the Philistine in his hand. King Saul said to him: Whose son are you, young man? David answered: I am the son of Jesse. When David had finish speaking with King Saul, **the soul of Jonathan was knit with the soul of David, because Jonathan loved him as his own soul. Jonathan and David made a covenant, because he loved him as his own soul. Then Jonathan stripped himself of the robe that was upon him and gave it to David, and his garments, even his sword, bow, and girdle.**

King Saul's Jealousy

1 Samuel 18:5 – 9

David went where King Saul sent him, and behaved himself wisely: and King Saul set him over the men of war, and David was accepted in the eyes of all the people including Saul's servants. Then it came to pass that the women came out of all the cities of Israel, singing and dancing, to meet King Saul, with instruments of music. As they played, they would say, King Saul has slain his thousands, and David his ten thousands. King Saul was very angry, because the saying displeased him; and he said, they have ascribed to David ten thousands, and to me they have ascribed only thousands; what more can David have, other than the kingdom? King Saul eyed David from that day forward…

1 Samuel 19:1 – 10

Then King Saul spoke to Jonathan, his son, and all his servants, saying they should kill David. However, Jonathan delighted much in David. So, Jonathan told David, that his father sought to kill him. Then Jonathan spoke well of David to his father, saying, let not the king sin against his servant, David, because he has not sinned against you. King Saul listened to his son and swore, as the LORD live, David shall not be killed. Then Jonathan brought

David to King Saul, and he was in his presence, as in times past. Then an evil spirit from the LORD was upon King Saul, as he sat in his own house with a spear in his hand; he sought to nail David to the wall with it, but David slipped away out of King Saul's presence, and the spear went into the wall: and David fled, and escaped that night.

Jonathan stood by David

1 Samuel 20:1 – 13

David fled and went to Jonathan and said: What have I done? What is my iniquity? What is my sin before your father, that he seeks my life? Jonathan said to him, God forbid; you shall not die: My father will do nothing either great or small without letting me know. Why would, my father hide his intentions from me? Then David swore and said, **your father certainly know that I have found grace in your eyes; and he says, let not Jonathan know, least he be grieved, but truly as the LORD live and as your soul shall live, there is but a step between me and death. Then Jonathan said to David, whatsoever your soul desire, I will do it for you.**

Then David said to Jonathan, tomorrow is the new moon, if your father misses me, then say: David earnestly asked leave of me that he might return to Bethlehem his city. If he say, it is well; I shall have peace: but if he is very angry, then be sure that evil is determined by him against me. **Therefore you should deal kindly with me; for you have brought me into a covenant of the LORD with you.** Jonathan replied, if I knew for certain that evil were determined by my father against you, would I not tell you? Then send you away that you may go in peace and the Lord be with you as he has been with my father.

Jonathan's love for David Challenged

1 Samuel 20:25 – 34

The king sat upon his seat, by the wall, and David's seat was empty. King Saul noticed David's seat was empty, but said nothing. The next day which was the second day of the month, again David's seat was empty and King Saul said to Jonathan: Why has David not come to eat with us, neither yesterday, nor today? Jonathan said to his father: David earnestly asked leave of me to go to Bethlehem to be with his family, therefore, he is not at the king's table. **Then King Saul's anger was kindled against Jonathan, and said to him, you son of the perverse rebellious woman, I know that you have chosen the son of Jesse to your own confusion, and to the confusion of your mother's nakedness?** For as long as the son of Jesse [David] live upon the ground: you shall not be established, nor your kingdom. Now fetch him, for he shall surely die. Jonathan answered his father, and said to him: Why should he die? What has he done? Then King Saul cast a javelin at Jonathan to smite him: Jonathan knew at that point his father was determined to kill David. So, Jonathan arose from the table in fierce anger and did not eat for he was grieved for David, because his father had done him shame.

The Secret Tryst

1 Samuel 20:35 – 42

In the morning, Jonathan went out into the field to meet David at the appointed time, accompanied by a young lad [to practice shooting arrows, as a deception]. But the lad knew nothing: only Jonathan and David knew the matter…. As soon as the boy was gone, **David appeared and fell on his face to the ground and bowed himself three times and they kissed one another, and wept one with another, but David wept even more. Then Jonathan said to David go in peace, we have sworn both of us in the name of the LORD, saying, the LORD be between me and you, and between my seed and your seed forever. David rose up and departed and Jonathan returned to the city.**

The Second Covenant

1 Samuel 23:15 – 18

David saw that King Saul had come again to seek his life, while he was in the wilderness. **Then Jonathan went to David and strengthened his hand in God and said to him, fear not: the hand of my father shall not find you and you shall be king over Israel, and I shall be next to you and that, King Saul, my father already knows. Then they made a covenant before the LORD....** [king Saul and Jonathan went to war against their enemy and they both died**].**

The Death of Jonathan

2 Samuel 1:1 – 5, 11 – 12

On the third day [following the death of Jonathan and King Saul], a man came from Saul's camp with his clothes rent, and earth upon his head and fell to the earth and bowed at David's feet. David said to him, where did you come from? He replied I escaped out of the camp of Israel.... David said how did it go? I pray that you tell me. He answered, the people fled from the battle, and many of them are injured and dead; and Saul and Jonathan were among the dead....

Then David took hold on his clothes, and rent them; and likewise all the men that were with him: they mourned, wept, and fasted, for Saul and Jonathan... because they had fallen by the sword.

David's lamentation over Jonathan and King Saul

2 Samuel 1:22 – 27

From the blood of the slain, from the fat of the mighty, the bow of Jonathan turned not back, and the sword of King Saul returned not empty. King Saul and Jonathan were lovely and pleasant in their lives, and in their death they were not divided: they were swifter than eagles, they were stronger than lions. Daughters of Israel, weep over King Saul, who clothed you in scarlet, with other delights, who put ornaments of gold upon your apparel.

How are the mighty fallen in the midst of the battle! O Jonathan, you were slain... I am distressed because of you: my brother Jonathan, very pleasant have you been to me: **your love to me was wonderful, passing the love of women.**

Note: This is a short version of the love story of Jonathan and David, intertwined between *1 Samuel 17:57 - 2 Samuel 21:14.*

About Jonathan

When you closely examine the love story of Jonathan and David from Jonathan's perspective, you will see that the relationship between them was of a sexual nature. Their love story began with Jonathan's soul being knit with the soul of David because Jonathan was in love with David. The very next thing that happened was Jonathan and David made a covenant. The details were never mentioned, but the reason for the covenant was love. What follows their covenant is what makes it sexual in nature. When Jonathan stripped naked before David, removing his princely robe, which was an outer covering over his garments. Then Jonathan removed his garments, including his sword, bow, and girdle. Now ask yourself: What man strips naked before another man after professing his love for him and it's not sexual?

Many will rely upon the fact that the story of Jonathan does not say explicitly that he had sex with David. However, the Bible does not say explicitly that Adam and Eve had sex, yet they had a son named Cain. In fact, the scripture used the word "knew" to imply a sexual interaction between Adam and Eve.

Genesis 4:1

> Adam knew Eve his wife; and she conceived, and bare Cain, and said, I have gotten a man from the LORD.

Therefore, in the same vein that you would accept the word "knew," which implied sex between Adam and Eve, could be the same frame of mind to accept David's own words toward Jonathan saying, "your love to me was wonderful, passing the love of women," which could imply a sexual relationship.

Now the question is: Why a covenant? Perhaps, the word "covenant" was used to show that David was in agreement with the love Jonathan gave him; however, it still does not explain why they made a covenant. Now, could this covenant between Jonathan and David be their attempt at a same-sex marriage? A covenant, by definition, is an agreement. So are marriages, where the man and the woman, both agree to love, honor and cherish each other, in sickness and in health. When you take a closer look at the relationship between Jonathan and David, their covenant could resemble that of a same-sex relationship or marriage. In 1 Samuel 18:1, the word "knit" was used to describe the souls of Jonathan and David to imply that their souls were intertwined or had become as one. It's another way of saying they were soul mates. This resembles what Jesus said concerning marriage itself.

Matthew 19:5 – 6
> **For this cause shall a man leave father and mother, and shall cleave to his wife: and they two shall be one flesh? Wherefore they are no longer two, but one flesh.**

The man and his wife are not physically joined together. What is being said is figurative, meaning their hearts and souls are in agreement and they become as one, in other words "knitted." What follows in 1 Samuel 18:3 was the covenant between Jonathan and David because he loved him. Then in 1 Samuel 18:4, Jonathan stripped naked before David. Could this be the beginning stages of them consummating their same-sex marriage? If no, what other reason could there be for Jonathan to make a covenant of love with David and then remove *all* his clothing?

What gives credence to a relationship on David's part between him and Jonathan, was his own words. Why compare the love of another man to the love of all women except to make a distinction?

2 Samuel 1:26
> "Your love to me was wonderful, passing the love of women."

What could further support the relationship between Jonathan and David as a same-sex relationship or marriage is based on who Jonathan was. When King Saul was angry and challenged his son, Jonathan, and his relationship with David, calling him "confused" and then comparing his confusion with a woman's naked body, this statement alone could imply that King Saul understood his son, Jonathan's relationship with David to be of a sexual nature.

1 Samuel 20:30
> You son of the perverse rebellious woman, do not I know that you have chosen the son of Jesse to your own confusion, and to the confusion of your mother's nakedness?

Nevertheless, Jonathan was a man who stood in his own truth. He was willing to separate himself from David forever, if that was what it took to save his life. Jonathan cemented his love for David when they made the second covenant, that David would be king over Israel, while his own father was yet the king of Israel. Jonathan was not confused: he had chosen the son of Jesse, because he loved him. He remained steadfast and stood with David, protected him, gave him comfort, and would have laid down his own life, for his love. The love story of Jonathan and David is exactly what Jesus taught to his disciples in the gospel of John.

John 15:12 – 13
> **This is my commandment, that you love one another, as I have loved you. Greater love has no man than this: that a man lay down his life for his friends.**

Jesus did not quantify how or whom you should love, but, that you love. Notice, Jesus did not say that a man lay down his life for his wife, mother, father, sister, brother, or children, but "friends." Jonathan and David were friends who loved one another.

Now, if what Paul wrote in Romans 1:26 – 27 about 'God' giving up of "them," meaning men and women in a same-sex relationship was true, then why would the NT reveal that 'God' appoint David king over Israel and say that David was a man after God's own heart?

Acts 13:21 – 23

>They desired a king: God gave them Saul the son of Cis, a man of the tribe of Benjamin, for forty years. When he had removed him, he raised up David to be their king; to whom he gave testimony, and said, I have found David the son of Jesse, a man after my own heart, which shall fulfill all my will. Of this man's seed has God according to his promise raised to Israel a Savior, Jesus.

According to the scriptures, God not only loved, protected, and supported David throughout his entire life (before and after he became king), but after his death, appointed his son, Solomon, to reign as king after him.

Among the masses God is seen as omnipresent, meaning God is everywhere; the Alpha and the Omega, meaning God is the beginning and the end; and all-knowing, meaning God knows all things, including the heart of David, and yet, did not give up on him after he entered into a covenant of love with another man. Now, on the other hand, what about Jesus? Paul began his letter to Rome saying that Jesus was made after the seed of David.

Romans 1:3

>Concerning his Son Jesus Christ our Lord, which was made of the seed of David, according to the flesh.

If David was wrong for being in love with another man, would Jesus, said to be the Son of God, have stood by him? In the book of Revelations, it is written that Jesus wanted everyone to know that he was of the seed of David. According to the scriptures, Jesus gave a declaration from heaven concerning David, saying:

Revelations 22:16

>**I Jesus have sent my angel to testify to you these things in the churches. I am the root and the offspring of David, and the bright and morning star.**

Therefore, in the NT, God and Jesus did not have a problem with David (a man chosen to become the king of Israel) for making a covenant of love with another man; yet, the Church today continue to teach against same-sex relationships when it comes to the masses. Why?

3

The Covenant

The reason for this chapter is to show how the *Wycliffe Bible Encyclopedia* (WBE) interpreted Jonathan and David's relationship and how far they would go to try to explain it.

Searching the WBE for additional information about the covenant between Jonathan and David, what you will find is vague and ambiguous information or nothing at all.

When you search the word "covenant" in the WBE, there are approximately six pages on the subject; however, the covenant between Jonathan and David was not mentioned. When you search the name "Jonathan" for information related to the covenant between him and David, this is a portion of what you will find.

Jonathan

- *"His friendship with David.* Jonathan and David's friendship is a most inspiring epic. After David slew the Philistine giant Goliath and won for himself a permanent place in the royal court, Jonathan loved the shepherd lad with all his soul. He recognized that David was a man chosen for the throne of Israel. He acquiesced to this by making a covenant and presenting to David his own princely robe and armor (1 Sam 18:1- 4)."

- "The final and romantic conference between these friends took place in the wilderness. There they made a pact that when David became

- the next king, Jonathan would be his prime minister, and they renewed their covenant to protect each other's posterity forever."

If you only read the first paragraph, you may walk away with the understanding that Jonathan and David were just friends. However, once you look further to the next paragraph, the author/writer used the word "romantic" in describing what took place between friends. The word "romantic" is defined in different ways, however, it usually means one thing when one confesses his love toward the other and it leads to a covenant of love.

> "**Romantic:** 1. involving sexual love: involving or characteristic of a love affair or sexual love, especially when the relationship idealized or exciting and intense. 2. suitable for love: characterized by or suitable for lovemaking or the expression of tender emotions"
> *–EWED*

The WBE appears to be saying that the covenant between friends was based on David becoming king and Jonathan, his prime minister. First of all, nowhere in the KJV or the NIV Bibles does the title "prime minister," appear. Secondly, what Jonathan actually said to David was this, "and you shall be king over Israel, and I shall be next to you," which meant forfeiting his place to the throne for David. Jonathan being the son of the king of Israel would have been next in line to the throne; therefore, Jonathan putting David first implied they would be together, hence the phase "I shall be next to you." Now ask yourself: What man would make a covenant to relinquish the power and prestige of being a king, for just a friend?

When you search the name "David" in the WBE for information related to the covenant between him and Jonathan, this is what you will find:

David

- "There friendship was of one soul in two bodies. The bond which united Jonathan and David was - mainly their common faith in the covenant of love of God for Israel. This unity of spirit won Jonathan to David, and he made with him a covenant of friendship and exchanged gifts in token of that friendship (1Sam 18:1- 4)."

In searching the name David, you are given a different answer from when the name Jonathan was searched. The WBE appears to be saying Jonathan and David made a covenant of friendship because of their love for Israel," which was why they exchanged gifts. The only problem with this scenario is there was no exchange of gifts. According to the scriptures, Jonathan stripped naked before David, giving him *all* his clothing. What did David give to Jonathan?

Why make up different answers, is it because the WBE refuse to acknowledge that Jonathan, a man, was in love with David, also a man? The WBE gave a more protected and yet subtle account concerning Jonathan and David's relationship, saying they were friends. Well, lovers can be friends and many are.

RAPE

4

The Laws

It is commonly preached that Leviticus 18:22 and Leviticus 20:13 relates to same-sex relations and that it is forbidden, in the OT. Not true!

Leviticus 18:22
> You shall not lie with a man, as with a woman: it is an abomination.

Leviticus 20:13
> If a man lie with another man, as he would with a woman, both of them have committed an abomination: they shall surely be put to death; their blood shall be upon them.

Now to truly believe that Leviticus 18:22 and Leviticus 20:13 were solely about consensual same-sex relations, then, same-sex relations among women should have been added to the law. Then again, maybe it was more acceptable for women to have sex with other women. King David had multiple wives and concubines, as well as his son Solomon who had seven hundred wives and three hundred concubines. To be clear, the OT does not mention women being with or wanting other women sexually or anything close to it within the KJV Bible. This is why it is important to take a closer look at each law thoroughly, first Leviticus 18:22 and then Leviticus 20:13, to understand why women were not included.

Leviticus 18:22

To be absolutely clear, Leviticus 18:22, is saying that a man should not have sex with another man, because it is an abomination. The use of the word "abomination" says to the reader that two men having sex is shameful, something horrible, disgusting, and immoral. Now Leviticus 18:23, the very next statute or ordinance says the following:

Leviticus 18:23

> Neither shall a man lie with any beast to defile himself: neither shall any woman stand before a beast to lie down with: it is confusion.

To be absolutely clear, Leviticus 18:23, is saying that a man or a woman should not have sex with a beast or an animal (bestiality), because it is confusion.

When comparing Leviticus 18:22 with Leviticus 18:23, you can see that the law pertaining to lying with a beast or an animal included both men and woman. Now this tells us, women having sex with other women could have been included in Leviticus 18:22, if it was necessary. Therefore Leviticus 18:22 is not about consensual same-sex relations, but something else.

When you take a closer look at Leviticus 18:23, by definition, confusion is a state of being confused. Being confused is a state of mind or a situation that lacks clarity. When you analyze Leviticus 18:23 as it is written, confusion is the reason given that a man or a woman should not have sex with a beast or an animal. Now the question is: Confusion for whom? A man having sex with a beast or an animal knows exactly what he is doing! Likewise, a woman having sex with a beast or an animal knows exactly what she is doing! Once again: Confusion for whom?

Now you would have to believe that the Lord said to his servant Moses, 'say to the masses, a man should not have sex with another man because it is shameful, something horrible, disgusting, and immoral. Neither should a man or woman have sex with a beast or an animal because it lacks clarity.' Now again, if there was no confusion concerning a man or woman having sex with a beast or an animal, would bestiality be accepted as the norm?

Genesis 2:18–24

> The LORD God said it is not good that the man should be alone; I will make a help mate for him. Then out of the ground the LORD God formed every beast of the field and every fowl of the air and brought them to Adam to see what he would call them, and what Adam called every living creature, that was their name…. but for Adam there was not found a help mate for him.
>
> Then the LORD God caused a deep sleep to fall upon Adam, and while he slept, he took one of his ribs and made the woman, and brought her to him. Adam said this is now bone of my bones, and flesh of my flesh: she shall be called Woman, because she was taken out of Man. Therefore shall a man leave his father and his mother, and shall cleave to his wife: and they shall be one flesh.

Was it the Lord God's intention for Adam to find a partner among the animals? It was Adam who did not find any beast of the field or creatures of the earth acceptable. Therefore, only as an afterthought did the Lord God make the woman, not from the dust of the earth, as he did with Adam and all the beast and creatures of the field and air, but separate, from the rib of a man. Then the Lord God brought the woman to Adam as he did all the beast of the field and creatures of the earth, and she was acceptable to him. So, why all the disdain as it relates to two men having consensual sex compared to bestiality?

Leviticus 20:13

To be absolutely clear, Leviticus 20:13, is saying that a man should not have sex with another man, and in doing so, they have done something shameful, horrible, disgusting, and immoral and should be put to death for their actions. Now looking forward to Leviticus 20:15 – 16 (a rewrite of Leviticus 18:23) which state the following:

Leviticus 20:15 – 16
> If a man lies with a beast, he shall surely be put to death along with the beast. If a woman approach any beast, and lie down, you shall kill the woman, and the beast: they shall surely be put to death; their blood shall be upon them.

To be absolutely clear, Leviticus 20:15 – 16, is saying a man or a woman should not have sex with a beast or an animal (bestiality), and in doing so, the man or woman, along with the beast or animal, should be put to death.

When comparing Leviticus 20:13 with Leviticus 20:15–16, you can see that the law pertaining to lying with a beast or animal included both men and woman. Once again this tells us women having sex with other women could have been included in Leviticus 20:13 (a rewrite of Leviticus 18:22), if it was necessary. Therefore Leviticus 20:13 is <u>not</u> about consensual same-sex relations, but something else.

Comparing Leviticus 18:22 with Leviticus 20:13, you would have to believe or accept that the Lord had a change of mind and said to his servant Moses, 'say to the masses, if a man has sex with another man, it is still an abomination: meaning it is shameful, something horrible, disgusting, and immoral, and both of them should be put to death.'

Then, comparing Leviticus 18:23 with Leviticus 20:15–16, you would have to believe or accept that the Lord changed his mind again and said to his servant Moses, 'Now say to the masses, if a man or a woman have sex with a beast or an animal, it is no longer confusion, but it is still <u>not</u> an abomination,' but for the act itself they should both be put to death. Now the question is: Why does the Lord consider a man having sex with another man an abomination, but, not a man or a woman having sex with a beast or animal?

Just as in modern times, laws are made to prevent or allow certain behaviors. In order to understand the laws of Leviticus 18:22 and Leviticus 20:13, it is necessary to know what the Bible says happened on the earth, which affected only the men and warranted death. Maybe Leviticus 18:22 and/or Leviticus 20:13 are to be taken literally. In the NT, Paul gives us another way of looking at the law.

Romans 3:20
> Therefore, by the deeds of the law shall no flesh be justified in his sight: for by the law is the knowledge of sin.

If this is true, that by the law is the knowledge of sin, meaning the law was created to bring sin to the light. Then the law itself exposes sin. So, what sin did Leviticus 18:22 or Leviticus 20:13 expose?

5

Sodom and Gomorrah

The story of Sodom and Gomorrah is one of the most epic and destructive acts in the Bible, which destroyed both human life and land. The one thing that comes to mind at the mentioning of Sodom and Gomorrah is the Lord's judgment, raining down fire and brimstone upon the wicked out of heaven like bombs, as a reminder that the Lord's wrath was against sinful, vile and vicious people.

Genesis 19:24–25

> The LORD rained upon Sodom and Gomorrah brimstone and fire from out of heaven; He overthrew those cities, and all the plain, and all the inhabitants of the cities, and that which grew upon the ground.

Much of what is preached from the pulpit and taught throughout the Christian community is that the Lord's wrath or vengeance was against consensual same-sex relations. This is simply not true. When you read the story of Sodom and Gomorrah, one thing is clear. It's not about men having or wanting consensual same-sex relations with other men. It is about rape.

The Story of
Sodom and Gomorrah

Genesis 19:1–19:29

There came two angels to Sodom. Lot seeing them rose up to meet them; and he bowed himself with his face toward the ground and said come into my house, and stay all night, and wash your feet, and in the morning go your way, and they said No, we will stay in the street all night. Then he pressed upon them greatly and they entered into his house…. Then the men of the city Sodom surrounded the house, both old and young. They called Lot, and said to him: Where are the men that came into your house this night? Bring them out to us, that we may know them. Lot went out to them and shut the door after him, and begged them not to do anything wicked.

Now, I have two virgin daughters, let me bring them out to you, and do to them what is good in your eyes: only to these men do nothing, because they came under the shadow of my roof. They said to Lot, stand back or we will do worse things with you, than with them as they came near to break down the door, but the men put forth their hand, and pulled Lot into the house with them, and shut the door. Then they struck the men outside the door of the house with blindness, both small and great that they could not find it.

The men said to Lot, are there any others here besides you: son-in-law, sons, or daughters? Bring them out: for we will destroy this place, because the cry of them is continuous before the face of the LORD and the LORD has sent us to destroy it. Take your wife, and two daughters, which are here and leave; least you will be consumed in the iniquity of the city….

Then the LORD rained upon Sodom and Gomorrah brimstone and fire out of heaven and overthrew those cities, and all the plain, and all the inhabitants of the cities, and that which grew upon the ground.

About the Laws

The story of Sodom and Gomorrah is not about men choosing to have consensual same-sex relations. It's about rape. Since the Lord intervened, technically what happened in Sodom can only be described as an attempted sexual rape. For clarity, when the statement is made in Genesis 19:5, "bring them out to us, that we may know them," it implied raping them. In this instance the word "know" in the biblical sense means "to have sex." In Genesis 19:5, the word "know" is used in the present tense, whereas in Genesis 4:1, it was used in the past tense.

Genesis 4:1
> And Adam <u>knew</u> Eve his wife; and she conceived, and bare Cain.

During the time of Sodom and Gomorrah, there were no statutes or ordinances, according to the scriptures. Biblically, it made sense for the Lord who destroyed life and land to include a commandment (You Shall Not Covet) and laws going forward that would tell his people what they should or should not do.

Leviticus 18:22
> You shall not lie with a man, as with a woman: it is (an) abomination.

Leviticus 20:13
> If a man lie with another man, as he would lie with a woman, both of them have committed an abomination: they shall surely be put to death; their blood shall be upon them.

What was happening in Sodom with men raping or wanting to rape other men was why Leviticus 18:22 and Leviticus 20:13 was needed. In the story of Sodom and Gomorrah, Lot protected the men, who were strangers, but offered both of his virgin daughters, in their place to be gang-raped by all the men of the city. This alone made it clear from the writer(s) point of view, that it was an abomination to rape a man, but more acceptable to rape a woman or a girl.

Therefore, according to the law, a man being raped would be seen as an abomination: something horrible, shameful, disgusting and immoral. In addition, the pervasive act of rape alone would explain the change of mind as to why death was warranted, in Leviticus 20:13.

Rape against men is a very important subject for the Bible to touch on, regardless of how fantastic the story is; and, they deserve to be protected along with the women. Now, the question is: Why does the OT Bible sanction rape against women and girls?

The Commandment
(You Shall Not Covet)

Looking closely at the commandments written in Exodus, chapter 20, they are a prohibitive set of commands stating what men should not do, with two exceptions of "Obey the Sabbath" and "Honor your mother and father."

- You shall have no other gods before me.
- You shall not make any graven image.
- You shall not bow down, nor serve them.
- You shall not take the Lord's name in vain.
- Obey the Sabbath.
- Honor your mother and father.
- You shall not kill.
- You shall not commit adultery.
- You shall not steal.
- You shall not bear false witness.
- You shall not covet.

What does the commandment, You Shall Not Covet, mean? This commandment is the cause of much confusion because it is poorly written and does not say what coveting actually is. When you look-up the word "covet" it is defined in different ways and can mean a variety of things. For example:

> **Covet:** 1. To want somebody else's property:
> to have a strong desire to possess something
> that belongs to somebody else 2. yearn to
> have: to want to have something very much
> –*EWED*

Taking definitions 1 and 2 into account, the commandment, Thou Shall Not Covet, is the desire to possess property that belonged to someone else. However, in the NT, Paul's letter to Rome made the commandment, You Shall Not Covet, about lust.

Romans 7:7

> For I had not known lust, except the law had said, you shall not covet.

Now the question is: Do the scriptures support both descriptions of the commandment, as it relates to property and lust? Yes. Looking closely at the commandment, You Shall Not Covet, it appears to be two separate commandments in one, meaning two different things.

Exodus 20:17 says,

> You shall not covet your neighbor's house, you shall not covet your neighbor's wife, manservant, maidservant, ox, ass, or anything that is your neighbor's.

(First Half - Property)

> You shall not covet your neighbor's house.

(Second Half - Lust)

> You shall not covet your neighbor's wife, manservant, maidservant, ox, ass, or anything that is your neighbor's.

Simply reading the first half of the commandment appears to make the entire commandment about property. This is where confusion comes in and many think of wrongful desire (to want or wish very strongly for someone or something), for the entire commandment. Thou Shall Not Desire, makes no sense. Desiring your neighbor's house or anything that belongs to them is not a bad thing. To desire what belongs to your neighbor to the point of taking ownership unlawfully is; however, that would fall under the commandment, You Shall Not Steal. If the commandment, You Shall Not Covet meant only strong or wrongful desire, there would be no need for any other commandment, because, no man commits adultery without having a strong or wrongful desire to do so. The same would be true for all the other commandments.

Therefore, to covet cannot simply be to desire wrongfully someone else's house or property. Nor can it be simply stealing, because You Shall Not Steal is a commandment already. You must physically do something in order to break the commandments. So the question is: How does one covet someone else's house or property? The scriptures give us two examples to help answer this question, the first in the book of Joshua and the second in the book of Micah.

#1

In the book of Joshua, a man by the name of Achan confessed his sin of violating the commandment of the Lord God, by coveting. What Achan did that was considered a sin in his confession was to wrongfully desire and possess property that belonged to someone else. What should stand out about Achan's confession is the phrase "among the spoils." The use of the word spoils implies the property was taken by force or violence.

Joshua 7:20-21 says,
> Achan said, indeed I have sinned against the LORD God of Israel, and thus and thus have I done: When I saw among the spoils a Babylon garment, and two hundred shekels of silver, and a wedge of gold of fifty shekels weight, I coveted them, and took them; and, behold, they are hidden in the earth under my tent, along with the silver.

#2

The book of Micah, is another example, where a man's property is taken by force or violence.

Micah 2:1-2 says,
> Woe to them that devise iniquity, and work evil upon their beds! When it is morning, they practice it, because it is in the power of their hand. They covet fields, and take them by violence; including houses, even a man's heritage.

Therefore, taking everything into account, the commandment, You Shall Not Covet, as it relates to property is to "take by force" wrongly what belongs to someone else. This is deviant behavior, which can be described as rape.

Rape: 4. an act of plunder, violent seizure, or abuse; despoliation; violation 5. the act of seizing and carrying off by force
–WEUD

In the NT, Paul's focus was not on the first half of the commandment, which relates to houses and land, but the second half, which relates to human beings and living things. The second half of the commandment states, you shall not covet your neighbor's wife, manservant, maidservant, ox, ass (donkey). It makes sense, as to how lust can be applied. Looking at the second half of the commandment from Lot's point of view makes things much clearer.

In the story of Sodom and Gomorrah, Lot had men with uncontrolled illicit sexual desires at his door, threatening him with violence and wanting to take hold of the two men that had entered into his house, so they could rape them.

Therefore, taking everything into account, You Shall Not Covet as it relates to lust is to "take by force" sexually what belongs to someone else. This is deviant sexual behavior, which can also be described as rape. In the case of Sodom and Gomorrah attempted sexual rape.

Rape: 1. The crime of having sexual intercourse with a person forcibly and without consent
–WNWD

Rape: 1. is the unlawful compelling of a person through physical force or duress to have a sexual interaction.
–WEUD

Changing the word "Covet" to "Rape" for the entire tenth commandment, then, you shall not rape your neighbor of his house or property; and you shall not rape your neighbor's wife, manservant, maidservant, ox, ass, or anything that is your neighbor's.

6

The Concubine

In the book of Judges (in the OT), there is a story about a Levite and his concubine. This story will seem very familiar to you because it mirrors the story of Sodom and Gomorrah in many aspects, but with a totally different outcome.

In the story of Sodom and Gomorrah, the Lord heard their cries and acted by raining down fire and brimstone on the ungodly. After which, the Lord gave the commandment, You Shall Not Covet to prohibit that behavior. The story of the Levite and his concubine is twofold: First, it establishes that the commandment, You Shall Not Covet, is limited in it protection of women and girls; and secondly, to start indentifying the characters for which the Bible is based on.

Overall, The Concubine is heartbreaking and yet eye-opening. The only thing that comes to mind after reading this story is: Where was the Lord?

An Important Note: This story has been simplified. When you read the story of the Levite and the concubine in the KJV, it would appear that the writer(s) could not decide if the woman or girl would be the Levite's concubine or wife. In the first three sentences, the woman or girl is referred to as his concubine twice, and the Levite is referred to as her husband, both cannot be true, because, if he is her husband, then she must be his wife. The woman or girl is referred to as a damsel, but never referenced as the Levite's wife; therefore, leaving the impression that she is his concubine. Nevertheless, this mislabeling is important, but confusing and continues back and forth in different forms, throughout the story. So, as you read the story in its entirety in the KJV Bible, be aware of this inconsistency. The Concubine: Book of Judges 19:1-29.

The Story of the Concubine

Judges 19:1–29

There was a certain Levite who had a concubine out of Judah. His concubine played the whore against him, and ran away to her father's house. The Levite went after her, to speak friendly to her, and to bring her back. When he arrived: She invited him into her father's house, and when her father saw him, he rejoiced to meet him....

When the Levite began to leave, with his concubine, her father, said to him, stay another night… but the man would not stay any longer, and as he traveled home, the sun went down upon them in the land of Benjamin…. An old man looked up and saw the Levite, a wayfaring man, in the street. So he brought him into his house…and they washed their feet, and did eat and drink. As they were making their hearts merry, the men of the city surrounded the house and beat on the door, and spoke to the old man, saying: bring out the man that came into your house, that we may rape him.

The old man, went out to them, and said, don't do anything wicked; seeing that this man has come into my house, don't be foolish. Here is my daughter a maiden [unmarried woman or girl] and his concubine; now I will bring them out, and do whatever you want with them: but, do not touch this man.

The men who surrounded the old man's house, would not listen to him, so the Levite took his concubine, and gave her to them; and they knew her, and abused her all night until the morning. When the sun began to rise, they let her go.

The concubine came and fell down at the door of the old man's house. When the Levite woke up the next morning, and opened the doors of the house, to go his way, he found the concubine dead at the door of the house, and her hands were upon the threshold. He said to her, "Get up and let's go." No answer. Then the man put her upon an ass, and headed home.

When the Levite came into his own house, he took a knife and divided his concubine, into twelve pieces, and sent a piece of her to the other twelve tribes in Israel [also known as the children of Israel]....

Judges 20:3–6

The children of Israel said, tell us, how this wickedness happened? The Levite answered; I came into Gibeah [which belonged to the tribe of Benjamin], with my concubine to lodge for the night. The men of Gibeah surrounded the house during the night and wanted to kill me: they raped my concubine and now she is dead. I took my concubine, and cut her in pieces, and sent her throughout all of Israel: because the men of Gibeah have committed lewdness and folly in Israel....

Where was the Lord?

The story of the Concubine focuses on the actions of a man who was identified as a Levite but not named. A certain Levite who followed after a woman or girl he believed to have cheated on him (played the whore) and ran away to her father's house. He stayed for days to "speak friendly to her," in hopes that she would come back with him, which she did. He entered into a stranger's house and became the original target of an angry mob of men who wanted to rape him. He sacrificed his concubine to save himself and charged all twelve tribes of Israel to revenge his concubine's rape and death, which led the children of Israel to war against one of their own, the tribe of Benjamin.

In telling the story of a woman or girl being raped, the writer(s) captures your attention within one verse, with a vague statement, "they knew her, and abused her all the night until the morning," implying she was sexually gang-raped. Rape all by itself is very, very ugly. Nevertheless, the writer(s) chose to dirty up the concubine in the beginning of the story (although this happens to rape victims to this very day) to make her an unsympathetic character by saying "she played the whore" as though she had done something wrong and to imply that she was not a virgin.

If the concubine was the man's wife or a virgin girl engaged to be his wife, and she had sex with another man (played the whore), under the OT law, she would have been worthy of death (not to be raped).

Deuteronomy 22:23 – 24 (NIV)
> If a man happens to meet in a town a virgin pledged to be married and he sleeps with her, you shall take both of them to the gate of that town and stone them to death--the girl because she was in a town and did not scream for help, and the man because he violated another man's wife. You must purge the evil from among you.

If the woman was only a concubine, she is a single woman and may be called a wife, but she is only an instrument used for the purposes of having sex or bearing children and nothing more. For example, consider the story of Abraham (formerly known as Abram) and his wife Sarah (Sarai) who gave her servant Hagar to her husband for the purpose of giving them a child, because Sarah was barren and Abraham had no heir. Hagar conceived and did give birth to a son named Ishmael.

Genesis 16:15

> Now Sarai Abram's wife had an Egyptian handmaid, whose name was Hagar. Sarai said to Abram the LORD has prevented me from bearing children; it may be that I may obtain children by my handmaid. Abram listened to the voice of Sarai and she took Hagar her maid and gave her to her husband Abram to be his wife (Genesis 16:1–3)… Hagar and Abram had a son who they named Ishmael.

According to the scriptures, the Lord later blessed Sarah and Abraham, and Sarah conceived and gave birth to a son, whom they named Isaac. The scriptures tell us that Isaac inherited everything from his father and received the honor and blessing of continuing the bloodline as his son. However, Abraham's son Ishmael was considered the son of his concubine, and he only received gifts from his father and was sent away (Genesis 25:5).

The Levite went after a single woman to "speak friendly to her" to convince her to come back and be with him, but, not as his wife, or a servant. Therefore, the commandment, You Shall Not Covet which is very specific, would not have helped the concubine because she did not belong to the Levite: she was not his wife, his servant, or an animal.

Exodus 20:17 – Lust (Second Half)

> You shall not covet your neighbor's wife, manservant, maidservant, ox, ass, or anything that is your neighbor's.

In addition, the Law of Moses provided no protections for a single woman or girl who was raped.

Deuteronomy 22:25 – 29 (NIV)

> But if out in the country a man happens to meet a girl pledged to be married and rapes her, only the man who has done this shall die. Do nothing to the girl; she has committed no sin deserving death. This case is like that of someone who attacks and murders his neighbor, for the man found the girl out in the country, and though the betrothed girl screamed, there was no one to rescue her.
>
> If a man happens to meet a virgin who is not pledged to be married and rapes her and they are discovered, he shall pay the girl's father fifty shekels of silver. He must marry the girl, for he has violated her. He can never divorce her as long as he lives.

Now biblically, it should not matter whether the woman or girl was the Levite's wife or his concubine, or even a virgin, because she was of the tribe of Judah, a descendant of Abraham, Isaac, and Jacob.

God's Chosen People

God said to his servant Moses, "I am the God of your father, the God of Abraham, Isaac and Jacob" (Exodus 3:1 – 6). It is this Jacob, who had twelve sons with four different women: Leah, her sister Rachel, and their handmaids (women or girl servants) Zilpah and Bilhah.

Genesis 35:23–26

> The sons of Leah: Reuben, Simeon, **Levi**, **Judah**, Issachar, and Zebulun.
> The sons of Rachel: Joseph and Benjamin.
> The sons of Bilhah: Dan and Naphtali.
> The sons of Zilpah: Gad and Asher.

According to the scriptures, Jacob's name was changed to Israel and his 12 sons and their descendants became the children of Israel, also known as, the twelve tribes of Israel, or the Israelites. It was to Jacob's descendants (the children of Israel) that the Lord gave the Ten Commandments and laws for them to live by.

The scriptures reinforce the Lord God as the God of the children of Israel. For example:

Exodus 3:15

God said to his servant Moses, say unto the children of Israel, The LORD God of your fathers, the God of Abraham, the God of Isaac, and the God of Jacob, hath sent me to you.

Exodus 29:45

And I will dwell among the children of Israel, and will be their God.... I am the LORD their God.

The Levite and the Concubine were both descendants of Abraham, Isaac and Jacob, and therefore, the children of Israel. So, why didn't the Lord protect and save his Concubine from being raped and murdered, as he protected and saved Lot, his wife and two daughters, who were the only survivors of the Lord's wrath upon Sodom and Gomorrah, but, were not of the bloodline of the children of Israel, the Lord's chosen people?

7

Why the Destruction?

Many ministers preach and teach from the pulpit using Sodom and Gomorrah assuring the masses of the Lord's protection over their lives based on these three tenants: the Lord hears the prayers and cries of the righteous; will always provide a way of escape (out of danger) for the righteous in any situation; and lastly, the righteous will be saved from all damnation. In the story of Sodom and Gomorrah this is not entirely the case; the Lord's wrath is demonstrated against the wicked and the innocent.

Until there is a clear understanding of why the Lord destroyed Sodom and Gomorrah, many may continue to believe or accept what is often taught from the pulpit that it is all about consensual same-sex relations.

There are actually two different reasons given for the destruction of Sodom and Gomorrah: the cries of the righteous and a lack of ten righteous souls.

The Cries of the Righteous

The cries of the righteous, was how the story began, and was the basis for the destruction of Sodom and Gomorrah.

Genesis 18:20

> The LORD said, because the cry of Sodom and Gomorrah is great, and because their sin is very grievous; I will go down now, and see

whether they have done altogether according to the cry of it, which came to me; and if not, I will know.

In the story, the Lord did not actually go down to investigate, but sent two witnesses in the form of angels to Sodom.

Genesis 19:1
> There came two angels to Sodom…

What is not clear, at this time, is why the Lord destroyed Gomorrah, because no witnesses were sent to investigate, if the cries in Gomorrah were true or not. In Genesis 19:13, the reason given by the Lord's witnesses for the destruction of Sodom and Gomorrah was "because the cry of *them*, is continuous before the face of the LORD." The writer(s) did not make known the reason for the righteous crying out; however, one could conclude that perhaps it involved rape. Now, what is interesting is who was crying out.

Genesis 19:12–13
> The men [angels] said to Lot: Are there any others here besides your, son-in-law, sons, or daughters? Bring them out: For we will destroy this place, because the cry of them is continuous before the face of the LORD; and the LORD has sent us to destroy it.

Only four people were saved out of Sodom: Lot, his wife, and their two daughters. It is clear that Lot did not cry out because the witnesses were speaking to him and told him that they were going to destroy Sodom "because the cry of them is continuous before the face of the LORD." They did not say to Lot that the Lord heard *his* cries or prayers. The only other people who could have cried out were Lot's wife and/or daughter(s). therefore, it would appear that the Lord destroyed Sodom and Gomorrah because of the cries of "them," women? Yet, for his own chosen concubine who surely cried out, and was brutality raped and murdered, nothing! The only other explanation is, the men did cry out, and the Lord decided that a man who is raped was also an abomination to him and should be put to death; hence the phrase "both of them" in Leviticus 20:13.

Ten Righteous Souls

When you analyze the scriptures closely, a different story emerges concerning the destruction of Sodom and Gomorrah, which ends with Abraham bargaining with the Lord to spare Sodom, if there were a minimum of ten righteous people found there.

Genesis 18:17, 20, 23 – 32

> The LORD said: shall I hide from Abraham that thing which I do… because the cry of Sodom and Gomorrah is great, and because their sin is very grievous…
>
> Abraham said to the Lord, will you destroy the righteous with the wicked? What if there are fifty righteous people within the city; and the LORD said: if I find in Sodom fifty righteous people within the city, I will spare all for their sakes. Then Abraham said what if there are five less than fifty, will you destroy the city? Then the Lord said: If I find forty five, I will not destroy it. What if there are only forty found there; and the Lord said, I will not destroy it, if I find forty. What if there is only thirty to be found there; and the Lord said, I will not destroy it, if I find thirty there. What if only twenty are found there; and the Lord said, I will not destroy it. Do not be angry and I will speak yet again: What if only ten shall be found there; and the Lord said, I will not destroy it for ten's sake.

The Lord was going to act from the beginning. What other reason is there for Abraham to ask the Lord if he was going to destroy the righteous with the wicked, if the Lord was not bent on destroying something or someone? This leaves some with the impression that the Lord destroyed Sodom and Gomorrah, because there were not ten righteous people within two cities. Now, if Sodom and Gomorrah were so sinful that the Lord could not find ten righteous people, then why was Sodom and Gomorrah saved in the War of the Kings from their enemies through Abram (later known as Abraham)?

The War of the Kings

There were four kings who went to war and prevailed against the five kings. Among the five kings were Sodom and Gomorrah.

Genesis 14:11–12, 14, 16, 18–23
> The four kings took all the goods of Sodom and Gomorrah and went their way. They took Lot, Abram's brother's son, who lived in Sodom, and his goods, and departed… When Abram heard that Lot was taken captive, he armed his trained servants, born in his own house, three hundred and eighteen, and pursued them… Then he brought back all the goods, and also brought back Lot and all his goods, the women, and all the people… Then Melchizedek king of Salem [a priest]…said, blessed be Abram of the Most High God, possessor of heaven and earth: and blessed be the Most High God, which has delivered your enemies into your hand.

The city of Sodom did not consist of men alone. The very reason that Lot came to live in Sodom was because he was very wealthy along with Abram, together they had too many possessions and were unable to live in the land of Canaan together. Lot chose Sodom because it appeared pleasing to his eyes. He came to Sodom with all his cattle, herdsmen, and tents when he separated from Abram.

When Abram (Abraham) saved Lot during the War of the Kings, there was no mention of Lot having a wife or children, even though women and other people were mentioned as being saved. Therefore, this leaves an impression that Lot met, married his wife, and had children while living in Sodom. Also both of Lot's daughters were married, which shows the people were going about their lives as normal. Surely some of Lot's herdsmen brought their wives or concubines with them when they settled in Sodom. The point here is: Even if, all the men of Sodom were wicked, there would still be other women, and children living there. What the scriptures tell us is that only Lot, his wife, and two daughters were saved, meaning everyone else and all their possessions were left behind and destroyed. What happened to the other women and children saved in the War of the Kings? They were clearly not counted among the righteous with Lot's wife and daughters because, if only six additional righteous souls were found, then the Lord would not have destroyed the city.

What did the innocent women and children do? What did the animals do? What did every seed-bearing tree, shrub, or plant do that they were all worthy to be destroyed? God said they were all good.

Genesis 1:10–12, 25, 31

> God called the dry land Earth; and the gathering together of the waters he called Seas: and God saw that it was good. The earth brought forth grass and herb yielding seed after its kind, and the tree yielding fruit after its kind: God saw that it was good….
>
> God made the beast of the earth after its kind, and cattle after their kind, and everything that creep upon the earth after its kind: and God saw that it was good….
>
> God saw everything that he had made, and, behold, it was very good.

Now, the question is: Why would the Lord allow Abram to save Sodom and Gomorrah, and all the people and all their possessions, if he was going to destroy them anyway? Just maybe there is something more to story of Sodom and Gomorrah other than covetous behavior.

Fornication

8

Jude

When it comes to the NT views on consensual sex, the story of Sodom and Gomorrah was used mainly as a comparison or an example of the Lord's wrath against any and every one for not believing in the teachings of God and Christ, which is meant to cause fear among the masses. For example,

2 Peter 2:6
> Turning the cities of Sodom and Gomorrah into ashes... making them an example to those who live ungodly.

The book of Jude goes one step further, which causes confusion because it is the only book in the NT that even tries to explain what Sodom and Gomorrah was all about, but, it misses the mark completely.

Jude is one of the shortest books in the entire Bible with only one chapter containing twenty-five verses. It is not clear whether Jude is the writer. In fact, theologians have written that it is probably Jude, meaning they don't know. The purpose of the book of Jude is threefold.

The first: is to convince the masses who may not continue to believe as they once did to stay committed to the faith; and to blame those as ungodly, who do not accept the Church teachings about their God and Christ.

Jude 1:3–4
> Beloved, it was needful for me to write to you, and exhort you to earnestly contend for the faith which was once delivered to the

saints. For there are certain men who crept in unaware, who were before of old ordained… ungodly men, turning the grace of our God into lasciviousness, and denying the only Lord God, and our Lord Jesus Christ.

The second is: to cause fear. The book of Jude is full of fantastic stories of angels, devils, and the Lords wrath against the masses. For example:

Jude 1:14-15
> Behold, the Lord cometh with ten thousands of his saints, to execute judgment upon all, and to convince all that are ungodly of their ungodly deeds which they have ungodly committed, and of all their hard speeches which ungodly sinners have spoken against him [the Lord].

The third and most important purpose for the book of Jude is: to convince the masses that the Lord is against consensual sex.

Jude 1:7
> Even as Sodom and Gomorrah, and the cities about them in like manner, giving themselves over to fornication, and going after strange flesh, set forth an example, of suffering the vengeance of eternal fire.

Many may believe and cite Jude's assertion that Sodom and Gomorrah was about fornication and "going after strange flesh" because it is in the Bible; although, they could read the story for themselves and know that it's not. Now what is meant by "going after strange flesh" would depend upon the reader's interpretation. Some may say bestiality, others may say something else.

Fornication: 1. sexual intercourse between two consenting adults who are not married to each other 2. sexual behavior considered immoral: in the Bible, sexual intercourse between a man and woman who are not married, or any form of sexual behavior considered to be immoral
–EWED

In the Book of Jude the OT story of Sodom and Gomorrah was rewritten to make it about consensual sex, which is much broader than an attempted gang rape of men by men, which would affect far less; making the change to consensual sex would affect just about everyone.

Therefore, what the book of Jude was attempting to do is convince the masses that the Lord's wrath upon Sodom and Gomorrah came about because of consensual sex, and to make it even more abominable he included "going after strange flesh" which is more than likely, bestiality.

Jude's misrepresentation of the story of Sodom and Gomorrah is conveniently beneficial to the Church, because it opened the door for ministers to preach and teach abstinence (no sex until marriage), which is adverse to human nature, causing true believers to sin and seek forgiveness.

9

Strange Flesh

The reason for this chapter is to show why many may have a negative view of fornication in general.

Many people use reference materials such as dictionaries and encyclopedias and believe that they provide factual information about a subject, title, or word. This is not always the case, in some instances, they are actually trying to persuade you the reader or researcher to believe or accept a certain point of view, not always the truth, which can be more misleading and harmful rather than informative.

Biblical Reference

Searching the *Holman Bible Dictionary* (HBD) for addition information, on "Sodom and Gomorrah" what you will find is a very short description of the events concerning their destruction. Then the reader is steered toward the word "sodomy."

Sodom and Gomorrah

- "Sodom and Gomorrah were renowned for their wickedness. Despite Abraham's successful plea not even ten righteous men could be found in Sodom, and the cities were judged by the Lord, then destroyed by brimstone and fire."

- "The unnatural lusts of the men of Sodom (Gen. 19:4-8; Jude 7) have given us the modern term sodomy..."

There are two things which need to be addressed in order to have a clearer understanding of what the truth really is. First, it is not true that the destruction came about because there were not "ten righteous <u>men</u>" found in Sodom. In fact, Abraham argued on behalf of the righteous. He did not specify men or women. The question that Abraham asked the Lord in Genesis 18:23 was: "Will you destroy the righteous with the wicked?" Therefore women were included among the righteous because Lot's wife and daughters were saved.

The HBD appear to be trying to shape their readers perception about the men of Sodom who in all appearances were inherently evil, wicked, and unrighteous and then to relate that perception to actual men today in or desiring a same-sex relationship. What supports this view is the second point, where the "modern term sodomy" is introduced in the second paragraph.

When you search for the word "sodomy," it's not in the HBD dictionary. However, what you will find is the word "sodomite," which simply means a person who practices sodomy.

Sodomite

- "Originally a citizen of the town of Sodom… The term came to mean a male who has sexual relations with another male. The wickedness of Sodom became proverbial (see Gen. 19:1-11). **See Homosexuality**"

Therefore, taking everything into account, the HBD appears to be saying that the men of Sodom had an unnatural lust for one another; however, with the use of the word sodomy, in this case sodomite, it implies that what took place in Sodom was not rape, but consensual same-sex relations, which is fornication.

Now the word "sodomite" steers you to "see homosexuality." When you search for the word "homosexuality," this is what you will find.

Homosexuality

- "Biblical references to homosexuality are relatively few. Genesis 19:1-11 tells the story of an attempted homosexual gang rape at the house of Lot by the wicked men of Sodom."

It is absolutely clear that the HBD knew Sodom was about a gang rape all along; so, why the deception? The HBD appear to be outright manipulating, deceiving, and lying to the readers. It takes determination and effort on their part to steer their readers to the belief that Sodom was about fornication and not rape using one word: sodomy.

The Words Sodomy and Sodomite

When you search non-biblical reference materials for the words "sodomy" or "sodomite," here are two examples of what you will find:

"**Sodomy:** 1. an offensive term for anal intercourse 2. an offensive term for sexual intercourse with an animal."

"**Sodomite:** an offensive term for somebody who practices anal intercourse."
–*EWED*

"**Sodomy:** 1. Anal or oral copulation with a member of the opposite sex. 2. Copulation with a member of the same sex. 3. Bestiality"

"**Sodomite:** 1. an inhabitant of Sodom. 2. A person who engages in Sodomy."
–*WEUD*

What took place in Sodom was not fornication or bestiality. In fact, the entire story of Sodom and Gomorrah never mentions or names any beast or animal. Therefore, using the words "sodomy" or "sodomite" to describe the actions of the men of Sodom or any man is wrong. The HBD does not say explicitly that Sodom and Gomorrah had anything to do with bestiality directly; however, they cited the words "unnatural lust" and Jude 7, before steering their readers to the word sodomy. Why?

When you apply the definitions 2 and 3 for the word sodomy, using a non-biblical dictionary such as *Webster's Encyclopedic Unabridged Dictionary* (WEUD), to Jude 7; definitions 2 equate to fornication, whereas definition 3, bestiality, could only be attributed to "going after strange flesh."

Jude 1:7 say,

"Even as Sodom and Gomorrah, and the cities about them in like manner, giving themselves over to fornication, and going after strange flesh, are set forth for an example, suffering the vengeance of eternal fire."

Now, it would also appear the only purpose for the deception is for you (the reader) to believe or accept that the Lord wrath upon Sodom was about consensual same-sex relations and that consensual same-sex relations is wrong, inherently evil, wicked, and unrighteous and need to be destroyed.

The word Sodomite in the Bible

The word "sodomy" does not appear in the KJV Bible. However, the word "sodomite" is mentioned once in Deuteronomy, and the word "sodomites" is mentioned four times within First and Second Kings.

Deuteronomy 23:17-18 says,

There shall be no whore of the daughters of Israel, or a sodomite of the sons of Israel. You shall not bring the hire of a whore, or the price of a dog, into the house of the LORD your God for any vow: both are an abomination to the LORD your God.

1 Kings 14:24

There were also sodomites in the land: and they did according to all the abominations of the nations which the LORD cast out before the children of Israel.

1 Kings 15:12

He took away the sodomites and removed all the idols that his fathers had made from the land.

1 Kings 22:46

The last of the sodomites, which remained in the days of his father he removed from the land.

2 Kings 23:7

> He tore down the houses of the sodomites that were near the house of the LORD…

In the book of Deuteronomy, the words "whore" and "sodomite" were both used as labels to define certain men and women of Israel as prostitutes. Therefore, First and Second Kings must also be referring to Sodomites as prostitutes.

> **"Prostitute:** 1. Somebody who is paid to provide sexual intercourse or other sex acts"
> *–EWED*

A prostitute is someone who has consensual sex with men or women for a fee. It should be clear from Deuteronomy that they were not referring to sex with animals (bestiality) because of the phrase, "you shall not bring the hire of a whore, or the price of a dog, into the house of the LORD your God for any vow" which refers to money earned via prostitution and animals do not pay for sex. Therefore, the word sodomite would only refer to a male prostitute, who sales his body for financial gain.

The reference materials listed prior and many others do not define the words "sodomy" or "sodomite" as being related to male prostitution. Therefore, based on the KJV Bible, the definitions for the words "sodomy" and "sodomites" (with the exception of the EWED) are built on lies and should be seen as offensive, ignorant, malicious, and hateful.

10

The Church

Paul said, follow him.

1 Corinthians 4:16
> I implore you, be followers of me.

And,

1 Corinthians 11:1-2
> Be followers of me, even as I am of Christ. Now I praise you, brethren, that you remember me in all things, and keep the ordinances, as I delivered them to you.

It is church leaders who build Paul up as being equal to God, quoting him as though he was God, and making everything he wrote (written on his behalf, or to him), God-driven and purposeful, because, he provides the yoke needed to control and indoctrinate the masses into believing that everything they feel or do, as it relates to sexual attraction, desire, and activity is wrong, in other words, something shameful, disgusting and immoral, when it comes to social issues, namely, same-sex relations, adultery, fornication, and divorce.

Same-Sex Relations

Romans 1:26–32
> For this cause God gave them up to vile affections: for even their women did change the natural use into that which is against nature: And likewise also the men, leaving the natural use of the woman, burned in their lust one toward another...

Paul used the words "the natural use," to imply or plant the seed that there is something unnatural about men and women who have same-sex relations. When you ask a believer or follower of the faith who are against same-sex relations why they oppose it, they tend to use the word "unnatural." Some believe Paul's assertion that God is against men and women who have same-sex relations and believe their affections are unnatural. Others are against same-sex relations because same-sex couples cannot procreate, as they believe God intended, meaning they cannot have children, which happens to be the same reason they are against same-sex marriage.

"**Unnatural:** 1. Contrary to expected behavior:
contrary to habit, custom, or practice."
–EWED

"**Unnatural:** 2. At variance with the character or
Nature of a person, animal or plant"
–WEUD

The word "unnatural" is not a bad word from one's own perspective. For men and women who are only attracted to individuals of the opposite sex, it would be unnatural for them to be with someone sexually of the same sex. The same would be true for men and women who are only attracted to individuals of the same sex; it would be unnatural for them to be with someone sexually of the opposite sex. Paul's words matter, because they destroy lives. Not just the lives of men and woman in a consensual same-sex relationship but, the lives of those who are taught to believe that a consensual same-sex relationships are wrong and worthy of death.

For those who justify their stance against same-sex relationships or marriage based on the fact that same-sex couples cannot procreate, should understand that for many people, having children is a choice. Not every man or woman who come together sexually desire to procreate. There are many men and women who want to have children but can't. Therefore, are men and women in a same-sex relationship or marriage any less natural than a sterile man and his wife, or a woman who is unable to conceive with her male companion? The problem with what Paul wrote is this: he is condemning men and women to death for having consensual sex, and even those who don't, but find pleasure in someone else who does.

Adultery and Fornication

A common theme in Paul's letters is that he considered consensual sex, such as: fornication and adultery to be unrighteous, in other words, a sin. When Paul mentioned them in his letters, he included despicable things, such as murder, lasciviousness, covetousness, idolatry, and many others to make his point that consensual sex is unrighteous and God and Christ are against it. For example:

1 Thessalonians 4:1–3 says,
> …We implore you, brethren, and exhort you by the Lord Jesus, that you have received of us how you ought to walk and to please God, so you would abound more and more. For you know what commandments we gave you by the Lord Jesus. This is the will of God, even that you should abstain from <u>fornication</u>.

Galatians 5:19–21 says,
> Now the works of the flesh are manifest, which are these; <u>Adultery</u>, <u>fornication</u>, uncleanness, lasciviousness, Idolatry, witchcraft, hatred, variance, emulations, wrath, strife, seditions, heresies, envying, murders, drunkenness, reveling, and others: I told you before, that they which do such things shall not inherit the kingdom of God.

1 Corinthians 6:9–10 says,
> The unrighteous shall not inherit the kingdom of God? Be not deceived: neither <u>fornicators</u>, nor idolaters, nor <u>adulterers</u>, nor effeminate, nor abusers of themselves with mankind, nor thieves, nor covetous, nor drunkards, nor revilers, nor extortioners, shall inherit the kingdom of God.

Ephesians 5:2–6 says,
> Be followers of God, as dear children; walk in love, as Christ has loved us, and has given himself for us. But <u>fornication</u>, and all

uncleanness, or covetousness, let it not be once named among you, as saints; Neither filthiness, nor foolish talking, nor jesting, which are not convenient: but rather giving of thanks. For this you know, that no whoremonger, nor unclean person, nor covetous man, who is an idolater, has no inheritance in the kingdom of Christ and of God. Let no man deceive you with vain words: because of these things the wrath of God is upon the children of disobedience.

Colossians 3:5–7 says,
Mortify your members which are upon the earth; <u>fornication</u>, uncleanness, inordinate affection, evil concupiscence, and covetousness, which is idolatry...the wrath of God cometh on the children of disobedience...

Hebrews 13:4 says,
Marriage is honorable in all, and the bed undefiled: but whoremongers and <u>adulterers</u> God will judge.

When you analyze Paul's letters his stance against consensual same-sex relations among the Romans was the same position he held against consensual sex between men and women among the Colossians, Corinthians, Ephesians, Galatians, Hebrews, and Thessalonians. Paul's writing are the tools used by the Church to segregate the masses.

- Same-sex against opposite-sex
- The single man or woman against the married
- The married against the divorced
- The adulterer against all other women
- The family man against all other men
- Woman with children against woman without

Therefore, the Church gets to control what outcome they want in the lives of many by preaching and teaching that no one should have sex unless it is done their way through marriage between a man and a woman, if at all. This is why abstinence is being taught in the church and spread throughout the world today.

1 Corinthians 7:1–2

> It is good for a man not to touch a woman. Nevertheless, to avoid fornication, let every man have his own wife, and let every woman have her own husband.

Being against consensual sex, married or not, among masses is the same as being against human nature. Even the beast of the fields; birds of the air; and the fish in the sea, are fruitful: beneficial, and do multiply: but, they don't marry? In other words, they don't make covenants that are legal and binding?

Divorce

1 Corinthians 7:10 – 11

> To the married I command, yet not I, but the Lord, let not the wife depart from her husband, if she depart, let her remain unmarried, or be reconciled to her husband and let not the husband put away his wife.

Paul, in essence, is blaming the woman, by not allowing a woman to marry another man in the eyes of the Church, in the event of a separation, regardless of the cause; which in turn, would make life harder for the women to leave their abusive and/or unloving husbands and find someone more suitable to their own liking, without judgment. Now think about it, why does the Church, care so much about who someone marries or love; and not be concerned about the earth as it relates to pollution and contamination of our water, air, and soil which is needed to sustain and prolong all life and will affect everyone.

Human beings are sexual being by nature. This is why Paul is using consensual sex to control his followers, by creating the mindset that God is against it. There is no logical reasoning, such as, a plague or disease upon the earth that affected the people in some way that would require them to abstain from sex. The point here is: who does Paul, think he is, to tell others how and with whom they should or should not have consensual sex, which is a private matter, Jesus!

COVETEOUS
BEHAVIOR

11

About Paul

Many churches under the banner of Christianity try to project Paul's gospel onto the masses around the world today, to indoctrinate and control them, by making them believe that they are sinners and in need of forgiveness. However, Paul's private letter to Rome was never meant to be read by the masses, because it demonstrates Paul's mental weakness, sexual immorality, and how he chose to push back at what he perceived to be the OT, commandments, one in particular: You Shall Not Covet, therefore, creating for himself and those in authority a way of escape from all their unrighteousness, by blaming someone else or something.

Paul began his letter to Rome saying disparaging things about "them," meaning men and women in or desiring a same-sex relationship. After making known God's vengeance toward his creation, using the OT to make his point, Paul expressed his views concerning same-sex relations saying:

Romans 1:18
> For the wrath of God is revealed from heaven against all ungodliness and the unrighteousness of men…

Romans 1:24–27
> Wherefore God also gave them up to uncleanness through the lusts of their own hearts, to dishonor their own bodies between themselves: Who changed the truth of God into a lie, and worshipped and served the creature more than the Creator, who is blessed forever. Amen. For this cause God gave them up to vile affections: for even their women did change the natural use into that which is against nature: likewise also the men, leaving the natural use of the woman, burned in their lust one toward another; men

with men working that which is unseemly, and receiving in themselves that recompense of their error which was appropriate.

Looking at the entirety of what Paul wrote thus far in the first chapter of Romans, he seemed to be using men and women in a same-sex relationship to project his beliefs that same-sex relations is deviant sexual behavior. Paul included women in verse 26, to make the subject solely about same-sex relations and not just an issue with men.

Romans 1:26
> For this cause God gave them up to vile affections: for even their women did change the natural use into that which is against nature.

When you look at verse 26, Paul is referring to women in a same-sex relationship in around about way. Notice, Paul does not use the word "lust" in relation to the women. Now when you look just at the first half of verse 27, Paul used the word "lust" to describe a sexual interaction among the men. In the second half of verse 27, Paul purposely linked men who have sexual relations to the men of Sodom.

The first half - (Romans 1:27)
> Likewise also the men, leaving the natural use of the woman, burned in their lust one toward another;

The second half - (Romans 1:27)
> Men with men working that which is unseemly, and receiving the recompense of their error, which was appropriate

Paul began in Romans 1:18, making mention of God's wrath being revealed from heaven against the unrighteous. There is no other story in the entire Bible, where men wanted or desired other men sexually ("working that which is unseemly"), and received an appropriate punishment for their actions ("receiving the recompense of their error which was meet"), other than the story of Sodom and Gomorrah. It seems as though Paul want the masses to be reminded of the deviant sexual behavior of Sodom whenever they think of men in or desiring a same-sex relationship. Besides that, there is no other reason why the second half of verse 27 would be included.

Paul went even further in verses 28 through 32, projecting all deviant and ill behavior he could think of onto men and women in or desiring a same-sex relationship.

Romans 1:28-32

> Even as they did not like to retain God in their knowledge, God gave them over to a reprobate mind, to do those things which are not convenient; Being filled with all unrighteousness, fornication, wickedness, covetousness, maliciousness; full of envy, murder, debate, deceit, malignity; whisperers, backbiters, haters of God, despiteful, proud, boasters, inventors of evil things, disobedient to parents, Without understanding, covenant breakers, without natural affection, implacable, unmerciful: Who knowing the judgment of God, that they which commit such things are worthy of death, not only do the same, but have pleasure in them that do them.

Paul was not saying that God wanted him to say to men and women in or desiring a same-sex relationship, "stop or change your behavior." Paul was speaking for God or as God in condemning consensual same-sex relations. At the same time, Paul wanted the masses to accept or believe that his stance against same-sex relations was not his view, but God's, saying:

> God also gave them up to uncleanness…

> God gave them up to vile affections...

> God gave them over to a reprobate mind...

To say that God "gave them up" is to say that God wants nothing to do with men and women who have same-sex relations. The problem with Paul's assertions is: it defeats God's capacity for forgiveness, which true believers rely on. So, under what authority is Paul's pronouncement that God gave "them" up or God is against "them" warranted? Ask yourself:

How is it that Paul would know that God gave "them" up and why? Did he ask God about "them?" Did God appear in a dream to tell Paul about "them?" Perhaps, God just spoke to Paul in the cool of the day and said, "I, God, have given up on men and women in a same-sex relationship because of their sinful desires; shameful lusts; and depraved mind." It doesn't make sense, and it's not true. Now ask yourself: Why would God, a minister, a doctor, or anyone else say anything to Paul about sex, unless he had a problem?

You can surmise from Paul's own writings that he indeed had a problem with lust, which he dealt with deceptively by blaming his own actions on sin, the law, and the Lord. Paul gave us a look into his soul where everyone can examine how he dealt with his own issues with sin, in Romans (chapters 7, verses: 7–25). Paul wrote in detail concerning his conviction, his rationale for his own actions, his justification concerning the law, and how he chose to overcome his problem on his road to redemption.

Now, in order to understand Paul and get a clear picture of what he is saying about his problem, it is important to analyze his writings as it relates to "his sin" and then "the law," separately. The reason for this is Paul's writing skills were unique and somewhat difficult to follow. In one sentence, Paul would say several different things, at times unrelated, adding a little truth to capture your attention away from the bold lie that he wanted you to accept or believe. For example, Paul wrote about his problem with lust, this way.

Romans 7:7 says,
> I had not known sin, but by the law: for I had not known lust, except the law had said: You shall not covet.

When you pick apart what Paul is saying about his problem in verse 7, phrase by phrase, he is saying four different things. The first three could all be true, however, the fourth thing is the lie he wants you to accept or believe. For example:

1. **I had not known sin, but by the law:** Paul recognized that his sin was because of the law. The law brought Paul sin (wrongdoing) to the light.

2. I had not known sin, but by the law: **for I had not known lust:** Paul defined his sin as "lust."

3. For I had not known lust, **except the law had said: You Shall Not Covet:** Paul equated his "lust" to the commandment, You Shall Not Covet.

4. **Except the law had said, You shall not covet:** Here is the lie! You Shall Not Covet is a commandment and not a law. Paul wants you to accept or believe that the commandment, You Shall Not Covet, is under the law when, in fact, the law(s) and the commandment(s) are two separate things, and nowhere in the law does it say, "You Shall Not Covet." Paul clearly acknowledged this fact, later, in verse 12.

Romans 7:12
> Wherefore, 'the law' is holy, and 'the commandment' is holy, and just, and good.

Therefore, in order to layout a clear and precise pattern of Paul's problem and how he dealt with it, it is necessary to analyze his writings on "his sin" and "the law" from two separate perspectives. Then bring them together for a completed analysis about Paul.

Now, to clearly appreciate what Paul is saying about his problem, you must focus on the words "sin" and "law."

Romans 7:7–25 says,

> I had not known sin, but by the law: for I had not known lust, except the law had said: You shall not covet. But sin, taking occasion by the commandment, worked in me all manner of concupiscence. For without the law sin was dead. For I was alive without the law once: but when the commandment came, sin revived, and I died. And the commandment, which was ordained to life, I found to be unto death. For sin, taking occasion by the commandment, deceived me, and by it slew me. Wherefore the law is holy, and the commandment holy, and just, and good. Was then that which is good made death to me? God forbid. But sin, that it might appear sin, working death in me by that which is good; that sin by the commandment might become exceeding sinful. For we know that the law is spiritual: but I am carnal, sold under sin. For that which I do, I allow not: for what I would, that do I not; but what I hate, that I do. If then I do that which I would not, I consent to the law that it is good. Now then it is no more I that do it, but sin that dwell in me. For I know that in me (that is, in my flesh,) dwell no good thing: the will is present with me; but how to perform that which is good, I find not. For the good that I would, I do not: but the evil which I would not, that I do. Now if I do that I would not, it is no more I that do it, but sin that dwell in me. I find then a law, that, when I would do good, evil is present with me. For I delight in the law of God after the inward man: But I see another law in my members, warring against the law of my mind, and bringing me into captivity to the law of sin, which is in my members. O wretched man that I am! Who shall deliver me from the body of this death? I thank God through Jesus Christ our Lord. So then with the mind I serve the law of God; but with the flesh the law of sin.

Paul's Perspective on his Sin

Paul's perspective on his sin was to paint himself as a victim, while blaming his own actions on the Lord and sin. He defined his sin by making a direct link between the Lord's commandment, You Shall Not Covet and lust.

Now remember the commandment, Thou Shall Not Covet, has two elements:

Exodus 20:17 says,
> You shall not covet your neighbor's house: You shall not covet your neighbor's wife, manservant, maidservant, ox, ass, or anything that is your neighbor's.

1. Property: meaning "to take by force" property that belongs to someone else.
2. Lust: meaning "to take by force" sexually what belongs to someone else.

Paul was referring to the second element of the commandment, which relates to human being and living things.

When you analyze Paul's own writings, it is clear that his sin was coveting, which he defined as lust. The same lust he projected onto men in the first half of Romans 1:27, which made it sexual. He then linked this same lust to the men of Sodom (who attempted to rape other men), in the second half of Roman 1:27, which made it deviant behavior. Therefore, Paul clearly made his sin of coveting about sexual deviant behavior.

Romans 7:8 says,
> But sin, taking occasion by the commandment, worked in me all manner of concupiscence [lust]. For without the law sin was dead.

Romans 7:11 says,

> For sin, taking occasion by the commandment, deceived me, and by it slew me.

Paul gave us insight into how entrenched coveting was for him in verse 8, when he used the phrase 'sin – worked in me all manner of lust.' Paul seemed to imply that his every covetous desire was because of sin. What is strange is how he used the word sin, in verses 8 and 11, as though he was talking about another person or entity other than himself. At the same time, painting himself as a victim, when he implied that "sin" produced in him all manner of lust and deceived him.

Paul went even further, in verses 14 through 16, when he acknowledged his sinful nature as a physical one and not just one of desire.

Romans 7:14-16 says,

> For we know that the law is spiritual: but I am carnal, sold under sin. For that which I do, I allow not: for what I would, that do I not; but what I hate, that I do. If then, I do that which I would not, I consent to the law that it is good.

When you analyze closely what Paul wrote, he appeared to be crying out in agony over his sin of coveting, as though he could not stop himself, when he said, "For that which I do, I allow not: for what I would, that do I not; but what I hate, that I do." He is clearly expressing himself as one who had hit rock bottom when he acknowledged his condition as "carnal" and stated how far gone he was when he referred to himself as being "sold under sin," giving the impression that his sin of coveting was an addiction.

Now momentarily consider an alcoholic, a person who drinks all the time and way too much. This person may not understand why he or she continues to drink. Even though drinking may give the person a momentary high, afterward he or she becomes sick and depressed, and the cycle starts all over again. Nevertheless, for an alcoholic to overcome his or her problem, he or she must take a minimum of four basic steps to heart:

1. Acknowledge he or she has a problem.

2. Take responsibility for his or her actions.

3. Want to stop.

4. Seek help.

Acknowledge the problem

…I had not known sin, but by the law: for I had not known lust, except the law had said: You shall not covet.

Take Responsibility

Paul seemed to have acknowledged his sin of coveting. However, Paul taking responsibility for his own actions was another issue. In an early assessment Paul seem to blame his own actions on sin in verses 8 and 11. Further into chapter 7, Paul outright blamed his own actions on sin.

Romans 7:17–20 says,
> Now then it is no more I that do it, but sin that dwell in me. For I know that in me (that is, in my flesh,) dwell no good thing: the will is present with me; but how to perform that which is good, I find not. For the good that I would, I do not: but the evil which I would not, that I do. Now if I do that I would not, it is no more I that do it, but sin that dwell in me.

When you analyze closely Paul's rationale of his own action(s), his mental stability appears unstable. Paul clearly rejected the fact that he was responsible for his own "evil" actions of coveting. Instead he blamed his own actions on sin, as though he was possessed, when he said, "If I do that I would not, it is no more I that do it, but sin that dwells in me." Therefore,

Paul was not acknowledging his sin of coveting as it related to his own actions, he was acknowledging what was being done to him by "sin," as though he was a victim. Using, the devil made me do it, as a form of defense.

Now just imagine for a moment, if anyone other than Paul was to say that 'sin' was to blame for anything that he or she had done, such as: commit rape, murder, or armed robbery. Would you believe this person? For sure, you would think that person was mentally ill or delusive, in addition to not taking responsibility for his or her own action(s).

Want to Stop

Paul began his letter to Rome saying he was a servant of Jesus Christ (1:1) and that Jesus was declared to be the Son of God with power (1:4). Then in chapter 15, Paul openly acknowledged that he was given grace to become a minister of Jesus Christ to the Gentiles (non Jewish people).

Romans 15:15-16 says,
> Nevertheless, brethren, I have written more boldly to you in some sort, as putting you in mind, because of the grace that is given to me of God, that I should be the minister of Jesus Christ to the Gentiles, ministering the gospel of God.

Now let's just accept as fact, that Paul was possessed by sin, which caused him to do wrong: covet men, women, and children. It is clear, Paul knew that he was possessed by sin (which was contrary to God), because he tells us. However, if Paul was a servant and a minister of Jesus Christ, then he should have known that Jesus was a healer of the sick, possessed, and the mentally unstable.

Matthew 4:23–24
> Jesus went about all Galilee, teaching in their synagogues, and preaching the gospel of the kingdom, and healing all manner of sickness and all manner of disease among the people. His fame went throughout all Syria: and they brought all the people with diseases

and torments, those which were possessed with devils, those which were lunatic, and those that had the palsy; and he healed them.

Then he should have also known that Jesus established the twelve apostles (which Paul later claimed to be one) and gave them the power to do the same, heal the sick, raise the dead and cast out demons.

Mark 6:7

> Jesus called the twelve apostles, and began to send them out two by two; and gave them power over unclean spirits…

And,
Mark 6:12

> They went out, and preached that men should repent and they cast out many devils, and anointed with oil many that were sick, and healed them.

If, Paul truly believed he was possessed with evil, then one or more of the apostles could have healed him because he knew and met them all. In fact, they worked together to settle a dispute concerning circumcision (Act 15:22). Now just imagine what two or three apostles could have done in the name of Jesus, if they had known about Paul's problem. They could have laid hands on him or outstretched their hands toward him and prayed away the evil (also known as an exorcism).

> **Exorcism:** 1. driving out of evil spirits: the use of prayers or religious rituals to drive out evil spirits believed to be possessing a person or place.
> *–EWED*

If Paul wanted to stop, why didn't he seek healing from the apostles? Then again, the scriptures tell us in the book of Acts, that Paul himself performed outstanding miracles and healed others, just like Jesus.

Acts 14:8–11

> There sat a certain man being a cripple from his mother's womb, who had never walked: This same man heard Paul speak. Paul

perceived that the man had faith to be healed and said to him with a loud voice stand upright on your feet, and the man leaped to his feet and walked. When the people saw what Paul had done, they lifted up their voices and said: The gods have come down to us in the likeness of men.

And,

Acts 16:16–18

A certain damsel possessed with a spirit of divination which brought her masters much gain by telling the future [fortune teller]: She followed Paul and those with him crying out and saying: These men are the servants of the most high God, which show us the way of salvation. This she did many days. Then Paul, being grieved, turned and said to the spirit, I command you in the name of Jesus Christ to come out of her. He [the spirit] came out that same hour.

Jesus said in Matthew 17:20, **if you have faith the size of a grain of mustard seed, you shall say to this mountain, move from here to there, and it shall move.** Surely, Paul's faith was greater than that of a mustard seed. So, why didn't he heal himself? Remember, Paul said sin produced in him all manner of lust, making his actions equal to or far worse than the men of Sodom. Therefore, the only conclusion is, Paul did not want to stop, because if he did, he would have been healed.

Seek Help

Paul wrote in his second letter to the Corinthians that he sought help from the Lord to take away the thorn in his flesh. He never mentioned specifically what his thorn in the flesh was, however, he seemed to know that the thorn in his flesh came from Satan and why.

2 Corinthians 12:7-9

To prevent me from being exalted because of an abundance of

revelations, there was given to me a thorn in the flesh, the messenger of Satan to torture me. For this thing I sought the Lord three times, that it might depart from me. And he said to me: **My grace is sufficient for you: for my strength is made perfect in weakness.** Most gladly will I suffer with my infirmities; that the power of Christ may rest upon me.

"**Revelation:** 1. information that is newly disclosed, especially surprising, or valuable 3. disclosure: the revealing of something previously hidden or secret
–EWED

To be clear, Paul a minister of Jesus Christ was saying that he was given "a thorn in the flesh," by Satan to torture him, because of his "revelations." Now the question is: What were Paul's revelations?

2 Corinthians 12:1 – 5
> I will come to visions and revelations of the Lord. I knew a man in Christ more than fourteen years ago, (whether in the body, I cannot tell; or whether out of the body, I cannot tell: God knows). He was caught up to the third heaven and I knew such a man (whether in the body, or out of the body, I cannot tell: God knows). He was caught up into paradise and heard unspeakable words, which it is not lawful for a man to utter. In this man will I glory. Yet in myself I will not glory, except in my infirmities.

When you analyze what Paul called his "revelations," he makes absolutely no sense. He is writing as though he was a witness to this man he knew fourteen years earlier, who ascended into a third heaven or paradise. Paul repeated himself twice to make it clear to Rome that the revelations he spoke of really happened, and he saw it firsthand when he used the phrases, "whether in the body, I cannot tell; or whether out of the body, I cannot tell: God knows."

Now let's momentarily accept that the man Paul knew ascended into the third heaven or paradise. Paul would still be here on Planet Earth. How is it that Paul would know that the man he knew "heard unspeakable words, which is not lawful for a man to utter," unless, he ascended along with him and heard it himself or the man descended from the third heaven or paradise and told Paul. Either way you look at it, Paul appears delusional because what he is saying is highly implausible and does not make any sense.

What makes thing far worse for Paul's mental stability was the fact that he believed that his revelations, which he deemed came from the Lord, held some sort of value that Satan saw them as a threat and gave him a thorn in his flesh, in other words, infirmities or a weakness in his flesh, to torture him because of the revelations he could reveal. For this reason, Paul said he begged the Lord three times to take away the thorn in his flesh that Satan gave to him, and the Lord said to him "**My grace is sufficient for you: for my strength is made perfect in weakness.**" In a word, the Lord said NO, which makes no sense. This would be the equivalence of the Lord saying to Paul, "I want you to suffer physically in your flesh by the hand of Satan and, at the same time, preach to the masses my message of salvation." What is strange was Paul's reaction, even a child could express an emotion of sadness after being told no for the most simplest of things. Paul on the other hand, had no expressed sadness or disappointment for what he deemed tortured him. Rather it's the opposite, saying, in 2 Corinthians 12:9 "Most gladly will I rather glory in my infirmities, that the power of Christ may rest upon me," as though, he never wanted to be healed.

What Paul is saying, makes the Lord an ally with Satan against him. Paul appears to be making himself, the new Job (from the book of Job, in the OT) whom the Lord allowed Satan to torture financially, emotionally, mentally and physically.

Job 1:8
    The LORD said to Satan, Have you considered my servant Job…

Now the question is: Could Paul's sin of coveting be related to his thorn in the flesh? Yes. When you look at the actual order of the NT books in the KJV, Romans comes before 2 Corinthians. When you place the NT books in chronological order as they were written, then 2 Corinthians would come before Romans. When you analyze Paul's writings in 2 Corinthians together with Romans (chapter 7), a creative story emerges between the two of them that just might clear things up a bit.

Paul's explanation of the Lord not taking away or healing his "thorn in the flesh" ties directly with his addiction of coveting. In 2 Corinthians, Paul was laying the groundwork to blame the Lord for his sinful nature by saying the Lord chose not to heal the thorn in his flesh and as a result "sin," the messenger of Satan continued to exist in him. This same sin produced in him all manner of lust, in other words, his addiction.

Therefore for Paul, there was no reason for him to take responsibility for his own actions or stop his evil ways because, according to Romans 7:17 – 20, it was never him, it was "sin," the messenger of Satan, still living in him because the Lord did not take away the thorn in his flesh after he begged him three times to do so.

Paul's letters to the churches at Corinth and Rome was his way of trying to justify his own actions, which he deemed evil, by blaming the Lord and sin. Raping men, women, or children was Paul's addiction. He told you himself when he stated he was of the tribe of Benjamin.

Romans 11:1
    I am an Israelite, of the seed of Abraham, of the tribe of Benjamin.

The same tribe, that surrounded the Old Man's house (in the book of Judges 19), and wanted to rape the Levite inside. The same tribe, that took the Concubine and *abused her all the night until the morning.* The same tribe, that went to war against the other twelve tribes and was nearly wipe out, because they would not see justice done for the Concubine, who was gang raped to death. The same tribe, that never took responsibility for coveting her (the Concubine) and the same tribe which never repented. So, why would Paul? It is who he was.

Paul's Perspective on the Law

Paul's perspective on the law was to destroy it, because of his sin, which he defined as lust and tied directly to the commandment, You Shall Not Covet.

Romans 7:7 says,
> ...I had not known sin, but by the law: for I had not known lust, except the law had said: You shall not covet.

The law Paul spoke of in Romans 7:7, in actuality, was the commandment, You Shall Not Covet. To be clear, the law does not say, you shall not covet. The commandments and the laws were mentioned as two separate things. They are not interchangeable; nor are they the same. For example:

Genesis 26:5
> Abraham obeyed my voice, and kept my charge, my commandments, my statutes, and my laws.

Now the question is: Why was Paul trying to make the commandment, Thou Shall Not Covet, a part of the law? In Romans 8 through 11, Paul acknowledged his sin was because of the commandment; therefore, his problem was not with the law, but the commandment itself.

Romans 7:8-11
> Sin, taking occasion by the commandment, worked in me all manner of concupiscence [lust]. For without the law sin was dead. For I was alive without the law once: but when the commandment came, sin revived, and I died. The commandment, which was ordained to life, I found to be unto death. For sin, taking occasion by the commandment, deceived me, and by it slew me.

Paul needed a way to push back against the commandment, You Shall Not Covet, which he deemed deceived him and brought him death. It is well documented in several of Paul's own writings that he had long dismissed the law as being relevant in his life. He believed that the law, in essence, was no longer needed for the forgiveness of sin, because the law died with Jesus on the cross, and those who believed in Jesus Christ were now under grace. For example:

Galatians 2:19–21

> For I through the law am dead to the law, that I might live to God. I am crucified with Christ: nevertheless I live; yet not I, but Christ lives in me: the life which I now live in the flesh I live by faith in the Son of God, who loved me, and gave himself for me. I do not frustrate the grace of God: for if righteousness came by the law, then Christ is dead in vain.

And,

Romans 6:14

> For sin shall not have dominion over you: for you are not under the law, but under grace.

And,

Colossians 2:13–14

> You, being dead in your sins and the uncircumcision of your flesh, Jesus quickened you together with him, he has forgiven all your trespasses; blotting out the handwriting of ordinances [the Law] that was against us, which was contrary to us, and took it out of the way, nailing it to his cross.

In Paul's eyes the law was dead; however, he still had a problem with the commandment, You Shall Not Covet, which is defined and not dependent on any law. The commandment clearly states what you should not do.

Exodus 20:17

> You shall not covet your neighbor's house.

You shall not covet your neighbor's wife, manservant, maidservant, ox, ass, or anything that is your neighbor's.

Therefore, Paul needed to make one commandment a part of the law. Then he could tie all commandments to the law. Now, if Paul was to try to tie the commandment, You Shall Not Covet to the law, he would have had a far difficult time doing so, because the law says nothing directly concerning the commandment itself. That is why Paul chose adultery, in his example to make a commandment a part of the law. The commandment simply says, You Shall Not Commit Adultery, whereas, the law in Leviticus concerning adultery says the following:

Leviticus 20:10
> The man that commit adultery with another man's wife, even he that commit adultery with his neighbor's wife, the adulterer and the adulteress shall surely be put to death.

The word adultery is not defined in the commandment or the law. Strictly looking at the law, you must be willing to accept that the word "adultery," means a sexual interaction with a married woman.

In Romans 7:1–3, Paul is writing to those in authority in Rome (who would know the OT law) to persuade them that the commandment, You Shall Not Commit Adultery is under the law.

Romans 7:1–3
> Brethren (speaking to those that know the law), do you know that the law has dominion over a man as long as he lives? A married woman is bound by the law to her husband as long as he lives; but if her husband died, she is loosed from the law. If, her husband is still alive, and she married another man, she shall be called an adulteress: however, if her husband died, while she was still married to another man, she is free from that law; so that she is no longer an adulteress.

To be clear, what Paul was saying is this, when a man and a woman marry, they are bound to the law to stay married, as long as the husband lives. If the husband died, then, she is free under the law to marry someone else; however, if her husband was still alive and she married another man, she would be called an adulteress because she had broken the commandment, You Shall Not Commit Adultery. If her first husband died while she was still married to another man, then, the law would set her free from the commandment, You Shall Not Commit Adultery and she would no longer be an adulteress.

The problem with Paul's assertion to make the commandment, You Shall Not Commit Adultery, a part of the law is that adultery is not based on marriage, but a sexual interaction with a *married* woman. The OT law does not define marriage, so, there is no law that says a woman is bound to her husband as long as he lives. In fact, the law says just the opposite.

Deuteronomy 24:1–4
> When a man and a woman marries, and over time he no longer favors her, because he has found some uncleanness in her: then let him write her a bill of divorcement, and give it to her, and send her out of his house. When she had departed out of his house, she may become another man's wife. If, her second husband hates her and write her a bill of divorcement, and give it to her, and send her out of his house, or he dies; then her first husband, who sent her away, may not take her again to be his wife, because she is defiled.

According to the OT law, a woman is free from her husband with a bill of divorcement (a piece a paper), while her husband is still alive. When she marries another man, she is not called an adulteress nor becomes an adulteress. If a woman leaves her husband (without a bill of divorcement), she would still be married to him, although they were apart. Therefore, any sexual interaction between her and any other man (not her husband) would fall under the commandment, You Shall Not Commit Adultery and the law, Leviticus 20:10. Then, according to the law, she is an adulteress and could be put to death along with the man who committed adultery with her. If, Leviticus 20:10 no longer existed, it would have no affect on the commandment, You Shall Not Commit Adultery.

Nevertheless, Paul believed that he and other men in authority were completely delivered from the law and the commandments.

Romans 7:5 – 6

> When we were in the flesh, our sins, brought to light by the law, existed in our bodies to bring forth fruit unto death. But now we are delivered from the law; that we should serve in newness of spirit, and not in the oldness of the letter.

This is why in Roman 7:7 Paul added the commandment, You Shall Not Covet, under the law saying, , except the law had said, You Shall Not Covet.

Therefore, Paul solved his problem, he wrote his own deliverance. He believed he was able to tie one commandment, You Shall Not Commit Adultery, to the law; even though his reasoning to tie a commandment to the law was based on a lie: that a woman is tied to her husband all the days of 'his' life. As more proof, Paul later wrote his letter to the Ephesians and declared to them that all the commandments were "abolished" through the blood of Jesus Christ on the cross.

Ephesians 2:13–16 (NIV)

> But now in Christ Jesus you who once were far away have been brought near through the blood of Christ. For he himself is our peace, who has made the two one and has destroyed the barrier, the dividing wall of hostility, by abolishing in his flesh the law with its commandments and regulations. His purpose was to create in himself one new man out of the two, thus making peace, and in this one body to reconcile both of them to God through the cross, by which he put to death their hostility.

If, Paul believed that the commandments were really abolished, then why would he then resurrect the commandment, Honor your father and mother, four chapters later?

Ephesians 6:1

> Children, obey your parents in the Lord: for this is right. Honor thy father and mother, which is the first commandment with promise; that it may be well with you, and you may live long on the earth.

Paul was not always against the commandments. When he wrote his first letter to the Corinthians, concerning circumcision, he stated that keeping the commandments was most important.

1 Corinthians 7:19

> Circumcision is nothing, and uncircumcision is nothing, but the keeping of the commandments of God.

Paul being for the commandments then, makes it clear now that the commandment, You Shall Not Covet, actually caught him by surprise.

Romans 7:9–10

> For I was alive without the law once: but when the commandment came, sin revived, and I died, and the commandment, which was ordained to life, I found to be unto death.

This goes to show that Paul was not against all the commandments, only the one that personally affected him and others who were in authority in Rome. Remember, Paul said, "by the law is the knowledge of sin" (Romans 3:20). Then abolishing the law along with the commandment, You Shall Not Covet, was for his own purpose; so, he would not have to acknowledge his own evil actions as sin.

Romans 4:15

> The law brings wrath: where there is no law, there is no transgression (sin).

Now let's just say the OT law was bad and outdated with its animal sacrifices and blood rituals and no longer needed. Let's also say that Paul's reasoning for wanting the law destroyed was warranted because Jesus Christ redeemed all under the law to grace, in the NT. Now ask yourself: What is wrong with any of these commandments that they should be added to the law and abolished?

- Honor Your Mother and Father
- You Shall Not Commit Adultery
- You Shall Not Murder
- You Shall Not Steal
- You Shall Not Bear False Witness (Lie)
- You Shall Not Covet

Paul believed he was successful at linking a commandment to the law, the law to Jesus Christ, and Jesus Christ to the cross. That is why, Paul made up out of thin air;

- The "law of God," which encompassed all the OT laws and commandments.

- The "law of sin," which represented his sinful nature, which is, the thorn in his flesh: his addiction to coveting men, women, children, or animals.

- The "law of the Spirit of Life," which represented freedom, making all thing new again.

Now Paul gets the outcome that he chose for himself, redemption.

Romans 7:22–8:1–2
> For I delight in the law of God after the inward man: I see another law in my members, warring against the law of my mind, and bringing me into captivity to the law of sin which is in my members. O wretched man that I am! Who shall deliver me from the body of this death? I thank God through Jesus Christ our Lord. So with my mind I serve the law of God; but with the flesh, the law of sin. There is now no condemnation to them which are in Christ Jesus… because the law of the Spirit of life in Christ Jesus has made me free

from the law of sin and death.

Finally, there would be total absolution for all of Paul's actions, and in his mind, he was free from the commandment, You Shall Not Covet. In fact, Paul was free from all the commandments, including You Shall Not Kill and You Shall Not Steal, leaving him free to serve two masters the Lord and sin.

Therefore, Paul who was, in essence, establishing the Church is creating a way of escape for wrong doing, mainly covetous behavior, for himself and those in authority in Rome, to whom his letter was written, by instituting forgiveness as a remedy.

Romans 3:23 – 24
> For all have sinned, and come short of the glory of God; being justified freely by his grace through the redemption that is in Christ Jesus.

It's all about Paul

From the beginning, Paul made the focus about men and women in a consensual same-sex relationship, while at the same time justified his own evil actions of rape against men, women, or children by blaming sin.

Paul's overall perspective on his sin and the law was self-serving. His uncontrolled illicit sexual appetite appears to be the reason for all his lies. Paul lied repeatedly and often to achieve the goal or the outcome that he wanted for himself, to be free from the commandment, You Shall Not Covet. Therefore, Paul's letter to Rome was not written for you or the church today (as you may believe it to be), but for himself and others like him in Rome, to justify evil acts by creating a way of escape using Jesus Christ as a buffer, for all their unrighteousness.

Notice, in Romans 1:27, Paul said, "the men, leaving the natural use of the woman, burned in their lust one toward another." These men Paul was speaking of were choosing to be together, like any other couple in a good and healthy relationship. This was not the case with Paul, because coveting is evil, unhealthy, and not about choice.

What stands out more than anything in Romans 1:28, was Paul saying, "They did not like to retain God in their knowledge." How could Paul know that, unless, there was an inner personal struggle between him and God? Remember, in Romans 7:14, Paul said he was "carnal" and "sold under sin." Therefore, if what Paul said was true, which no one should doubt, then, it was Paul who did not always retain God on his mind.

When you take a closer look at Romans 1:29–32, a picture starts to develop about Paul that might make sense. You can surmise that Paul was more than likely talking about himself, because everything he wrote seemed to be very specific and of a personal nature. For example, Paul included three of the OT's commandments, You Shall Not Covet (covetousness), You Shall Not Kill (murder) and Honor your Father and Mother; and omitted You Shall Not Commit Adultery, You Shall Not Steal, and You Shall Not Bear False Witness (Lie). So, why were they not included? When you analyze what Paul wrote word for word, it is personal, specific, and appears to be a self-analysis of his own person life, which could all be summed up in his own words.

Romans 7:18 -19
> For I know that in me (that is, in my flesh,) dwells no good thing: for the will is present with me; but how to perform that which is good, I find not. For the good that I would, I do not: but the evil which I would not, that I do.

Some may conclude that God gave up on men and women who have consensual same-sex relations and believe they are unclean, and the affection they share is vile, because of what they were taught or somehow share that same view; however, no one should believe or conclude that God, the creator of heaven and earth, gave men and women who have same-sex relations over to a reprobate mind "*to do*" other immoral things. It's as though, Paul was saying that men and women who have consensual same-sex relations are predisposed to unrighteous and wicked acts, if this is the case, you must accept that fornication, which is sex between single men and women, is one of those unrighteous and wicked acts. Then those who commit fornication are also predisposed to acts, such as covetousness, maliciousness; being full of envy, murder, debate, deceitful, malignity; whisperer, backbiter, haters of God, despiteful, proud, boaster, inventors of evil things, disobedient to parents, without understanding, covenant breaker, without natural affection, implacable, unmerciful; and worthy of death.

12

Thorn in the Flesh

The main reason for this chapter is to show that Paul's mental stability is a factor, because he is the predominant writer of the NT. Also, to demonstrate two things: How others saw Paul's thorn in the flesh, and how far the *Wycliffe Bible Encyclopedia* (*WBE*), would go to explain Paul's own writings.

2 Corinthians 12:7–9
> **(7)**To prevent me from being exalted because of an abundance of revelations, there was given to me a thorn in the flesh, the messenger of Satan to torture me. **(8)**For this thing I sought the Lord three times, that it might depart from me. **(9)**And he said to me: **My grace is sufficient for you: for my strength is made perfect in weakness.** Most gladly will I suffer with my infirmities; that the power of Christ may rest upon me.

The *WBE* suggested four scenarios for Paul's thorn in the flesh, which they provided an explanation for only 1 and 2 .

1. "persistent carnal desires or fleshly temptation"
2. "feelings of guilt stemming from him having formerly persecuted the church"
3. "some form of physical or nervous ailment"
4. "a personal enemy who sought to slander and discredit him"

- "Regarding the first, he found victory through the indwelling Spirit of God (Rom 8:5-13). Regarding the second, he knew that the grace of Jesus Christ had fully absolved him of his past crime (1 Tim 1:13-

16). Whatever was the nature of his thorn, it did not prevent his continuing in an extremely active ministry which included long journeys on foot."

The first and third items seemed to be spot-on, whereas the second and fourth scenarios listed, are a farce in determining what Paul's thorn in the flesh really was. However, when reviewing the fourth item listed, the WBE opens the door to a better understanding as to why Paul wrote both Corinthian letters.

1 and 3

The first item listed: The *WBE* dismissed the idea that Paul's 'thorn in the flesh' was his persistent carnal desires, using his own writings, Romans 8:5–13. The *WBE* unintentionally defined Paul's problem when they stated that he had "found victory through the indwelling Spirit of God," which is a conclusion. Therefore, Paul's victory was over his 'thorn in the flesh', which was his persistent carnal desire, in other words, his addiction to coveting.

The third item suggest that others have formed an opinion that Paul suffered from some sort of physical ailment. The *WBE* listed a total of six possible diseases to explain his visions and revelations for which he received his thorn in the flesh.

1. "Epilepsy"
2. "Acute Ophthalmic or eye trouble"
3. "Malarial Fever"
4. "Hysteria or Melancholy"
5. "Sick Headache"
6. "Nervous Exhaustion"

Some of the sicknesses and diseases listed demonstrate that Paul more than likely had a brain injury or an illness that caused him to hallucinate. The fact that it included "hysteria," suggest that Paul could have suffered from a traumatic injury which caused him to become mentally unstable.

2 and 4

The second item listed, doesn't make much sense to suggest that Satan gave Paul a thorn in the flesh because he persecuted the church. One would think Satan would have rewarded Paul for his actions against the church; in the end, the *WBE* ruled it out, by again citing Paul's own writings for his absolution.

1 Timothy 1:12-15

> I thank Christ Jesus our Lord, who hath enabled me, he counted me faithful, putting me into the ministry; who was before a blasphemer, and a persecutor, and injurious: but I obtained mercy, because I did it ignorantly in unbelief. The grace of our Lord was exceeding abundant… This is a faithful saying, and worthy of all acceptation, that Christ Jesus came into the world to save sinners; of whom I am chief.

The fourth and final item listed, suggest that Paul's thorn in the flesh was a "personal enemy who sought to slander and discredit him." To support their theory, the *WBE* put forth two explanations.

- "In the OT a 'thorn' was a rather common idiom for a human enemy… (Numbers 33:55; Joshua 23:13). Ezekiel refers to the enemies of Israel as 'a pricking brier' and 'any grieving thorn.'"

- "A study of the phrase 'thorn in the flesh' and of its context in Paul's defense of his apostleship (2 Cor. 10–13) indicates that it probably refers to a person, not an illness."

The first paragraph: To support their enemy theory, they cited scriptures from the OT which were irrelevant, but contained the word "thorns."

The Second paragraph implied that Paul's 'thorn in the flesh' was him defending his apostleship, an enemy. To support this theory they cited the following:

2 Corinthians 12:10–13
> (10)Therefore I take pleasure in <u>infirmities</u>, in <u>reproaches</u>, in <u>necessities</u>, in <u>persecutions</u>, in <u>distresses</u> for Christ's sake: for when I am weak, then am I strong. (11)I am a fool in my achievements; you have compelled me: for I ought to have been commended of you: for in nothing am I behind the very chief apostles, though I be nothing. (12)Truly the signs of an apostle were done among you in all patience, in signs, and wonders, and mighty deeds. (13)What is it you were inferior to other churches, except that I myself was not burdensome to you? Forgive me this wrong.

Now to be clear, Paul's 'thorn in the flesh' story was concluded in verse 9. When you analyze all four verses 10-13, they have absolutely nothing to do with Paul's thorn in the flesh! However, they are very, very, interesting, because they provide insight as to why Paul wrote first and second Corinthians, which was money.

Verse 10 is the beginning of Paul's conclusion for his entire 2 Corinthians letter. Looking only at verse 10, it is a conclusion of a whole list of things that Paul wrote about in some detail in the prior chapter that he is saying happened to him during his ministry (2 Corinthians 11:20–33).

In Reproaches:
2 Corinthians 11:20-21
> For you suffer, if a man bring you into bondage, if a man devour you, if a man take of you, if a man exalt himself, if a man smite you on the face. I speak as concerning reproach…

In Infirmities:
2 Corinthians 11:24-25
> From the Jews five times I received forty lashes minus one. Three times was I beaten with rods, once was I stoned, three times I

suffered shipwreck, and spent a night and a day in the deep open
sea;

In Distresses:
2 Corinthians 11:26
> Journeying often, in perils: of waters, of robbers by my own
> countrymen, by the heathen, in the city, in the wilderness, in the sea,
> and among false brethren;

In Necessities:
2 Corinthians 11:27
> In weariness and painfulness, in watching often, in hunger and
> thirst, in fasting often, in cold and nakedness…

In Persecutions:
2 Corinthians 11:31-33
> The God and Father of our Lord Jesus Christ, which is blessed for
> evermore, know that I lie not. In Damascus the governor with
> stationed troops, desiring to apprehend me, and through a window
> in a basket I was let down by the wall, and escaped his hands.

When you look only at verse 11, what stands out is the word "you." Some
may conclude that Paul was referring to an enemy in opposition to his
teachings of God and Christ based solely on the word "you." Looking at
the entire verse in context, it seems less likely. In fact, the statement "for I
ought to have been commended of *you*" refers to whom Paul was writing
his letter:

2 Corinthians 1:1
> …To the church of God at Corinth with all the saints, in Achaia.

Analyzing verses 12 and 13, Paul wanted the church at Corinth to
recognize his authority and his apostleship.

2 Corinthians 12:12-13
> Truly the signs of an apostle were worked among you in all

patience, in signs, wonders, and mighty deeds. What is it that you were inferior to other churches, except that I myself was not burdensome to you? Forgive me this wrong.

Now, to put things in context it is important to establish why Paul wrote what appears to be his second letter to the church at Corinth; and there are three main reasons:

The first reason was money. In Paul's first letter to the church at Corinth, he ordered the church to take up a weekly collection of money among the saints for his own purposes. (Many, if not all, Christian churches today take up collections of money in the form of tithes, offerings, or gifts of love mainly on Sunday, the first day of the week.)

1 Corinthians 16:1-3

> Now concerning the collection for the saints, as I have given orders to the churches of Galatia, you also do the same. On the first day of the week let every one of you lay in store, as God has prospered him, in advance before I arrive. When I come, whomsoever you shall approve by your letters, them will I send to bring your liberality to Jerusalem.

Paul being challenged was why he began his second letter using a more calm and peaceful tone and laying out excuses for why he needed money (the gift).

2 Corinthians 1:8–11

> Brethren, we want you to be aware of our troubles which came to us in Asia, that we were pressed beyond our own strength, insomuch that we lost hope of staying alive: But we did not trust in ourselves, but in God which raise the dead. Who delivered us from so great a death, and whom we trust will continue to deliver us.

> You also helping together by prayer for us, and for the gift [weekly collections] bestowed upon us by the means of many persons, thanks may be given by many on our behalf.

Paul wrote in detail concerning the gift or bounty (money) he was expecting from the church at Corinth. For example:

2 Corinthians 9:5-7 (NIV)
> For I know your eagerness to help, and I have been boasting about it to the Macedonians, telling them that since last year you in Achaia were ready to give; and your enthusiasm has stirred most of them to action. But I am sending the brothers in order that our boasting about you in this matter should not prove hollow, but that you may be ready, as I said you would be. For if any Macedonians come with me and find you unprepared, we--not to say anything about you-- would be ashamed of having been so confident. So I thought it necessary to urge the brothers to visit you in advance and finish the arrangements for the generous gift you had promised. Then it will be ready as a generous gift, not as one grudgingly given. Remember this: Whoever sows sparingly will also reap sparingly, and whoever sows generously will also reap generously. Each man should give what he has decided in his heart to give, not reluctantly or under compulsion, for God loves a cheerful giver.

The second revealed that the church had challenged Paul sexual immorality in a prior letter, based on his response, to call out other who had sinned.

2 Corinthians 12:19 – 21 (NIV)
> Have you been thinking all along that we have been defending ourselves to you? We have been speaking in the sight of God as those in Christ; and everything we do, dear friends, is for your strengthening. For I am afraid that when I come I may not find you as I want you to be, and you may not find me as you want me to be. I fear that there may be quarreling, jealousy, outbursts of anger, factions, slander, gossip, arrogance and disorder. I am afraid that when I come again my God will humble me before you, and I will be grieved over many who have sinned earlier and have not repented of the impurity, sexual sin and debauchery in which they have indulged.

The third is: The church challenged Paul's authority by wanting proof that Christ was speaking through him, and here's how Paul responded:

2 Corinthians 13:1 – 5 (NIV)
> This will be my third visit to you. "Every matter must be established by the testimony of two or three witnesses." I already gave you a warning when I was with you the second time. I now repeat it while absent: On my return I will not spare those who sinned earlier or any of the others, since you are demanding proof that Christ is speaking through me. He is not weak in dealing with you, but is powerful among you. For to be sure, he was crucified in weakness, yet he lives by God's power. Likewise, we are weak in him, yet by God's power we will live with him to serve you. Examine yourselves to see whether you are in the faith; test yourselves. Do you not realize that Christ Jesus is in you--unless, of course, you fail the test?

Now, to sum up 2 Corinthians 12:10–13, Paul was saying that he should have been commended by the church at Corinth and all the saints for everything he suffered (infirmities, reproaches, necessities, persecutions, and distresses) in bringing them the gospel of God at no cost.

2 Corinthians 11:7-9
> Have I committed an offence in abasing myself that you might be exalted, because I have preached to you the gospel of God freely? I robbed other churches, taking wages of them, to do you service. When I was present with you, and wanted, I was chargeable to no man: for that which was lacking to me the brethren which came from Macedonia supplied: and in all things I have kept myself from being burdensome to you.

Paul was clearly responding to his authority being challenged on multiple fronts because he ordered the church at Corinth to take up a weekly collection of money for his use. Paul's authority to speak for Jesus Christ was also an issue being challenged and was more than likely the reason why he changed his title, to appear more authoritarian, between letters.

First Corinthians: Paul, called (*to be*) an apostle of Jesus Christ through the will of God

Second Corinthians: Paul, an apostle of Jesus Christ by the will of God

First and Second Corinthians were private letters Paul wrote to the church at Corinth to convince them of his authority he believed he had been given by Jesus Christ and God. His letters were never meant for anyone else, and that includes Christians today. It is clear from Paul's first letter to the Corinthians that he was responding to an earlier letter written to him:

1 Corinthians 7:1–2

> *Now concerning the things you wrote to me:* It is good for a man not to touch a woman. Nevertheless, to avoid fornication, let every man have his own wife, and let every woman have her own husband.

It is clear Paul was expecting a private written response from the church at Corinth:

1 Corinthians 16:1–3

> Now concerning the collection for the saints, as I have given order to the churches of Galatia, you also do the same…. When I come, whomever you shall approve by **your letters**, them will I send to bring your liberality to Jerusalem.

All written communications or letters related to First and Second Corinthians have not been revealed. There is no way of knowing whether Paul's first letter to the Corinthians was his first or his tenth. Ask yourself: Why would the church at Corinth seek proof of Jesus Christ speaking through Paul, in 2nd Corinthians 13:3, unless Paul told them that Jesus Christ was speaking through, by or in him, in one of his letters, which has not yet been revealed? Also, there is no way of knowing whether Paul received the money, gift, or bounty, which the letters were about. Now, the question is: How could Paul's private and incomplete communications, about money, sexual immorality, and his authority to speak for Jesus Christ, with the church at Corinth or any church become the Word of God?

Using the scriptures they provided, the *WBE* concluded that Paul's thorn in the flesh was a "personal enemy who sought to slander and discredit him." Maybe they should have concluded that Paul's thorn in the flesh was his persistent carnal desires, perhaps due to a physical or nervous ailment (mental defect).

1. "persistent carnal desires or fleshly temptation"
2. ~~"feelings of guilt stemming from his having formerly persecuted the church"~~
3. "some form of physical or nervous ailment"
4. ~~"a personal enemy who sought to slander and discredit him"~~

Nonetheless, the *WBE* closed with Paul's thorn in the flesh, which appears to be written directly to Christians, this way:

- "In his response to his thorn in the flesh Paul demonstrated the proper Christian response to frustration, whatever form it may take. After earnest prayer for its removal, he accepted it and made the best of the situation by the grace of Christ."

Therefore, regardless of what Paul's thorn in the flesh could have been, the proper Christian response is to accept it. Regardless of what *it* is.

The Truth

13

The True Standard-Bearer

The reason Paul gave for writing his letter to Rome was that he believed that 'God' had given him *grace*, to minister the "gospel of God" to the Gentiles, "non-Jews," in order to present the Gentiles, as an acceptable offering back to God.

Romans 15:15–16, 18–19

> Nevertheless, brethren, I have written more boldly to you in some sort, as putting you in mind, because of the grace that is given to me of God, that I should be the minister of Jesus Christ to the Gentiles, ministering the gospel of God, that the offering up of the Gentiles might be acceptable, being sanctified by the Holy Ghost…
>
> For I will not dare to speak of any of those things which Christ has not worked by me, to make the Gentiles obedient, by word and deed, Through mighty signs and wonders, by the power of the Spirit of God… I have fully preached the gospel of Christ.

The same grace that Paul believed that God had given him in Romans 15:15-16, to minister the gospel of God, is the same grace he believed God gave him in 2 Corinthians 12:9 ("<u>**My grace**</u> **is sufficient for thee: for my strength is made perfect in weakness"**), concerning his thorn in the flesh, which made absolutely no sense. Nevertheless, as a minister of the gospel of God, Paul believed that Jesus Christ was speaking through, by, or in him in order to make the Gentiles obedient. (Now remember, the church at Corinth challenged Paul, because they wanted proof that Jesus Christ was speaking through him, in 2 Corinthians 13:3). What Paul is saying was whatever he says should be considered the gospel of God or the absolute truth, because it would be Jesus Christ, the Son of God, who was speaking through, by, or in him. As a result, Paul seemed to believe that everything he said was in essence the word of God, therefore, he had the authority to speak for God or as God, against men and women in a same-sex relationship saying,

- God also gave them up to uncleanness…

- God gave them up to vile affections…

- God gave them over to a reprobate mind…

Everything Paul wrote in the first chapter of Romans continued on into the second chapter, where he stated that those who obey his truth seek eternal life or the promise of eternal life. Those who do not obey will receive indignation, wrath, tribulation and anguish, because God would judge all men based on *his gospel*.

Romans 2:7–11, 16 (NIV)

> To those who by persistence in doing good seek glory, honor and immortality, he will give eternal life. But for those who are self-seeking and who reject the truth and follow evil, there will be wrath and anger. There will be trouble and distress for every human being who does evil: first for the Jew, then for the Gentile; but glory, honor and peace for everyone who does good: first for the Jew, then for the Gentile…. This will take place on the day when God will judge men's secrets through Jesus Christ, as my gospel declares. For God does not show favoritism.

"**Gospel:** 1. set of beliefs: a set of beliefs held strongly
by a group or person 2. absolute truth: something believed
to be absolutely and unquestionably true"
–EWED

Is Paul the true standard-bearer? If Paul is saying to follow him and obey *his* gospel as a servant, minister, and an apostle, being sent by God; what exactly is he offering the Gentiles, for their obedience? Grace?

Grace: 7. gift of God to humankind: in Christianity, the infinite love, mercy, favor, and goodwill shown to humankind by God 8. freedom from sin: in Christianity, the condition of being free of sin, e.g. through repentance to God
–EWED

The problem with Paul as the standard-bearer is this: no one really knows who he is. For example, in the book of Acts, said to be written by Luke, Paul says he's a Jew.

Acts 21:39
> Paul said: I am a Jew of Tarsus, a city in Cilicia…

In first Corinthians, written by Paul, he pretends to be a Jew.

1 Corinthians 9:19–22
> I am free from all men, yet have I made myself servant to all, that I might gain the more. **To the Jews I became as a Jew**, **that I might gain the Jews**; to them that are under the law, as under the law, that I might gain them that are under the law; To them that are without law, as without law…that I might gain them that are without law. To the weak became I as weak, that I might gain the weak: I am made all things to all men that I might by all means save some.

Is Paul a Jew? One thing is clear, you don't have to pretend to be someone who you already are, unless, you are not who you say you are. With Paul it depended on who he was writing to that defined who he was. For example, his private letters to the Thessalonian and Philippian churches, Paul made no mention of being an apostle. In fact, he simply wrote to them as Paul. When he wrote his first letter to the Corinthian and Roman churches, he was called *to be* an apostle. Theologians adding the words "*to be*" changes how you see Paul. The statement "called *to be* an apostle" can mean one of two things: either Paul is an apostle or he would be one in the future. However, when you remove the words "to be," then, Paul was called an apostle, not that he was or would ever be an apostle. When Paul wrote his second letter to the Corinthian, Colossian, and Ephesian churches, Paul said he was an apostle of Jesus Christ by the will of God. When Paul wrote his first letter to Timothy, his son, he was an apostle of Jesus Christ by the commandment of God our Savior and Lord JesusChrist. Therefore, depending on whom Paul was writing to and trying to persuade, he tailored who he was for his own gain, because he believed he was all things to all men.

The Gospel Truth

Paul's private letters were never meant to be disseminated to the masses, especially, his letter to the Church at Colosse and his second letter to his son, Timothy, because they revealed that Paul knew at least two of the gospel writers: Luke and Mark.

Colossians 4:14

> Luke, the beloved physician, and Demas, greet you.

In Paul's letter to the Colossians he included Luke as part of his greeting. Also, in his second letter to Timothy, he mentions that Luke is with him and his plan to use Mark for the ministry.

2 Timothy 4:11

> Only Luke is with me. Take Mark, and bring him with you: for he is profitable to me for the ministry.

Now, if you include the book of Acts, written by Luke, Paul also knew John, all three worked with Paul in establishing the Church.

Acts 13:13

> When Paul and his company left Paphos… John departed from them and returned to Jerusalem.

If Paul knew 3 out of 4 Gospel writers, are the gospels independent of one another? It is believed that the gospels were originally written from 1 to 60 years after the death of Jesus, which is approximately more than 6,000 years ago:

Matthew	1-10 yrs.
Mark	25-30 yrs.
Luke	30-35 yrs.
John	50-60 yrs.

Now, for one moment, just accept all 4 gospel writers as being with Jesus the entire time he was said to be on the earth; and each independently wrote their own gospels based on what they heard and saw, one year apart following Jesus' death. How is it that Matthew, Mark, and Luke continuously wrote their gospel's telling the same stories and using the exact same phases and verses, at times, word for word? For example:

The Miracle of Jesus
feeding 5,000 with 2 fish and 5 loaves of bread

Matthew 14:15, 19 - 20

And when it was evening, his disciples came to him, saying, This is a desert place, and the time is now past; send the multitude away, that they may go into the villages, and buy themselves victuals…. And he commanded the multitude to sit down on the grass, and took the five loaves, and the two fishes, and looking up to heaven, he blessed, and brake, and gave the loaves to his disciples, and the disciples to the multitude. And they did all eat, and were filled: and they took up of the fragments that remained twelve baskets full.

Mark 6:35 - 36, 39, 41 - 43

And when the day was now far spent, his disciples came unto him, and said, This is a desert place, and now the time is far passed: Send them away, that they may go into the country round about, and into the villages, and buy themselves bread: for they have nothing to eat…. And he commanded them to make all sit down by companies upon the green grass…. And when he had taken the five loaves and the two fishes, he looked up to heaven, and blessed, and brake the loaves, and gave them to his disciples to set before them; and the two fishes divided he among them all…. And they did all eat, and were filled. And they took up twelve baskets full of the fragments, and of the fishes.

Luke 9:12, 15 - 17

When the day began to wear away, then came the twelve, and said unto him, Send the multitude away, that they may go into the towns and country round about, and lodge, and get victuals: for we are here in a desert place.... And they did so, and made them all sit down. Then he took the five loaves and the two fishes, and looking up to heaven, he blessed them, and brake, and gave to the disciples to set before the multitude. And they did eat, and were all filled: and there was taken up of fragments that remained to them twelve baskets.

Today this is called plagiarism. Now, considering that all four gospels were said to be written in the first century, it seems even less authentic or believable; nevertheless, this repetition continues throughout the NT.

Plagiarism: 2. something plagiarized: a piece of written work
or an idea that somebody has copied and claimed as his or her own
–EWED

It would appear that overall, the gospels of Mark and Luke were written to bolster the gospel of Matthew and to clarify, correct, and to make changes from the previous gospel. For example: In the gospel of Matthew, Jesus chose Matthew to be one of his 12 apostles. In the gospels of Mark and Luke, Matthew's name was changed to Levi, a more Jewish sounding name.

Matthew 9:9
> As Jesus passed by, he saw a man, named Matthew, sitting at the receipt of custom: and he said to him, **Follow me.** He arose, and followed him.

Mark 2:14
> As Jesus passed by, he saw Levi the son of Alphaeus sitting at the receipt of custom, and said to him, **Follow me.** He arose and followed him.

Luke 5:27 – 28
> Jesus went forth, and saw a publican, named Levi, sitting at the receipt of custom: he said to him, **Follow me.** He left all, rose up, and followed him.

(Note: The name Levi does not appear among the named 12 apostles handpicked by Jesus, but Matthew does in all three gospels (Matthew 10:2 – 4, Mark 3:14 – 19, Luke 6:13 – 16))

Therefore, everything Matthew, Mark, and Luke wrote about Jesus would have been sanctioned by Paul and the Church. Now, the question is: why was it necessary for Paul to have a fourth gospel?

There Must be Blood

In many of Paul's letters he focused on the blood of Jesus as the saving grace for forgiveness. For example:

Colossians 1:14

> In whom we have redemption through his blood, even the forgiveness of sins:

Ephesians 1:7

> In whom we have redemption through his blood, the forgiveness of sins, according to the riches of his grace;

Romans 5:9

> ... being now justified by his blood, we shall be saved from wrath through him.

Paul needed another gospel to demonstrate that Jesus was the ultimate blood sacrifice, the high priest, to do away with the OT once and for all; and to provide a way for the Jews to become true believers and followers of Jesus Christ, the Son of God.

The gospel of John focuses on the blood of Jesus; Jews; and the Son of God. These three issues provide the continuation of the OT into the New. In the OT there was no forgiveness of sin without blood, which included animal sacrifice and rituals. Paul explains this in the book of Hebrew.

Hebrew 9:18 – 22

> Neither the first testament was dedicated without blood. For when Moses had spoken every precept to all the people according to the law, he took the blood of calves and of goats, with water, and scarlet wool, and hyssop, and sprinkled the book, and all the people, saying, this is the blood of the testament which God has enjoined to you. Moreover he sprinkled with blood both the tabernacle, and all

the vessels of the ministry. Almost all things are by the law purged with blood; and without the shedding of blood there is no remission of sin [forgiveness].

Therefore, to satisfy the OT there needed to be blood. Only the high priest could enter into the second chamber called the holy place of the tabernacle with the blood of an animal for the forgiveness of sin. That is why in the NT it is through the blood of Jesus that all who believe and follow him receives forgiveness according to Paul's gospel.

Hebrew 9:6 – 7, 11 – 12

> [In the OT] the priests went always into the first tabernacle, accomplishing the service of God. But into the second went the high priest alone once every year, not without blood, which he offered for himself, and for the errors of the people…
>
> Christ being made a high priest of good things to come, by a greater and more perfect tabernacle, not made with hands, that is to say, not of this building; Neither by the blood of goats and calves, but by his own blood he entered in once into the holy place, having obtained eternal redemption for us.

In the gospels of Matthew, Mark, and Luke, the body and blood of Jesus Christ is symbolic, there is no actual blood. For example:

Communion

Matthew 26:26 – 29

> As they were eating, Jesus took bread, and blessed it, and gave it to the disciples, and said: **Take, eat; this is my body.** He took the cup, and gave thanks, and gave it to them [the 12 apostles], saying; **Drink all of it, for this is my blood of the New Testament, which is shed for many for the remission of sins.**

Mark 14:22 – 24

> Jesus took bread, and blessed it, and gave it to them, and said: **Take, eat,**

this is my body. He took the cup, and when he had given thanks, he gave it to them and they all drank of it. He said to them: **This is my blood of the New Testament, which is shed for many.**

Luke 22:19 - 20

He took bread, and gave thanks, and gave to them, saying: **this is my body which is given for you, this do in remembrance of me.** Likewise also the cup after supper, saying: **this cup is the New Testament in my blood, which is shed for you.**

The same is true with the crucifixion of Jesus Christ in the gospels of Matthew, Mark (15:15 – 46), and Luke (23:26 – 56) there is no blood; no mention of nails being put through his hands or feet; No one threw a stone at him; or physically beat Jesus in any way that caused him to shed blood.

Crucified: 1. execute somebody on cross: to execute somebody by crucifixion 2. criticize somebody harshly: to criticize somebody unsparingly 3. treat somebody cruelly: to defeat, torment, or victimize somebody in a thorough or cruel way.
–EWED

The crucifixion of Jesus, in Matthew is very similar to the gospel of John, until the very end.

The Crucifixion of Jesus - Matthew

Matthew 27:27 – 35, 37 – 42, 46 – 54

Then the governor's soldiers took Jesus into the common hall, and gathered the whole band of soldiers. They stripped him of his clothing and put on him a scarlet robe. When they had platted a crown of thorns, they put it upon his head, and a reed in his right hand: and they bowed their knee before him, and mocked him, saying, Hail, King of the Jews! They spit upon him, they took the robe off and put his clothing back on him, and led him away to crucify him.

When they reached Golgotha: a place called the skull, they gave him vinegar to drink mingled with gall: when he had tasted it, he would not drink. They crucified him, and parted his garments, casting lots... and set over his head a sign, THIS IS JESUS THE KING OF THE JEWS. Then two thieves were crucified with him, one on the right hand, and another on the left. People passed by reviled him, wagging their heads and saying: You who can destroy the temple, and build it again in three days, save yourself. If you are the Son of God, come down from the cross.

The chief priests mocked him, with the scribes and elders, saying, he saved others; himself he cannot save. If he is the King of Israel, let him now come down from the cross, and we will believe him....

About the ninth hour Jesus cried with a loud voice, saying, **Eli, Eli, lama sabachthani?** ...Which means, **my God, my God, why have you forsaken me?** Jesus, when he had cried again with a loud voice, yielded up the ghost [he died].

Behold, the veil of the temple was torn from the top to the bottom; and the earth did quake, and the rocks broke apart; and the graves were opened; and many bodies of the saints which slept arose and came out of the graves after Jesus' resurrection, and went into the holy city, and appeared unto many.

Now, when the centurion, and those with him, watching Jesus, saw the earthquake, and those things that were done, they feared greatly, saying, truly this was the Son of God.

The Crucifixion of Jesus - John

John 19:16 – 19, 23 – 24, 28 – 35

He delivered Jesus unto them to be crucified. They took Jesus, and led him away to a place called Golgotha, in Hebrew, where they crucified him, and two others with him, and Jesus in the midst. Pilate wrote a title, and put it on the cross and the writing was, JESUS OF NAZARETH THE KING OF THE JEWS....

Then the soldiers, when they had crucified Jesus, took his garments, and made four parts, to every soldier a part... They said therefore among themselves, Let us not tear it, but cast lots for it...

After this, Jesus knowing that all things were now accomplished, that the scripture might be fulfilled, said, **I thirst.** They filled a sponge with vinegar, and put it upon hyssop, and put it to his mouth. When Jesus therefore had received the vinegar, he said: **It is finished:** and he bowed his head, and gave up the ghost.

Then came the soldiers, and broke the legs of the first, and of the other which was crucified with him. But when they came to Jesus, and saw that he was dead already, they did not break his legs: But one of the soldiers with a spear pierced his side, and blood and water came out. He that saw it bare record and his record is true: and he knows that he spoke the truth that you might believe.

Therefore, Paul needed blood, and to get it, he manufactured another outcome for himself along with the Church, saying, *one* unnamed witness saw an unidentified soldier stab Jesus in his side after he was already dead, then to bring attention to the blood, the writer(s) concluded that water came out as well. The one common denominator between many if not all the characters of the NT Bible is Paul. Now the question is: Did the Roman Catholic Church ordained the gospels to be written for different reasons; one, being able to control and indoctrinate the masses by giving them a form of God to follow and believe in; another would be, to gain wealth from the masses, such as the poor, the broken hearted, down trodden, and guilt ridden through tithes, offerings, gifts of love, and/or indulgences?

4

Follow and Obey

Jesus said, follow me.

John 10:27-28

> My sheep hear my voice, and I know them, and they follow me: And I give to them eternal life; and they shall never perish, neither shall any man pluck them out of my hand.

Church leaders teach the masses to follow, believe in, and pray to Jesus Christ as their Lord and Savior, saying he represents an ideology of love, forgiveness, and redemption, in addition to giving them eternal life. Why? According to the gospel of Matthew, Jesus was very specific concerning who he came for.

Matthew 15:24

> I am not sent but to the lost sheep of the house of Israel.

In addition, the scriptures tell us why Jesus came and his purpose on the earth.

Matthew 10:34–38

> Do not suppose that I have come to bring peace to the earth. I did not come to bring peace, but a sword. For I am come to set a man at variance against his father, the daughter against her mother, and the daughter-in-law against her mother-in-law. A man's foes shall be of his own household. He that loves their father or mother more than me is not worthy of me: and he that loves their son or

daughter more than me is not worthy of me. He that does not take up his cross, and follow after me, is not worthy of me.

Jesus illustrated his teachings to his followers, true believers, two chapters later when he rejected his own mother (the Virgin Mary) and his brothers stating that his disciples (followers) was his family.

Matthew 12:46-50

> While he yet talked to the people, behold, his mother and his brethren stood without, desiring to speak with him. Then one said to him [Jesus], Behold, your mother and your brothers want to speak with you. But he replied: **Who is my mother? Who are my brethren?** Then he stretched forth his hand toward his disciples, and said: **Behold my mother and my brothers! For whosoever shall do the will of my Father which is in heaven, the same is my brother, sister, and mother.**

Jesus made it clear when he began to teach his followers to hate their own flesh and blood, including their own life, and to give up everything for him.

Luke 14:25

> There went great multitudes with him: and he turned, and said to them: **If any man come to me, and hate not his father, mother, wife, children, brethren, sisters, and his own life also, he cannot be my disciple. Whosoever do not bear his cross and come after me, cannot be my disciple…**

Luke 14: 33

> **So likewise, whosoever of you that forsake not all that he has, he cannot be my disciple.**

Jesus began his ministry in all Four Gospels saying, "Follow me." For example, in the gospel of Matthew, Jesus saw two brothers, Peter and Andrew who were fisherman. He said to them, "Follow me," and they did.

At that moment, they gave up everything without asking a question to follow after Jesus and became his disciples. James and John were two fishermen who were also brothers. Jesus said to them, "Follow me," and they abandoned their own father, equipment, and ship to follow after him without asking one question.

Matthew 4:18–22

>Jesus, walking by the sea of Galilee, saw two brethren, Simon called Peter, and Andrew his brother, casting a net into the sea: for they were fishers. He said to them, **Follow me, and I will make you fishers of men.** And they straightway left their nets, and followed him. And going on from there, he saw, James and John his brother, in a ship with their father, mending their nets; and he called them. They immediately left the ship and their father, and followed him.

Also Matthew, the tax collector gave up his livelihood and followed after Jesus, again without asking a single question.

Matthews 9:9

>As Jesus passed forth from there, he saw a man, named Matthew, sitting at the receipt of custom: and he said to him, **Follow me.** He arose, and followed him.

Until, followers of the faith begin to question what they believe, they may never have a full understanding of why they follow after the teachings of Jesus Christ, Paul, or anyone else. The scriptures bear this out. Even Peter, who was an apostle, did not know why he had forsaken all and followed after Jesus Christ, until he asked a question.

Matthew 19:27–29

>Then Peter said to him [Jesus], behold, we have forsaken all, and followed you; what's in it for us? Jesus replied, **Truthfully, I say to you that have followed me, in the regeneration when the Son of man shall sit in the throne of his glory, you also shall sit upon twelve thrones, judging the twelve tribes of Israel. Every one that has forsaken houses, brothers, sisters, father, mother, wife, children, or land for my name's sake, shall receive a hundredfold, and shall inherit everlasting life.**

Jesus' response to Peter in the gospels of Mark and Luke was slightly different, minus the twelve thrones and judging the twelve tribes of Israel.

Mark 10:28–30
> Then Peter said to him [Jesus], we have left all, and have followed you. Jesus replied, **There is no man that has left his house, brothers, sisters, father, mother, wife, children, or lands, for my sake, and the gospel's; he shall receive an hundredfold now in this time, houses, brothers, sisters, mothers, children, and lands, with persecutions; and in the world to come eternal life.**

Luke 18:28
> Then Peter said, we have left all, and followed you. Jesus replied, **Truthfully I say to you, there is no man that has left house, or parents, brothers, wife, children, for the kingdom of God's sake, who shall not receive many more in this present time, and in the world to come life everlasting.**

Looking at all three gospels: Matthew, Mark, and Luke for what they share in common, a follower of Jesus Christ, mainly the twelve apostles, were promised two things: One hundredfold and Eternal life

One Hundredfold

Every apostle who have left behind a mother, father, sister, brother, spouse, and/or children to followed after Jesus Christ, making him Lord and Savior of their lives, will receive one hundred times their loss, while on this earth, in this world, among like followers. Remember, Jesus said **"Whosoever shall do the will of my Father which is in heaven, the same is my brother, sister, and mother,"** in other words, likeminded followers will take the place or become like mothers, sisters, brothers, or children.

Therefore, if an apostle gave up or left behind property, such as a home or parcel of land he should receive one hundred homes or parcels of land in return, or he would receive a home or parcel of land that is one hundred times in value, while on this earth, in this world. Now the question is: When and how would the 12 apostle or like followers receive their hundredfold?

Eternal Life

Jesus promised his apostles that they will receive eternal life, 'not' on this earth, but, in the world to come, which will contain a new heaven and a new earth, based on a vision by someone named John, who is identified in the book of Revelations, as a servant.

Revelation 1:1

> The Revelation of Jesus Christ, which God gave to him [an angel], to show his servants things which must shortly come to pass; and he sent and signified it by his angel to his servant John: Who bare record of the word of God, and of the testimony of Jesus Christ, and of all things that he saw.

Revelations 21:1

> I [John] saw a new heaven and a new earth: for the first heaven and the first earth were passed away; and there was no more sea. I John saw the holy city, New Jerusalem, coming down from God out of heaven, prepared as a bride adorned for her husband. I heard a great voice out of heaven saying, behold, the tabernacle of God is with men, and he will dwell with them, and they shall be his people, and God himself shall be with them, and be their God. And God shall wipe away all tears from their eyes; and there shall be no more death, neither sorrow, nor crying, neither shall there be any more pain: for the former things are passed away.

Now, for those who believe they will receive eternal life in the world to come should ask themselves one simple question. Why is it that all people on this earth do not have eternal life already? In the beginning, man was meant to live forever in this world, according to Genesis 1:26, because man was made in God's likeness and image. The reason given by Paul for all citizens of this earth not having eternal life was that Adam, the first man the Lord God ever created, sinned, and because of his sin, death fell upon all.

1 Corinthians 15:21

> By man came death, by man came also the resurrection of the dead. For as in Adam all die, even so in Christ shall all be made alive.

And,

Romans 5:12, 18–21

> By one man sin entered into the world, and death by sin; and death passed upon all men, so that all have sinned… Therefore, by the offence of one, judgment came upon all men to condemnation; even so, by the righteousness of one, the free gift came upon all men unto justification of life.

> By one man's disobedience [Adam] many were made sinners, so by the obedience of one [Jesus] shall many be made righteous. Moreover the law entered, that the offence might abound. But where sin abounded, grace much more abound: because sin brought death, even so might grace reign through righteousness unto eternal life by Jesus Christ our Lord.

Adam's Transgression

According to the OT scriptures, Adam transgression (sin) was against the first commandment given by the Lord God:

Genesis 2:16 – 17

> The LORD God commanded the man [Adam], saying, of every tree of the garden you may freely eat: But of the tree of knowledge of

good and evil, you shall not eat of it: for in the day that you eat thereof you shall surely die….

The tree of knowledge in the garden is figurative, because knowledge does not grow on trees. Therefore, the Lord God commanded Adam not to partake of or seek knowledge for himself.

Knowledge: 1. information in mind: general awareness or possession of information, facts, ideas, truths, or principles 2. specific information: clear awareness or explicit information, e.g. of a situation or fact.
–EWED

Why this is important is because it is believed that the same death the Lord God pronounced upon Adam for seeking knowledge, is the same death that Paul says falls upon all men making them sinners; and the very reason the masses do not have eternal life today, but, why they need Paul and/or the Church; and a savior, Jesus Christ, to follow and obey without question, so that they *might* receive eternal life, in the world to come.

The point here is, if the Lord God did not prevent Adam from seeking knowledge (sinning) in this world, what precludes this same scenario from happening in the world to come. Clearly, the same Lord God that many serve and follow now on this earth, will be the same Lord God that they will serve and follow in the world to come.

Nonetheless, one would think that everyone is expected to love their mother, father, sister, brother, spouse, and children, and many do, regardless of what they believe or who they follow, not in order to move on to a new world, but because they are human beings.

Many churches use Jesus, 'the Son of God', as a mediator to hide behind, to take the spotlight away from them and their ministers who try to persuade the masses into accepting their dogma. Ask anyone: Who wrote the first five books of the Bible? Some would say "Moses," "probably Moses," "someone else," or "I don't know;" Ask, who wrote the first book in the NT? Many would say "Matthew," "probably Matthew," "someone else," or "I don't know." Again ask, who wrote Romans? Some would say "Paul," "probably Paul," "someone else," or "I don't know." This one thing is clear, no one would say God. Not one! Therefore, questioning, challenging, or rejecting any religion or their form of politics is not the same as questioning, challenging, or rejecting God, the Creator of heaven and earth; or a higher power, but man.

PART: 2

PROPERTY

AND

LAND

15

A Tale of Two Rapes

A fable is a fictional story that may contain supernatural, mythological, mystical, or legendary characters and events to teach a lesson. The story of Sodom and Gomorrah has all the characteristics of a fable: the mythological rain of fire and brimstone falling from a mystical heaven that destroys all human life and land within two cities by an all-powerful God, who sends two men (witnesses) toward the city of Sodom who enter as angels with superhuman abilities to blind men at will. Lot, who is legendary, is the main reoccurring character always in need of being saved. This is what some of the great fairy tales are made of.

What further supports the fact that Sodom and Gomorrah is nothing more than a fable is the story: The Concubine. Comparing Sodom and Gomorrah to The Concubine, they appear to be two separate stories, yet, verse by verse; they are the same with one central theme in both stories.

Both stories begin with a homeowner inviting in strangers. The wicked men of the city surround the house where the strangers were lodging. They demanded the stranger(s) be brought out so they could covet them sexually. The homeowners plead for the stranger(s) not to be harmed. The homeowners, who are fathers, offer up their daughter(s) to be gang-raped in defense of the male stranger(s). Looking at both stories very carefully, they appear to be mirror copy of each other in many aspects, even though one version may be more dramatic than the other.

When you analyze each fable individually, they appear to be about sexual immorality, men wanting to gang-rape other men; however, nothing is as it seems. When you analyze both fables together as to how they may relate to each other, they open the door to understanding what the Protestant's OT Bible is all about, which is property and land.

16

Women and Girls

The writer(s) of both fables, 'Sodom and Gomorrah' and 'The Concubine,' demonstrated that women and girls had no rights, that they were instruments to be used by and for men; and biblically, with one statement, women and girls were made worthless:

Lot (Sodom and Gomorrah): "Let me bring them out to you, and you can do what you like with them."

Old Man (The Concubine): "Behold, here is my daughter a maiden, and his concubine; them I will bring out now, and humble them, and do with them what seem good to you"

The writer(s) never explained why Lot or the Old Man, fathers, put forth their daughter(s) as property, in defense of men who were strangers to be gang-raped by all the men in the city. However, the *Holman Bible Dictionary* (HBD) tries to explain Lot's behavior toward his daughters, as "the lesser of two evils," under the term "homosexuality."

Homosexuality

- "Sexual preference for and sexual behavior between members of the same sex, considered to be an immoral life-style and behavior pattern throughout the biblical revelation. Only heterosexual preference and behavior patterns are approved in Scripture as conforming to God's plan in the creation of man and woman. Moreover, all sexual behavior is to take place in the context of marriage. Sex is considered good so long as it takes place within these parameters."

- "(v. 5) mentions specifically the homosexual intentions of the men of Sodom. Lot considers this behavior wicked (v. 7). Raping his daughters was considered the lesser of two evils (v. 8)."

To be clear, the *HBD* appears to be saying that a women being gang-raped is "the lesser of two evils" when compared to a man being gang-raped, because they believe that sex between a man and a woman conforms to God's plan.

The word "rape" does not appear in the King James Version of the Bible. However, statements such as "forced her," and "abused her" are used to describe a sexual assault, which is rape. Whereas, consensual sex between a man and a woman would mean both or all parties are in agreement with the sex or type of sex they would have. If the man took the woman and defiled her, forced her, and/or abused her, it is rape; the same would be true if it was between two men instead of a man and a woman. It's not who is raped that makes it rape. Rape is rape!

There is no greater example in the entire Bible of what rape really is other than the story, The Concubine, where the men of city came for the Levite to defile him, force him, and abuse him sexually. The Levite may have been their preference to dominate sexually; however, they took what was given, the woman, and raped her to death, forever solidifying that rape is about lust, anger, physical control, and violence.

It would appear the writer(s) chose rape as their theme in both fables, to first capture your attention and then to make it clear to men, that they are dominant compared to the women. Using the daughters demonstrated the man's dominance in the human hierarchy, even to the extent of a father discarding his own daughter(s) for the protection and well-being of a male stranger. The writer(s) made it clear in the story of Sodom and Gomorrah that men should always be protected over women. In the story, The Concubine, the writer(s) clearly demonstrated that men should always be protected over the women, even if it kills them.

Therefore, the lesson here was not same-sex relations (to be specific), fornication, and definitely not bestiality, but male dominance.

Different but Equal

Most, if not all depictions of God is of a male; and many today believe that God is male. In the first chapter of Genesis, the writer(s) used a plural statement, "let us," to identify who God was. So, how is it that the word *us* became male only?

Genesis 1:26
> God said; let us make man in our image, after our likeness…

Ministers commonly teach that the word *us* in Genesis 1:26 represented the Holy Trinity: God, the Father; God, the Son/The Word; and God, the Holy Spirit. To support this view many church leaders cite the writings of John in the NT.

John 1:1 – 3
> In the beginning was the Word, and the Word was with God, and the Word was God. The Word was with God from the beginning. All things were made by him; and without him was nothing made that was made.

1 John 5:7
> For there are three that bear record in heaven, the Father, the Word, and the Holy Ghost: and these three are one.

Therefore, one could see the image of God in Genesis 1:26, as that of a male, based solely on the NT scriptures. However, when you take a closer look at the actual OT scripture, the word *us* is defined. God said "let us make man in our image, after our likeness" the word *us* represented God or Gods, which is defined as both male and female, in verse 27. Many church leaders who are predominantly male focus on the pronouns *his, him* and *he,* in Genesis 1:27 and mistakenly assume that God is only male.

Genesis 1:27

> So God created man in <u>his</u> *own* image, in the image of God created <u>he</u> <u>him</u>; male and female created <u>he</u> them.

When you search for the word *his* within the same chapter, it refers to a variety of things, but, it is not gender specific, for example:

Genesis 1:11

> God said, let the earth bring forth grass, the herb yielding seed, and he fruit tree yielding fruit after **his** kind, whose seed is in itself upon the earth and it was so.

And,

Genesis 1:21

> God created great whales and every living creature that move, which the waters brought forth abundantly, after their kind, and every winged fowl after **his** kind and God saw that it was good.

The same would be true for the pronoun *he* and *him*, they are not gender specific. In Genesis 1:26, God said "let us make "***man***" in our image and likeness." Then in verse 27, it says "God created "***man***" in his own image, in the image of God created <u>he</u> <u>him</u>; male and female created <u>he</u> <u>them</u>." The words <u>*he*</u> <u>*him*</u> equates directly to the words <u>*he*</u> <u>*them*</u>; therefore, God created himself (*him*) male and female in the creation of *them*.

The pronoun *he* in verse 27, is not gender specific, but represent both masculinity and femininity, for example, the word *he* is represented in the words <u>he</u> and s<u>he</u>; the same is true in words such as <u>male</u> and fe<u>male</u>, <u>man</u> and wo<u>man</u>, and, <u>men</u> and wo<u>men</u>. Therefore, mankind was created to be different, but equal.

Corrupting the Woman

Many believe that the first five books of the Bible were written by one person, Moses, and believe in only one God, who is defined as the creator of heaven and earth. Throughout the Protestant's OT Bible there are three titles or deities: God, Lord God, and Lord that appear over and over again, at times together within the same verse or chapter.

The second chapter of Genesis appears to be a continuation of the first chapter, but it's not. In the second chapter the man is seen as the head of the woman, instead of both of them being equal.

Genesis 2:7

> The <u>LORD God</u> formed man from the dust of the ground, and breathed into his nostrils the breath of life; and man became a living soul…

Genesis 2:18–25

> The LORD God said it is not good that a man should be alone; I will make a help meet for him. Out of the ground the LORD God formed every beast of the field and every fowl of the air; and brought them to Adam... but Adam did not find a help meet. Then the LORD God caused a deep sleep to fall upon Adam, and as he slept the LORD God took one of his ribs, and closed up his flesh. The rib, which the LORD God had taken from Adam, he made a woman, and brought her to him.

LORD: 1. Christian God: in Christianity, God or
Jesus Christ 2. Jewish God: in Judaism, God
–EWED

The writer(s) of Genesis appear to be making a distinction by labeling them differently; notice, in chapter 1, God *created* man: male and female; in chapter 2, the Lord God *formed* or shaped the man from the dust of the earth, meaning from nothing, into their image and took what they formed and made a woman to the man's liking.

Therefore, telling the tale of who was formed first and how, was to establish male superiority and to gives rise to a false narrative that women were made as a lesser and non-consequential being.

When it comes to the unkind treatment of women, it's not just the fables: 'Sodom and Gomorrah' and 'The Concubine;' or that women were considered an after-thought in the eyes of the Lord God that should be worrisome. It is the entire Bible, that objectifies women as law breakers, disobedient, mischievous, in need of being put in their place, and worthy of death; in many instances by diminishing, blaming, punishing, and outright lying about them. For example, the following four stories:

Eve

The Lord God said to the man (Adam) you shall not eat or partake of the tree of knowledge. When Adam sinned, he blamed the woman (Eve) for his transgression. As a result, the Lord God physically punished the woman, and diminished and threatened the serpent, but, Adam who transgressed the commandment of the Lord God was not punished. (The story of Adam and Eve: Genesis 2:9, 15 – 17, 3:1 – 19)

The Commandment given to Adam

Out of the ground the LORD God grew every tree that was pleasant to the sight, and good for food; the tree of life and the tree of knowledge (of good and evil) were in the middle of the garden. Then the LORD God commanded the man, saying, of every tree of the garden you may freely eat: But of the tree of knowledge, you shall not eat of it: in the day that you do, you shall surely die....

The Enticement of Eve

Now the serpent was more subtle than any beast of the field which the LORD God had made. He said to the woman, has God said, you shall not eat of every tree of the garden? The woman replied we may eat of the fruit of the trees of the garden: but of the fruit of the tree which is in the middle of the garden, God has said, you shall not eat of it, neither shall you touch it, least you die. Then the serpent said to the woman, you shall not surely die, for God knows that in the day you eat thereof, then your eyes shall be opened, and you shall be as gods, knowing good and evil.

Eve Received Knowledge

When the woman saw that the tree was good for food, and that it was pleasant to the eyes, and a tree to be desired to make one wise, she took of the fruit thereof, and did eat, and gave also to her husband with her; and he did eat. Their eyes were opened, and they knew that they were naked; and they sewed fig leaves together, and made themselves aprons.

Adam Blamed Eve

Then Adam and Eve heard the voice of the LORD God while they were walking in the garden in the cool of the day and Adam and his wife hid themselves from the presence of the LORD God among the trees of the garden. The LORD God called out to Adam and said: Where are you? He replied, I heard your voice in the garden and I was afraid, because I was naked so I hid myself. The Lord God said: Who told you that you were naked? Have you eaten of the tree I commanded you not to eat?

Then Adam replied, the woman who you gave to be with me, she gave me of the tree, and I did eat. The LORD God said to the woman: What is this you have done? The woman said, the serpent beguiled me, and I did eat.

The Serpent Diminished and Threatened

The LORD God said to the serpent, because you have done this, you are cursed above all cattle, and above every beast of the field; upon your belly shall you go, and dust shall you eat all the days of your life: I will put enmity between you and the woman, and between your seed and her seed; it shall bruise your head, and you shall bruise his heel.

Enmity: - Hostility: the extreme ill will or hatred
that exists between enemies.
–EWED

Eve's Punishment

The Lord God said to the woman, I will greatly multiply your sorrow and your conception; in sorrow you shall bring forth children; and your desire shall be to your husband, and he shall rule over you.

Adam was not Punished

The Lord God said to Adam, because you have hearkened unto the voice of your wife, and have eaten of the tree, which I commanded you not to eat of: cursed is the ground for your sake; in sorrow shall you eat of it all the days of your life; Thorns and thistles shall it bring forth to you; and you shall eat the herb of the field; In the sweat of your face shall you eat bread, till you return to the ground; for out of it were you taken: for dust you are, and to dust shall you return.

The story of Adam and Eve is not about eating fruit (what many believe to be an apple) from a tree, it's about knowledge. The tree of Knowledge in the middle of the garden is figurative, because knowledge does not grow on trees. The Lord God allowed Adam to partake of the tree of life, whatever it entailed, yet commanded him not to partake or seek knowledge for himself. Why?

About Adam

After Adam sinned he gained knowledge, he knew that he was naked. Now what was also true is that the Lord God knew Adam was naked all along and did not tell him. It would appear that the Lord God wanted Adam to remain unvarnished, unadulterated, simple, and defenseless, in another word, naked, so that, he would not know good and evil, or the truth from a lie; therefore, making it much easier for the Lord God to indoctrinate and control him.

It is clear that Adam was not punished, after he transgressed the Lord God's commandment, because he did not die, the scripture say Adam lived to be 930 years old. Many ministers believe and preach that Adam died the same day he sinned, and to support their belief they cite 2nd Peter in the NT.

2 Peter 3:8

> Beloved, be not ignorant of this one thing, that one day with the Lord is, as a thousand years, and a thousand years as one day.

In Genesis 2:17 the Lord God said to Adam, concerning the tree of knowledge, *"you shall not eat of it: in the day that you do, you shall surely die."* After Adam sinned, he did not die, because in Genesis 3:17 the Lord God had a change of mind and cursed the ground for Adam in place of him dying that day, saying, "cursed is the ground for your sake; in sorrow shall you eat of it *all the days of your life,*" which means more than one day. Also, according to the 1st chapter of Genesis, a day was defined this way:

Genesis 1:5 – 31

> The evening and the morning were the first day.
> The evening and the morning were the second day...
> The evening and the morning were the third day.
> The evening and the morning were the fourth day.
> The evening and the morning were the fifth day.
> The evening and the morning were the sixth day.

The evening, being the end of a day, then the morning would be the start of a new day. Many believe that God created the heavens and the earth (the world) in 6 days, not in or approximately 6,000 years.

After the Lord God cursed the ground for Adam's sake he said "thorns and thistles shall it bring forth to you; and you shall eat the herb of the field," this too was not a punishment. Before Adam sinned it was the plan from the beginning that man would eat from the trees and herbs of the field (the ground). It was also the Lord God's plan that the man would work the ground and take care of it.

Genesis 2:5 – 7, 15

> No plant or herb of the field in the earth had grown: because the LORD God had not caused it to rain upon the earth, and there was no man to till the ground.

> A mist from the earth came and watered the whole face of the ground. Then the LORD God formed man of the dust of the ground, and breathed into his nostrils the breath of life; and man became a living soul…. The LORD God took the man, and put him into the Garden of Eden to dress it and to keep it.

Many ministers use 2nd Peter 3:8, in the NT, to help make the point that Adam was punished for his transgression, which is dishonest, because this belief can be disproven by reading the actual scriptures in Genesis, which are clear, Adam did not pay the price of death for his transgression, nor was he punished for it.

Now, it is commonly taught that the reason for the trees: Life and Knowledge, in the middle of the garden was that man had *free will*. The choices given to Adam was: life without knowledge or having knowledge until death, which originally was to be less than one day. Adam chose knowledge, therefore death. As a result, the Lord God took away Adam's ability to continue to have free will; he barred Adam from partaking of the tree of Life to prevent him from continuing to live forever having knowledge and knowing: good and evil.

Genesis 3:22 – 24

> The LORD God said, Behold, the man has become as one of us, to know good and evil: and now, lest he take also of the tree of life, and eat, and live forever. Therefore the LORD God banished Adam from the Garden of Eden, to till the ground from where he was taken. So he drove out the man; and he placed at the east of the Garden of Eden cherubim's, and a flaming sword which turned every way, to keep him away from the tree of life.

Therefore, based on the scriptures Adam did not receive death as a punishment because of his transgression, but, because he chose knowledge, in other words, to become educated.

Education: 2. knowledge: the knowledge
or abilities gained through being educated.
–EWED

About Eve

The Protestant's OT Bible tells us two things about Eve to make it clear that she was punished. First, she was Adam's wife; and secondly, she conceived and had a son (Genesis 4:1).

Genesis 3:16
> To the woman the Lord God said, I will greatly multiply your sorrow and your conception; in sorrow you shall bring forth children; and your desire shall be to your husband, and he shall rule over you.

Unlike Adam, Eve acknowledged that the serpent beguiled her; meaning he enticed her with his words to seek knowledge, which she did. The Lord God said the same thing in Genesis 3:17, concerning Adam listening to the *voice* of his wife; meaning, Eve enticed Adam with her words to seek knowledge, which he did.

The serpent did not press Eve to accept his truth, he barely spoke and when he did he asked her one question and made one statement.

The serpent: "Has God, said you shall not eat of every tree of the garden?"

Eve replied: "We may eat of the fruit of the trees of the garden: but of the fruit of the tree which is in the middle of the garden, *God* has said, you shall not eat of it, neither shall you touch it, least you die."

The serpent: "You shall **not** surely die, for *God* knows that in the day you eat, your eyes shall be opened, and you shall be as gods, knowing good and evil."

Eve originally believed a lie, based on her reply, because *God*, the creator, did not say that they (Adam and/or Eve) were not to eat of the tree in the middle of the garden, the Lord God did. It is commonly preached to the masses that the serpent was a liar because he added one word, the word *not*; therefore, based on the serpent adding the word *not* many define the serpent, as the devil, a deceiver, or a liar; and to help make that point, they turn to the NT.

Revelation 12:9
> The great dragon was cast out, that old serpent, called the Devil, and Satan, which deceived the whole world.

The serpent is believed to be many things, an actual talking snake, the devil, Satan, a dragon, a fallen angel, or just pure evil, but never a man who was referenced *as* a serpent.

Searching for additional information about the serpent, this is what you will find under the heading: Devil, Satan, Evil, Demonic.

- Satan, the chief of the fallen angels, is mentioned in a number of places in the OT. It is clear that from the very moment of the creation of this world that Satan and fallen angels were on the scene, rebels against God. Satan was evidently perfect in his original state. Pride seems to have been the cause of his fall. Disguised as a serpent, he was the agent of temptation for the first man and woman...
  –HBD

Now, based on the scriptures the serpent did not deceive Eve, so, it hard to see the serpent as evil because he did not mislead or lie to her. He said two things to Eve which can be proven were not lies.

1. **She would not die:** Nowhere in the entire Bible does it say that Eve died. The scriptures tell us Adam died (Genesis 5:5); Abraham died (Genesis 25:8); his wife Sarah died at the age of 127 (Genesis 23:1 - 2), and many other men and women, but not Eve. Why not say Eve died, except to prove that the serpent was not a liar.

2. **Her eyes shall be opened and she will be as gods, knowing good and evil:** Figuratively, Eve's eyes were opened and she became wise, and knew something she did not know before, that she was naked. Also, she would have known she was lied to, but, not by the serpent.

Genesis 3:7
> The eyes of them both were opened, and they knew that they were naked…

The serpent simply told Eve the truth that God, the creator, did not say what she believed he had said. So, what did the serpent do wrong? If he did not lie, then it would appear the serpent was diminished and threatened by the Lord God for telling Eve the truth and enticing her to seek knowledge.

In the NT, Eve's name is mentioned twice, by Paul, in two of his letters, 1st Timothy and 2nd Corinthians, to diminish her and women altogether.

1st Timothy

Paul wrote a private letter to Timothy, his son, who was to establish the principles of the church at Ephesus, in his absence. Paul outlined for Timothy, a minister, his gospel for him to preach to the masses.

The Men

1 Timothy 2:1 – 8
> I urge that, first of all, supplications, prayers, intercessions, and giving of thanks, be made for all men; for kings, and for all that are in authority; that we may lead a quiet and peaceable life in all godliness and honesty. This is good and acceptable in the sight of God our Savior; who will have all men to be saved, and to come unto the knowledge of the truth.
>
> There is one God, and one mediator between God and men, the man Christ Jesus; who gave himself a ransom for all, to be testified of in due time. Whereby, I am an ordained preacher, and an apostle (I speak the truth in Christ, and lie not), a teacher of the Gentiles in faith and verity. I want men to pray everywhere, lifting up holy hands, without wrath and doubting.

About the Women

1 Timothy 2:9 – 15

> In like manner women should adorn themselves in modest apparel, with shamefacedness and sobriety; not with braided hair, gold, pearls, or costly array; But (women professing godliness) with good works. Let the woman learn in silence with all subjection. But I suffer not a woman to teach, nor to usurp authority over the man, but to be in silence. For Adam was formed first, then Eve. Adam was not deceived, *but the woman being deceived was in the transgression.* Notwithstanding she shall be saved in childbearing, if they continue in faith, charity and holiness with sobriety.

The men Paul is talking about in 1 Timothy 2:1 – 8 (who are to receive request and prayers…) are not all men, but, kings and other men in authority, which would include him and his son, that is why Paul mentioned that he was a preacher, an apostle, and a teacher, to be seen as one who has authority, which could be why Paul included the phrase "that *we* may lead a quiet and peaceable life," when writing to his son.

In verses 9 through 15, Paul is saying women are subject to all men (in authority or not). In describing how the women were to be treated in his letter, Paul used words such as shamefacedness and subjection to diminish them and for men to put them in their place, even if physical force was necessary.

Shamefaced: 1. showing a feeling of shame
or embarrassment 2. timid or easily embarrassed
–EWED

Subjection: domination: the bringing of a person or
people under the control of another, usually by force
–EWED

Paul continued to say that women shall be saved in giving birth, if they follow and obey. Now the question is: What is a woman being saved from, is it death, hell, or the devil? Not pain! Remember, the Lord God said "I will greatly multiply your sorrow and your conception; in sorrow you shall bring forth children," as a punishment for the woman. This appears to be Paul's attempt at aligning all women with the belief that they have done something wrong, and are in need of being saved.

Now notice, Paul changed the subject from *Eve* being beguiled, which was acknowledged, to being deceived. Paul's use of the word *deceived* in his letter to Timothy was not actually about Eve, but all women. Paul used Eve in order to make a distinction that women were less than smart, in other words, easily misled and prone to believe a lie.

> **Beguile**: 1. charm somebody: to win and hold somebody's attention, interest, or devotion
> *–EWED*

> **Deceive**: 1. intentionally trick or mislead somebody: to mislead or deliberately hide the truth from somebody
> *–EWED*

For a moment, let's just accept that Paul is correct and Eve's punishment applied to all women. Eve's punishment is specific based on Genesis 3:16, it would only be a punishment if the woman married and/or had children. This is why Paul wrote in many of his letters that God is against men and women who have sex outside of marriage, because it is his belief and/or the Church that all women be punished or at best accept the same punishment as Eve, so that they would be subject to their husbands rule over them.

1 Timothy 5:14
> I want the younger women to marry, bear children, guide the house, and give no occasion to the adversary to speak reproachfully.

Therefore, Paul's gospel concerning women throughout his letter was for woman to know their place. Now the question is: How are women to adorn themselves with shamefacedness today? Is it being silent and only speak when allowed to? Are women to hold their heads low in disgrace, while their husbands rule them? Are women to no longer pursue a career or have an opinion that is different from a man? Why it is important to ask these questions is because many accept the Bible as the Word of God and not of men.

2nd Corinthians

Analyzing Paul's second letter to the Corinthians he knew Eve was not deceived, because he acknowledged that Eve was beguiled by the serpent in this letter, which was written before 1st Timothy.

2 Corinthians 11:2 – 4

> I have espoused you to one husband that I may present you as a chaste virgin to Christ. I am afraid that as the serpent beguiled Eve through his subtlety, that your minds could be corrupted from the simplicity that is in Christ. If anyone come preaching another Jesus, whom we have not preached, or receive another spirit, or another gospel, which you have not accepted from us, you might believe him.

Paul wrote about Eve being beguiled by the serpent because he was afraid. The church at Corinth was already challenging his authority to speak for God and Christ, so he used Eve to make a point as to why the masses should not listen or believe what anyone else might preach or teach that does not align with his gospel.

Therefore, it should be clear that Adam blamed Eve for his transgression; then the Lord God punished her; and Paul lied about her, in order to make it appear as though it was the woman's fault from the very beginning.

Lot's Daughters

Toward the end of the story of Sodom and Gomorrah (in the OT) the witnesses physically laid hands on Lot, his wife, and two daughters and removed them from the city of Sodom for their own safety. They demanded that Lot and his family not look back to see the destruction; however, Lot's wife disobeyed and look back, and as the story goes, turned into a pile of salt. Lot, not knowing what had happened to his wife continued on with his two daughters and lived alone with them, in the mountains (Genesis 19:15 – 17, 26)

The tale of Lot's two daughters is a story about incest. In telling this account the writer(s), in Genesis, managed to somehow blame the daughters, by making the story about rape: nonconsensual sexual abuse, of their father, Lot.

Incest alone is often buried and entangled with lies, and this story is no different. This story minimized the incestuous relationship between Lot and his daughter's, who were both virgins and married (child brides), by saying they were both impregnated after only one sexual encounter each, with their father (Genesis 19:8 and 19:14). According to the scriptures, in the span of two nights both daughters made their father drink wine and as he slept his daughters had sex with him without his knowledge and became pregnant, one on the first night and the other on the second.

Genesis 19:30 – 36

> Lot went and dwelt in the mountain with his two daughters… The firstborn said to the younger, our father is old and there is no other man in the earth to have sex with: Come, let us make our father drink wine, and we will lie with him, that we may preserve the seed of our father. They made their father drink wine that night: and the older daughter went in and lay with her father; and he did not know when she laid down, or when she got up.

It came to pass the next day, that the older daughter said to the younger, behold, last night I laid [had sex] with my father: let us make him drink wine this night also; and you go in, and lie with him, that we may preserve the seed of our father. They made their father drink wine that night also: then the younger daughter lay with him; and he did not know when she laid down, or when she got up. Therefore, both the daughters of Lot were with child by their father.

The writer(s) completely exonerated Lot, but, blamed his daughters, in essence by saying; they plotted, manipulated, and sexually abused their own father without his knowledge. In telling this story as to why it happened you are given two different reasons: The first reason was, "there is no other man in the earth to have sex with," which meant they wanted children and there were no other men available. The second reason was, the daughters wanted to preserve their father's seed because he had no male heirs. Both reasons given make it appear as though Lot's daughters were desperate to fulfill a duty to have a child, even to the point of sexually assaulting their own father. Both of Lot's daughters had sons, Moab and Ammon.

In the NT the apostle Peter wrote about Lot as though he was a victim and knew him personally.

2 Peter 2:6 – 9

Turning the cities of Sodom and Gomorrah into ashes condemned them, making them an example to those that live ungodly; and delivered just Lot, vexed with the filthy conversation of the wicked: (For that righteous man living among them, vexed his righteous soul from day to day with their unlawful deeds). The Lord knows how to deliver the godly out of temptations, and to reserve the unjust unto the Day of Judgment to be punished.

This is the same Lot who offered up both his married daughter who were virgins to be gang-raped by all the men of the city of Sodom to protect two male strangers. Lot had no concern for the sanctity of his daughter's marriages, which many believe the Bible teaches.

1 Peter 3:1 – 7

> Likewise, wives, be in subjection to your own husbands; if any obey not the word, he may be won over by the conversation of their wives…
>
> The wives adornment; let it not be an outward adorning of plaiting the hair, wearing of gold, or putting on of apparel, but let it be the hidden man of the heart, which is not corruptible, the ornament of a meek and quiet spirit, in the sight of God is a great price.
>
> In the past holy women who trusted in God, adorned themselves, being in subjection to their own husbands: Even as Sara obeyed Abraham, calling him lord…. Likewise, husbands, dwell with them according to knowledge, giving honor to the wife, as unto the weaker vessel, and as being heirs together of the grace of life; that your prayers be not hindered.

Peter believed that a husband should have dominion over his wife, the same as Paul. Now notice, Peter made no mention of Lot's daughters or his treatment toward them while in Sodom, nor him impregnating both of them, even though, the law tells us if a man has sexual relations with his daughter-in-law, they would both be worthy of death.

Leviticus 20:12

> If a man lie with his daughter-in-law, both of them shall surely be put to death: they have worked confusion; their blood shall be upon them.

An incestuous relationship between close family members were identified in chapter 18:6 – 18 and part of 20, and forbidden in many aspects. For example:

Leviticus 18:6 – 10

> You shall not approach anyone that is near of kin to him, to uncover

their nakedness: I am the LORD. (7)The nakedness of your father, or the nakedness of your mother, shall you not uncover: she is your mother; you shall not uncover her nakedness. (8)The nakedness of your father's wife shall you not uncover: it is your father's nakedness. (9)The nakedness of your sister, the daughter of your father, or daughter of your mother, whether she be born at home, or born abroad, even their nakedness you shall not uncover. (10)The nakedness of your son's daughter, or of your daughter's daughter, even their nakedness you shall not uncover...

(Note: In Leviticus uncovering the nakedness of another is considered a sexual relationship in the NIV Bible (Leviticus 18:6–18)).

Naked: The phrase "to uncover the nakedness of"
means to have sexual intercourse
–HBD

What is being said in Leviticus 18:7-10, is from a male perspective, because the Bible was written to and for men, which means that a man should not have sexual relations with his father or mother; his father's wife (remember: men had more than one wife); his sister; his grand-daughter, and so forth. Nowhere in Leviticus, chapters 18 or 20, does it say that a man should not have sexual relations with *his* daughter(s).

Therefore, in telling the story of a sexual interaction between a father and his virgin daughters without disdain, consequences, or punishment: Is the Bible supporting incest, a man's right to have sexual relations with his own daughter(s)?

Bathsheba

King David committed adultery with Bathsheba, a married woman, and she became pregnant as a result. When David found out that Bathsheba was pregnant he plotted to send her husband, Uriah, who was a soldier in his army, home from the field in hope that he would have sex with his wife in order to disguise the fact that she was pregnant by anyone other than her own husband. However, as the story goes, Uriah would not go home and have sex with his wife after two different attempts by King David.

2 Samuel 11:6 - 13

> David sent to Joab [captian of his army], saying, send me Uriah the Hittite. When Uriah arrived, David made small talk with him concerning Joab, the people, and the war. Then David said to Uriah, go down to your house, and wash your feet. Uriah departed out of the king's house, and sent with him plenty of meat from the king. But Uriah slept at the door of the king's house with all the other servants, and did not go to his house.

> When they had told David, saying, Uriah did not go to his house, David said to Uriah, why didn't you go home? Uriah replied, the ark, Israel, and Judah, live in tents; and my captain Joab and his men, are encamped in the open fields; shall I then go home, to eat and drink, and to lie with my wife? As you live, and as my soul live, I will not go home. David said to Uriah, stay here today and tomorrow I will let you leave. So Uriah stayed in Jerusalem that day, and the next day. When David had called him, he did eat and drink with him; and he became drunk: in the evening he went out to lie on his bed with the servants, but did not go home.

2 Samuel 11:14 – 21, 26 – 27

> David wrote a letter to Joab, and sent it by the hand of Uriah. In the letter, he said, set Uriah in the forefront of the hottest battle, and retire from him that he may be wounded, and die.

When Joab observed the city that he assigned Uriah to, was a place where he knew that valiant men were… and Uriah the Hittite was killed.

Then Joab sent and told David all the things concerning the war; and charged the messenger, saying, when you have finished telling the matters of the war unto the king... then say your servant Uriah the Hittite is dead.

When Bathsheba heard that her husband was dead, she mourned for him and when the mourning was past, David sent and fetched her to his house, and she became his wife, and she gave birth to a son. But the thing that David had done displeased the LORD.

Therefore, King David's attempt at fixing his own problem failed, killing Uriah and marring Bathsheba was for his own protection, because the law of adultery says that a man should not have sex with a married woman and if he does, both of them should be put to death.

In David's case the Lord did not kill or physically punish him in any way. However, when it came to Bathsheba, the Lord not only physically punished her by making her first give birth, but punished her again along with her son by making the newborn sick for seven days, then killing him.

In addition to Bathsheba, the Lord punished all David's wives, by having them publicly sexually assaulted in broad daylight, while David watched.

2 Samuel 12:9 - 23

> You have despised the commandment of the LORD, to do evil in his sight? You have killed Uriah the Hittite with the sword of the children of Ammon [Lot's descendants], and have taken Uriah's wife to be yours. Now the sword shall never depart from your house…. The LORD said, behold, I will raise up evil against you out of your own house, and I will take your wives before your eyes, and give them to your neighbor, and he shall lie with your wives in sun. For you did it secretly: but I will do this thing before all of Israel, and before the sun.

David said to Nathan [the prophet], I have sinned against the LORD. Nathan replied the LORD has put away your sin; you shall not die. Howbeit, because of your deed you have given great occasion to the enemies of the LORD to blaspheme, and the child that is born to you shall surely die....

The LORD struck the child that Uriah's wife had with David, and it was very sick. David begged God for the child; and David fasted, and went in, and lay all night upon the earth... and ate nothing. Then on the seventh day the child died.

It is commonly taught that the baby Bathsheba had would have been Uriah's child, because she was his wife and conceived the child while they were married. Therefore, the Lord removed all David's sin including the child that would have served as a reminder of his transgression: the killing of Uriah.

More importantly, why tell this story at all, of sanctioning the rape of women; and the torture and killing of an infant? One would think that most people would be against the rape of another regardless of rather it is a man, women, or child. Even, for those who are against the abortion of a fetus, would concede that bringing a child into the world, then torturing and killing him or her, is far worse!

Mariam

Mariam's story details the unfairness of how a woman is treated and punished compared to a man, for doing the exact same thing. The story of Mariam begins with her and her brother Aaron speaking disparagingly against Moses their oldest brother for marrying an Ethiopian woman.

1 Chronicles 6:3

>   The children of Amram; Aaron, and Moses, and Miriam.

As the story goes the Lord heard both Aaron and Mariam speaking against Moses, but punished only Mariam with leprosy for seven days.

Numbers 12:1 – 15

>   Miriam and Aaron spoke against Moses because of the Ethiopian woman whom he had married: for he had married an Ethiopian woman. They said, has the LORD indeed spoken only by Moses? Has he not spoken also by us? The LORD heard it. (Now Moses was very meek, above all the men which were upon the face of the earth.)
>
>   Then the LORD spoke suddenly to Moses, Aaron, and Miriam, come out to the tabernacle of the congregation, and they came out. The LORD came down in the pillar of the cloud, and stood in the door of the tabernacle, and called Aaron and Miriam: and they both step forward. He said hear now my words: If there be a prophet among you, I the LORD will make myself known to him in a vision, and will speak to him in a dream. My servant Moses not so, who is faithful in my house. With him will I speak mouth to mouth… Therefore why were you not afraid to speak against my servant Moses? The anger of the LORD was kindled against them; and he departed.
>
>   Then the cloud departed from off the tabernacle; and, behold, Miriam became leprous, white as snow: and Aaron looked upon Miriam, and she was leprous. Aaron said to Moses, My lord, I beg

you, forgive us, we have done foolishly, and have sinned.... Moses cried to the LORD, saying, heal her now, O God, I beg you. Then the LORD said to Moses, if her father had spit in her face, would she not be shamed seven days? Let her be shut out from the camp seven days, and after that let her be received in again.

The scriptures clearly state that "the anger of the LORD was kindled against *them*," yet nothing happened to Aaron, a priest, and a man of authority, even after he acknowledged that he and Mariam had both sinned. Now, Mariam, on the other hand, was shamed as well as physically punished with Leprosy for doing the exact same thing as her brother.

What can one learn from these four stories other than women are to be blamed regardless of what they do or do not do; and should not be in control of their own image or body. Telling these stories over and over again is corruption, because it diminishes woman and girl in the eyes of many who believe that the Bible is the Word of God. This is the same corruption you find within both fables 'Sodom and Gomorrah,' and 'The Concubine' that women are property, non-consequential beings, and should be treated lesser than an animal, if necessary. Therefore, based on actual scriptures one may surmise the Bible to be anti-woman.

17

The Children of Israel

The writer(s) of both fables, 'Sodom and Gomorrah' and 'The Concubine,' demonstrated that the Lord, is not who he says he is.

It is the characters in both stories that stand out. In the story of Sodom and Gomorrah you learned that Lot was Abraham's nephew; however, no information was given about his wife or two daughters.

In the story, The Concubine, the writer(s) identified the characters; by labeling the man as a Levite and saying that the woman was from Bethlehem Judah. The writer(s) made the story about the children of Israel, the Lord's chosen people the descendants **Abraham, Isaac, and Jacob**. If the Lord is who he says he is, then, why would he say early on in Exodus 29:45 "I will dwell among the children of Israel, and will be their God," and, in their time of need, do nothing?

The Name Israel

The biblical name "Israel" means different things to many people. To some, the name Israel is the name the Lord gave to Jacob in the Bible as a blessing. To others, the name Israel represented the Lord's chosen people. Many believe the name Israel in the Bible is the same as the State of Israel in the Middle East. This is not the case, because the State of Israel did not become a nation until May 14, 1948, whereas the KJV Bible was said be printed in 1611. To be clear, they are not the same!

Biblically, there is a major dilemma concerning the name Israel, which theologians and historians have ignored. The Bible gives two different accounts as to how the name Israel came to be. When you analyze both accounts of Jacob's name being changed to Israel, one thing is clear: both cannot be true; however, together they reveal a hidden mystery in the Bible, concerning Abraham, the covenant, and land.

The First Account

Genesis 32:22–30

> Jacob rose up that night, and took his two wives, two women servants, and his eleven sons and sent them and all that he had over the brook. Jacob was left alone; and there a man wrestled with him until the breaking of the day. When the man saw that he was losing against Jacob, he touched the hollow of his thigh; and it was out of joint, as he continued to wrestle with him.
>
> The man said let me go, for it is daybreak. Jacob said I will not let you go, except you bless me. The man said to him: What is your name? He replied, Jacob. Then the man said your name shall no longer be called Jacob, but Israel: for as a prince you have power with God and with men, and have prevailed…. At sunset he halted upon his thigh. Therefore <u>the children of Israel</u> do not eat the tendons in the hollow of the thigh, to this day.

This account seemed to have been dropped in the middle of the story of Jacob leaving his father-in-law and returning home and meeting up with his brother Esau. Two things standout in the above account, the first thing is: Jacob had eleven (11) sons when his name was changed to Israel; and secondly, because Jacob's name was changed to Israel, the title given to his son was: the children of Israel; other than these two bits of information, this narrative still defies common sense.

The Second Account

Genesis 35:9 - 12

> God appeared before Jacob again, and blessed him. God said to him, your name shall no longer be called Jacob, but Israel shall be your name: and he called his name Israel.

> God said to him, I am God Almighty: be fruitful and multiply; <u>a nation and a company of nations</u> shall you become, and kings shall come out of your loins; and the land which I gave Abraham and Isaac, to you will I give it, and to your seed after you.

Now, what stands out in this account of Jacob name being changed to Israel is the phrase, "<u>a nation and a company of nations </u>shall you become." When you separate them, they mean two different things: a nation; and a company of nations.

The words "a nation" refers only to Jacob. According to the scriptures, Abraham's son Isaac and his wife Rebekah had twins, Jacob and Esau, who were referred to as two separate nations. Therefore, the Lord saw Jacob as "a nation."

Genesis 25:23

> The LORD said to Rebekah, two nations are in your womb…

The words, "a company of nations" would then represent Jacob's descendants, his sons, who were to become many nations, based on the covenant the Lord made previously with Abraham (Abram).

The Covenant

Genesis 17: 1 – 11

> When Abram was 99 years old, the LORD appeared to him, and said I am the Almighty God; walk before me, and be perfect. I will make my covenant between me and you, and will multiply thee exceedingly.... Your name shall no longer be called Abram, but, Abraham. A father of many nations have I made you and I will make you exceeding fruitful, and I will make nations of you, and kings shall come out of you.
>
> And I will establish my covenant with you and your seed after you in their generations for an everlasting covenant, to be a God to you, and to your seed after you.
>
> And I will give to you and to your seed after you, the land of Canaan, for an everlasting possession; and I will be their God. This is my covenant, which you shall keep, between me and you and your seed after you; every male among you shall be circumcised. You shall also circumcise the flesh of your foreskin; and it shall be a token of the covenant between me and you.

Notice, in Genesis 17:1 – 11, the 'LORD' appeared before Abram and referred to himself as an 'Almighty God' as a seductive lure followed by his many promises. The covenant the Lord made with Abram was to become his God and the God of his descendants, this would include Jacob and all his sons; in return the Lord agreed to give Abram and his descendants the land of Canaan, forever. In other words, the Lord made a land deal with Abraham and his descendants to become their God. It would appear that the now 'God' of Abram changed his name to Abraham to reflect the covenant that was made.

Now notice, in Genesis 35:9 – 12, the LORD appeared before Jacob, as his 'God,' and again referred to himself as an 'Almighty God' and reiterated pretty much the same things the LORD said to Abraham; including changing Jacob's name to Israel to reflex that a covenant had taken place.

The problem with both accounts is the name change itself. After Abram's name was changed to Abraham he was no longer referred to as Abram. This is not the case with Jacob. In Exodus 3:6, the Lord said to Moses, "I am the God of thy father, the God of Abraham, the God of Isaac, and the God of Jacob." It is this same Jacob, whose name was changed to Israel, back in Genesis twice. So why didn't the Lord say to Moses, "I am the God of thy father, the God of Abraham, the God of Isaac, and the God of Israel?" Did the Lord, forget his covenant and that he had changed Jacob's name to Israel?

In the NT, Jesus, said to be the Son of God, did not refer to Jacob as Israel.

Matthews 8:11

I say to you, that many shall come from the east and west, and sit down with Abraham, Isaac, and Jacob, in the kingdom of heaven.

As a result, it would appear that the Lord did not change Jacob's name to Israel, per se, based on two facts:

1. The scriptures did not always refer to Jacob as Israel.
2. There are two different accounts of how the name Israel came to be.

If you set aside Jacob's name being changed to Israel, what you learn is that both accounts focus on the descendants of Jacob, his sons. In the first account Jacob's eleven sons were called, the children of Israel. Then in the second account, 'God' said to Jacob "a nation and a company of nations shall you become, and kings shall come out of your loins" meaning his sons. Now the question is: Who are the children of Israel and how would they become a company of nations?

18

The Lord's Army

The commandments were the pillars for the Lord's chosen people to live by, which says:

Exodus 20:12 – 17

> Honor your father and your mother: that your days may be long upon the land which the LORD thy God will give you.

> You shall not kill

> You shall not commit adultery

> You shall not steal

> You shall not bear false witness

> You shall not covet: property

> You shall not covet: Lust

The most important commandment throughout the entire Bible is: You Shall Not Covet. It is because of this commandment that the Lord's army came to light. Every story in the Bible is there for reason, however, not for the reasons that are commonly preached to the masses on a daily basis. Many of the OT stories are multifaceted, when you begin to remove the fantastical layers in many of the stories, such as, Noah, Joseph, and Moses the scriptures reveal a playbook of destruction: Why the Lord needed an army? How the Lord's army came to be? What was the purpose for the Lord's army?

The Story of Noah

The story of Noah that is commonly preached from the pulpit, is an exaggerated fable about a 500 year old man named Noah whom the Lord had chosen to build a boat (called an ark), to save himself and his family (a total of eight souls); and every animal species of the world, to repopulate the earth, after the Lord destroyed it with a flood, by making it rain 40 days and 40 nights, because he deemed the entire earth to be corrupt.

About Canaan

Noah had three sons: Shem, Ham, and Japheth. Abraham, Isaac, and Jacob were descendants of Shem. Canaan was Noah's grandson, whom he cursed, because his father, Ham, looked upon Noah's naked body while he slept in his tent, drunk from the wine of his own vineyard. It is believed that the reason why Noah could not curse his own son, Ham, who violated him with his eyes, was because God had blessed Noah and his three sons upon leaving the ark (Genesis 9:1), therefore, Noah cursed Ham's son Canaan. Why Canaan? Ham had several sons, why Noah chose to curse Canaan to be a slave is not clear, but what is clear from the scriptures, is that Canaan did nothing wrong.

Genesis 9:20 – 27

> Noah planted a vineyard and became drunk from the wine and fell asleep uncovered in his tent. Ham, the father of Canaan, saw his father's naked body, and told his two brother. Shem and Japheth took a garment, and laid it upon both their shoulders, and walked backwards and covered their father's naked body.
> Noah awoke from his wine and knew what Ham had done to him and cursed his son. Noah said, cursed be Canaan; a servant of servants shall he be to his brothers. He said, blessed be the LORD God of Shem; and Canaan shall be his servant. God shall enlarge Japheth, and he shall dwell in the tents of Shem; and Canaan shall be his servant.

Genesis 10:6, 15

The sons of Ham were; Cush, Mizraim, Phut, and Canaan….

Canaan sons were; Sidon his firstborn, Heth, the Jebusite, Amorite, Girgasite, Hivite, Arkite, Sinite, Arvadite, Zemarite, and the Hamathite: were the beginning of the Canaanites.

The writer(s) of Genesis never stated why anyone was against Canaan, that the land belonging to him and his descendants were to be taken away and given to Abraham and his descendants (with his wife Sarah), prior to the Lord's covenant with him. Was it to honor Noah's curse? If you look at Canaan from the standpoint that every good story needs a villain, then telling the story about Ham's descendants, mainly Canaan, as slaves was the writer(s) way of identifying an adversary.

Now the question is: When the Lord made his covenant with Abraham to give him and his descendants the land of Canaan and he would be their God, Abraham was only the tenth generation from Noah and the flood, in other words, the earth would have been uninhabited, so, why would Abraham sell his birthright and the birthright of his descendants for land that belonged to someone else when the whole earth was sparsely populated and land was plenteous?

The Making of an Army

Before the Lord changed Abram's name to Abraham the scriptures foretold of the cost that would come upon Abraham's descendants in order for them to receive the Promised Land: the land of Canaan, which was four hundred years of slavery in Egypt.

Genesis 15:7–8, 13–14

> I am the LORD that brought you out of Ur, from among the Chaldeans, to give you this land as an inheritance. Then Abram said Lord GOD, how will I know that I shall inherit it? …The Lord replied know for sure that your seed shall be a stranger in a land that is not theirs, and they shall enslave them for four hundred years; and that nation, whom they shall serve, I will judge: and afterward they shall come out with lots of material possessions.

The stories of Joseph and Moses, they are not random fables all by themselves; they have meaning and a purpose as to why they were included in the Bible. These two fables tell the story of how the Lord created an army out of Abraham's descendants, in essence, slaves, in order to fulfill the Covenant that he supposedly made with Abraham, to give his descendants the land of Canaan.

The story of Joseph

The story of Joseph is a very interesting one, which details how the children of Israel, were enslaved in Egypt (Genesis 37 – Genesis 50:26).

Joseph was Jacob's favorite son, born to his second wife Rachel, who he loved more than the others, she died after giving birth to her second son, Benjamin, in the city of Bethlehem, in the land of Canaan (Genesis 35:16 – 19). Now, at this point, Jacob had twelve sons.

Joseph's older brothers despised him because their father's favor toward him. When Joseph was seventeen year old, his brothers plotted to get rid of him and sold him to the Midianites, then, the Midianites sold Joseph to a wealthy Egyptian who enslaved him in Egypt.

From this point on, the story of Joseph chronicles his many highs and lows until, his ultimate triumph to become the Pharaoh's second in command of all the land of Egypt; after he alone was able to interpret the Pharaoh's reoccurring dream, which foretold that Egypt would have seven years of prosperity in which they were to store up food for the seven years of famine that was sure to follow.

It was during the seven years of famine that Joseph reunited with his brothers who sold him. They initially came to Egypt in search of food, because the famine had spread throughout the region and Egypt had more than enough….

As the story goes, the God of Abraham spoke to Jacob in a vision and enticed him to go to Egypt because of the famine, saying "I will go down with you."

Genesis 46:2 – 7, 26

> God spoke to Israel in a vision and said, Jacob, Jacob and he replied, here I am; and a voice said, I am God, the God of your father: fear not to go down into Egypt; for I will make you a great nation: I will go down with you into Egypt; and I will also surely bring you out. Jacob and his sons along with their wives and children took their cattle, and all their goods, which they had gotten in the land of Canaan, and went into Egypt… There were a total of 66 people that came with Jacob into Egypt, which came out of his loins, besides his sons.

Genesis 48:3 – 5

> Jacob said to Joseph, God Almighty appeared unto me in the land of Canaan, and blessed me and said to me, I will make you fruitful and to multiply, and I will make of thee a multitude of people; and will give   this land to your seed after you for an everlasting possession.

Now your two sons, Ephraim and Manasseh, which were born to you in the land of Egypt, before I came here, are mine; as Reuben and Simeon, they shall be mine.

As a result, Joseph was to receive a double portion (in the land of Canaan), over his other brothers, because Jacob had in essence adopted Ephraim and Manasseh, as his own, in place of Joseph; and Jacob and his now thirteen sons and their descendants, prospered in Egypt.

Exodus 1:6 –14

Joseph and all his brothers of that generation died, and their descendants: the children of Israel were fruitful, strong, and the land was filled with them.

Over time there came a new king in Egypt, which knew not Joseph. He said to the Egyptians, behold, the children of Israel are more and mightier than us: Come, let us deal wisely with them; lest they multiply even more, and when there is war, they join our enemies, and fight against us…

Therefore they set taskmasters over the children of Israel to cause them anguish, but the more they troubled them, the more they multiplied and grew. The Egyptians made the children of Israel to live under strict rules and made their lives bitter with hard bondage: with very little to no wages, in brick and mortar, and in all manner of service in the field.

Therefore, Jacob's thirteen sons became the 'children of Israel,' who were enslaved in Egypt, living under what would be considered today as Jim Crow laws.

Moses and Aaron

The book of Exodus chronicles the children of Israel's exit from Egypt after a little over 400 years of enslavement.

Exodus 3:7 – 8

> The LORD said, I have surely seen the affliction of my people which *are* in Egypt, and have heard their cry by reason of their taskmasters; for I know their sorrows; I will deliver them out of the hand of the Egyptians, and bring them up out of that land into a good and large land, flowing with milk and honey….

Moses and Aaron were sent to the house of Pharaoh, to relay the Lord's message, "let my people go" with great fanfare: visiting plague after plague upon the Egyptians, to torture them, all the while, *not* wanting the people to be let go, to bring attention to the Lord might; the same Lord who allowed the descendants of Jacob to be in slavery for over four hundred years, in the first place.

Exodus 6:26

> It was Aaron and Moses, to whom the LORD said, Bring out the children of Israel from the land of Egypt according to their armies….

In order for the children of Israel to become a nation or a community of nations they would need their own land. When they were freed from slavery in Egypt, they wandered through the wilderness, because they had no land of their own. The covenant the Lord made with Abraham and his descendants: the children of Israel (also known as, the twelve tribes of Israel), was to give them the land of Canaan, also known as the Promised Land, to become nations. Now the question is: How would the children of Israel come to possess the land the Lord promised them?

After wandering in the desert the Lord established his army within twelve of the tribes of Israel with assigned captains to lead them into war, in addition to tribe of Levi, also known as, the priestly tribe.

Numbers 1:1–4, 45–46

> The LORD spoke to Moses early in the second year after they came out of the land of Egypt, saying, take a count of all the tribes of Israel, include the names of every male from twenty years old and upward, who are able to go to war in Israel: you and Aaron shall number them by their armies. With you there shall be a man of every tribe; everyone of them the head of his house.
>
> All those that were numbered of the children of Israel, from twenty years old and upward, that were able to go to war in Israel were 603,550.

Therefore, setting aside the Levites (the thirteenth tribe): which contains the priesthood; eligible males twenty years and older among the twelve tribes of Israel, represented the Lord's army.

The Plan

The book of Numbers not only established the Lord's army, it also outlined two specific purposes as to why an army was needed. The first was to covet all the land that belonged to Canaan and his descendants initially. The second purpose revealed an even darker side of the Lord's plan for his army, which was based on race, religion, and pure greed.

Coveting the Land of Canaan

When the Lord initially established his covenant with Abraham he said, "I will *give* to you and to your seed after you, the land wherein you are a stranger, all the land of Canaan, for an everlasting possession; and I will be their God." Again, the Lord said repeatedly in the books of Genesis, Exodus, and Leviticus that *he* alone would give the land that was flowing with milk and honey, the land of Canaan, also known as the Promised Land to the descendants of Abraham. For example:

Exodus 13:5

> The LORD shall bring you into the land of the Canaanites, Hittites, Amorites, Hivites, and the Jebusites, which he swore unto their fathers to give them, a land flowing with milk and honey…

And,

Leviticus 20:24

> I have said unto you, you shall inherit their land, and I will give it to you to possess it, a land that flows with milk and honey: I am the LORD your God, which has separated you from other people.

The Spies

It is clear from the scriptures that the Lord knew nothing about the Promised Land he said he would give to the descendants of Abraham, because he ordered Moses to send in spies, one man from each of the twelve tribes of Israel, to determine if the land was worth coveting and to report back specifics concerning the land and the people.

Numbers 13:1 – 3

> The LORD spoke to Moses, saying, send a man from every tribe to search the land of Canaan, which I give to the children of Israel. Moses by the commandment of the LORD sent men from the wilderness....

The Reconnaissance

Numbers 13:17 – 24

> Moses sent them to spy out the land of Canaan, and said to them go southward, and go up into the mountain and see what the land is like; Are the people strong or weak, few or many? What kind of land do they live in: Is it good or bad? What kind of cities do they live in? Do they live in tents, or in houses? Is the land fat or lean? Are there trees or not? Be of good courage, and bring back the fruit of the land.

> So they went up, and searched the land from the wilderness…and they ascended toward the south… They came to the brook of Eshcol, and cut down a branch with one cluster of grapes, and they carried it between them upon a staff; and they took of the pomegranates, and of the figs.

The Report

Numbers 13:25 – 33

They returned from searching the land after forty days. They came to Moses, and Aaron, and to all thirteen tribes of Israel in the wilderness and brought back word unto them saying, we came from the land where you sent us, and surely it flows with milk and honey; and this is the fruit of it. Nevertheless, the people were strong that live in the land and the cities are walled, and very great: The child-Ren of Anak live in the south; The Hittites, Jebusites, and Amorites, live in the mountains; and the Canaanites live by the sea, and by the coast of Jordan. Then Caleb quieted the people before Moses, and said, let us go up at once, and possess it; for we are well able to take the land. The men that went up with Caleb said, we are not able to go up against them; they are stronger than us and gave an evil report of the land which they had searched to the children of Israel, saying, the land, we searched is a land that eats up the inhabitants thereof; and all the people that we saw in it are men of a great stature. There we saw the giants, the sons of Anak… and we were in our own eyes as grasshoppers, and so were we in their eyes also.

The Fear

The children of Israel were initially in fear of coveting the land of Canaan, based on the negative report. This report angered the Lord, because his army feared the descendants of Canaan (who were living in their own land), so much so, that they were willing to return to Egypt. Nevertheless, the Lord's anger continued against the children of Israel for forty years (the sole reason why they remained in the wilderness), until that generation had died, because they refused to covet the land which belonged to Canaan and his descendants, and for speaking out against the Lord for not honoring the Covenant he supposedly made with Abraham and with them, to 'give' them the Promised Land which flowed with milk and honey as an everlasting possession.

Numbers 14:22 – 34

> Those men which had seen my glory, and my miracles, which I did in Egypt and in the wilderness, have tempted me ten times, and have not listened to me; surely they shall not see the land which I swore to their fathers, neither shall any of them that provoked me see it: except my servant Caleb, because he had another spirit within him, and has followed me fully, him will I bring into the land of Canaan; and his seed shall possess it...
>
> The LORD spoke to Moses and Aaron, saying: How long shall I bear with this evil congregation, which speak against me? Say to them, as truly as I live, said the LORD, as you have spoken against me, so will I do to you; everyone of you, from twenty years old and upward, which have spoken against me. You shall not come into the land, which I swore to you, except Caleb and Joshua the son of Nun. Your little ones, will I bring in and they shall know the land which you have despised. As for this generation, your children shall wander in the wilderness forty years, one year for every day they spied out the land, so that you shall know my breach of promise.

The Lord was a liar! Now, the question is: Why did the Lord blamed and punished the children of Israel continuously for his own breach of the covenant he made with Abraham? If the Lord is who he says he is and who many believe him to be, their God, then why did he not honor the covenant he made with Abraham and give his descendants the Promised Land? According to the scriptures, when Abraham supposedly made the covenant with the Lord, he honored it the same day.

Genesis 17:23 – 24

> Abraham took Ishmael his son, and everyone born in his house or bought with his money, and circumcised the flesh of their foreskin the same day, God had spoke with him. Abraham was 99 years old, when he was circumcised.

Many of the children of Israel were put to death for challenging and complaining to and about Moses, Aaron, and the Lord, himself, for taking them from Egypt, a land which flowed with milk and honey, into the desert and not giving them the land that the Lord had promised. For example in chapter 16, when a group of 250 men led by a Levite named Korah spoke out saying:

Numbers 16:13 – 14, 31 - 34

> Is it a small thing that you have brought us from a land that flows with milk and honey, to kill us in the wilderness, and then make yourself a ruler over us? Moreover you have not brought us into a land that flows with milk and honey, or given us inheritance of fields and vineyards…
>
> When Korah had finished speaking, the ground caved in under them and the earth opened up and swallowed them all, and they perished from among the congregation, and all of people that were around them fled.

To control his army, the Lord lied, blamed others, and spread fear among the remaining children of Israel, so much so, that they acknowledged that they were sinners and were willing to do anything to curry favor with the Lord, even going to war against the Canaanites.

The many wars of the Lord

The first conflict recorded among the children of Israel (who were now being referred to as just Israel) came about when a Canaanite King heard that the children of Israel had sent spies into their land, so he went after them and arrested them. Now the question is: How would the Canaanites know that spies came into their land, unless someone told them? It would appear that the Lord used deceptive tactics in order to instigate a conflict between the children of Israel (who were meek) and the Canaanites.

Numbers 21:1 – 3

> When king Arad the Canaanite, which lived in the south, heard that Israel sent spies into their land; they fought against Israel, and took some of them prisoners. Israel vowed a vow to the LORD, and said: if you will indeed deliver these Canaanites into our hands, then we will utterly destroy their cities. The LORD listened to the voice of Israel, and delivered up the Canaanites…

According to the scriptures, the children of Israel strategically moved throughout the desert provoking, killing, and taking the land of the Canaanites under the guide of Moses until his death, then, the Lord appointed Joshua as taskmaster to continue coveting the land of Canaan and other lands.

The book of Joshua (chapter 12:1–13:14) chronicles all the land that was coveted during both Joshua and Moses' reign as taskmasters over the children of Israel and what lands was yet to be coveted.

Moses coveted two kingdoms with Aaron (the high priest) and the Lord's army; and all of the spoils were divided up among 2 ½ tribes

Joshua coveted thirty one kingdoms with Eleazer the new high priest (after the death of his father Aaron) and the Lord's army; and all the spoils taken with Joshua were divided up among the remaining 9 ½ tribes.

Joshua 12:7 – 10, 24

> These are the kingdoms which Joshua and the children of Israel coveted on the west side of the Jordan from the Hittites, Amorites, Canaanites, Perizzites, Hivites, and the Jebusites: Jericho... and Jerusalem... thirty one kings in all.

The only lands coveted from the descendants of Canaan by Moses and Joshua that stands out today were Jericho and Jerusalem, many of the others names, for the most part, appear to be placeholders.

Jericho was given to the tribe of Benjamin, according to Joshua 18:21, the same tribe Paul claimed as his own, in the NT; and Jerusalem, was listed among the land given to the tribe of Judah, according to Joshua 15:1 – 12; which is the same tribe belonging to Jesus.

Jericho: Town in the West Bank, in the Jordan Valley;
It is regarded as the world's oldest town…
–EWED

Jerusalem: Historic city lying at the intersection of Israel
and the West Bank; The whole of the city is claimed by Israel
as its capital, but this is disputed internationally.
–EWED

Jerusalem is mentioned in the Bible 811 times in 764 versus, more than any other actual city, state, country that exist today including Israel (excluding titles, people, and references to fictitious land: such as, the land of Israel), Egypt, Syria, Lebanon, and Jordon.

Land to be Coveted

Joshua 13:1 – 2

> The LORD said to Joshua, you are old and stricken in years, and there remains much land to be coveted. This is the land which remains: all the borders of the Philistines, and Geshuri…

The land that was yet to be coveted did not belong to Canaan or his descendants, but his brother Mizraim whose descendants were the Philistines.

Genesis 10:6

> The sons of Ham; Cush, **Mizraim**, Phut, and Canaan.

1 Chronicles 1:11 – 12

> Mizraim begat Ludim, Anamim, Lehabim, Naphtuhim, Pathrusim, Casluhim, **(of whom came the Philistines)** and Caphthorim.

The name Philistine is commonly referred to as Palestine.

> **Palestine:** Particularly land west of Jordan River God allotted to Israel for an inheritance (Josh. 13-19)…. Palestine is derived from the name Pelishtim or "Philistines."
> *–HBD*

It was David who fought both the Philistines (which made him the great warrior he was known for, because he killed Goliath, a giant, with a slingshot and cut off his head and brought it before King Saul); and the

Geshurites, in the land of Geshuri, who appear to be related to Canaan, because David coveted and killed them along with the Amalekites who were descendants of Canaan.

1 Samuel 27:8 – 9

> David and his men went up, and invaded the **Geshurites,** and the Gezrites, and the Amalekites: for those nations were of old inhabitants… David coveted the land, and left neither man nor woman alive, and took away the sheep, oxen, asses, camels, and the apparel, and returned…

Therefore, it would appear that the Lord was not just interested in coveting all the land of Canaan, his plan for the children of Israel was for them to covet all the land belonging to the descendants of Ham.

19

Race, Religion, and Pure Greed

The book of Numbers details the horrific story of the Midianites who were betrayed and killed at the hands of the Lord and Moses, based on race, religious beliefs, and pure greed.

About Moses

Moses was a Hebrew raised from a child under Egyptian rule. At this point in the story of Moses, the children of Israel were still enslaved in Egypt. (Here is a little more of Moses back story, which is necessary to understand his actions as they relate to his family and the Lord.)

Exodus 2:11 – 15

> When Moses was grown, he went out among his brethren, and looked on their burdens: he saw an Egyptian beating a Hebrew, one of his brethren, and when he was sure that no one was looking, he killed the Egyptian, and hid his body in the sand. When he went out the second day, and saw two Hebrew men fighting, Moses said to the one in the wrong: Why are you fighting your brother? He replied, who made you a prince and a judge over us? Will you kill me, like you killed the Egyptian? Moses became fearful that his crime was well known. Later when Pharaoh heard what Moses had done, he sought to kill him, but Moses fled Egypt and Pharaoh, and went to live in the land of Midian.

The Midianites were an established people with land of their own. Moses lived among the Midianites and married the daughter of the priest of Midian, Zipporah, and they had two sons.

Exodus 3:1 – 8, 4:10 –15, 18–20

Now Moses kept the flock of Jethro his father-in-law, the priest of Midian: he led the flock to the backside of the desert, and came to the mountain of God, Horeb. The angel of the LORD appeared unto Moses in a flame of fire out of the midst of a burning bush, and said, Moses, Moses. He replied, here I am. Then the Lord said I am the God of thy father, the God of Abraham, the God of Isaac, and the God of Jacob. I have surely seen the affliction of my people which are in Egypt… and I will send you to Pharaoh that you may bring the children of Israel out of Egypt.

Moses said to the LORD, I am not eloquent; I am slow of speech, and have a slow tongue. The LORD replied: "Who made man's mouth? Who make the deaf, dumb, the seeing, and the blind? I did." Now go, and I will be with you, and teach you what you shall say. Moses replied, O my Lord, send someone else. The LORD became angry with Moses, and said, let your brother Aaron speak for you; I know he can speak well and I will be there for both of you and to teach you what you shall say and do.

Moses went and returned to Jethro his father-in-law, and said to him, let me go, and return to my brethren which are in Egypt, and see whether they are alive. Jethro said to Moses, go in peace.

The LORD said to Moses in Midian, go, return to Egypt: for all the men are dead which sought your life. Moses took his wife and his sons, and set them upon an ass, and he returned to the land of Egypt to set the children of Israel free.

The Midianites

Now remember, when the children of Israel left Egypt they had no land of their own, so they remained in the desert or on land which belonged to other people or nations. While the children of Israel were in the land of Moab some of them begin to have sexual relations with the Moabites (descendants of Lot) and the Midianites; and worshipped the gods of Moab. Their actions were so egregious to the Lord, because some of the children of Israel did not segregate themselves from everyone else, the Lord had them brutally killed, based on nothing more than religious and moral grounds.

Numbers 25:1 – 8

> ...The children of Israel began to commit whoredom with the daughters of Moab. They invited them to the sacrifices of their gods: and they did eat, and bowed down to their gods: Baalpeor. The LORD was angry with them and said to Moses, cut off the heads of the people which joined in, so that the fierce anger of the LORD may be turned away from Israel. Moses said to the judges of Israel, slay everyone that joined in.

> Then behold, one of the children of Israel brought a Midianite woman among his brethren in the sight of Moses, and in the sight of all the congregation of the children of Israel... When Phinehas, the grandson of Aaron the priest, saw it, he rose up from among the congregation, and took a javelin and went after the man in his tent and thrust it through both of them; through the man and into the belly of the woman.

The Continuation of the Priesthood

The descendants of Levi were known as the Levites, the priestly tribe, and the thirteenth tribe. The Lord's servant Moses and his brother Aaron were Levites. The Lord chose Aaron and his sons to be priest over the land of Israel. The remaining Levites were not priests; nor could they become priests. They were given duties to assist the priest (Aaron and his sons) by maintaining the tabernacle (a portable tent use as a sanctuary to house the Ark of the covenant, which is said to contained the Ten Commandments written by the hand of God on two tablets of stone).

Numbers 3:6–9

> Bring the tribe of Levi near, and present them before Aaron the priest, that they may minister to him… give the Levites to Aaron and his sons: they are solely given to him out of the children of Israel.

The Sole Purpose of Tithing

According to the scriptures, tithing came about because of the Levites. In exchange for the work performed by the priest and the remaining Levites, they were to receive tithes from the other tribes of Israel as an inheritance from the Lord. Each of the tribes was to give a tenth of its first-fruits, such as grains, fruits, and spices to the Levites. In return, the Levites were to give a tenth of the best of all they received [the Lord's portion] and give it to the priest: Aaron and his sons.

Numbers 18:20-21, 28

> The LORD spoke to Aaron, you shall have no inheritance in the land of Israel, I am your inheritance among the children of Israel. And, behold, I have given the children of Levi all the tenth in Israel for an inheritance, for their service concerning the tabernacle of the congregation …
>
> [The Levites] shall offer a heave offering [10%] to the LORD of all your tithes, which you receive of the children of Israel; and you shall give the LORD'S heave offering to Aaron the priest.
>
> Originally the remaining Levites were to serve only the priest, Aaron and his sons, which meant, when Aaron and his sons died, the priesthood would end. There would be no priest to lead the children of Israel into war or carry the Ark of the Covenant from

place to place or from one war zone to another. Then, there would be no priest for the Levites to assist, no need to maintain the tabernacle, no need for tithing, and no forgiveness of sin following the death of Aaron's last living son, until, Phinehas. The killing of the Midianite woman and the Israelite man brought forth a change ofmind for the Lord.

Numbers 25:10 – 13

The LORD said to Moses, Phinehas [currently not a priest], has turned my wrath away from the children of Israel. Behold, I give to him my covenant of peace: he shall have it, and his seed after him, *even* the covenant of an everlasting priesthood; because he was zealous for his God, and made atonement for the children of Israel.

Originally, the offering for atonement was made with the blood of a sacrificed animal (a bullock or young bull).

Exodus 29:36

You [the priest] shall offer every day a bullock for a sin offering for atonement.

The killing of human beings as a sin offering for atonement was the basis for the continuation of the priesthood. Now, the priesthood would continue on through Phinehas and his descendants with no end.

The Lord's anger continued against the Midianites after the woman was killed by Aaron's grandson, Phinehas: now a priest. The Lord ordered Moses to again number his army from the age of twenty and up within all twelve tribes of Israel. The final count was 601,730 eligible men fit to go to war (less 1,820 from original count which included Korah and the 250 men who died because they spoke out against Aaron, Moses and the Lord).

Numbers 31:1 – 19

The LORD said to Moses, avenge the children of Israel of the Midianites: afterward you shall be gathered to your people. Moses spoke to the twelve tribes of Israel and said, arm yourselves for war; and go against the Midianites and avenge the LORD of Midian. Moses sent a total of twelve thousand men; one thousand from every tribe to war with Phinehas, the priest, leading the way against the Midianites. Together they killed all the males, including the five king of Midian. The children of Israel took all the women of Midian captive and their little ones and coveted all their cattle, flocks, and other goods. They burnt all their cities and brought the captives, to Moses, Eleazar the priest, and all thirteen tribes of Israel. Moses was angry with the officers: the captains over thousands, and hundreds, which came from the battle and said to them, have you saved all the women? Now, kill every male among the little ones, and kill every woman that is not a virgin. All the girls who are virgins keep them for yourselves.

Now, what appears to make the killing of the Midianites about racial identity is the story of Mariam. When you take another look at the story of Mariam, it appears to be just another story blaming and punishing the woman even though a man was caught doing the exact same thing. However, the story of Mariam, in actuality, is not so much about Mariam, but who Moses' wife was.

Numbers 12:1

Miriam and Aaron the priest spoke against Moses because he had married an Ethiopian woman.

Moses' wife was a Midianite, by labeling Zipporah as an Ethiopian changed the killing of the Midianites from just being about religion or forbidden sexual activity to their identity or race.

When the Lord said to Moses, "afterward you shall be gathered to your people" he meant the Levites; this phrase made it about identity or race, because Moses' two sons with his wife Zipporah (at this time she was already dead) would have been one half Midian or Ethiopian. What the Lord in essence was asking Moses to do was to choose between him and his sons; and Moses chose the Lord. Why?

The scriptures tell us that Moses was chosen and sent to lead the Lord army, not because he was strong, but because he was a man with no confidence (Exodus 4:10-14) and *very* meek (Numbers 12:3), in other words, one who would follow and obey.

Meek: 1. mild: showing mildness or quietness of nature
2. cowed: showing submissiveness and lack of initiative or will
–HBD

Therefore, when Moses followed the Lord's command and called for the ethnic cleansing of all the Midianites, which included his own flesh and blood, it demonstrated the Lord's dominance in the human hierarchy, that the Lord is above all men and should always be obeyed, even if it requires a father to kill his own sons.

The Great Divide

The Book of Numbers is truly a book about the numbers. Not only does it number the Lord's army of eligible males from the age of twenty and up, it also provides a breakdown of how the property coveted from the Midianites were to be divided among the children of Israel, priest, and the remaining Levites.

Numbers 31:25–54

The Lord ordered Moses and the priests [who are Levites] to divide everything that was coveted between the children of Israel that went to war [the Lord's army] and the remaining that did not. Everything the men of war had coveted was:

675,000 – Sheep
72,000 – Beeves (Oxen or Cows)
61,000 – Asses (Donkeys)
32,000 – Virgin girls

The priest, were to take their portion of 1/500 (one out of every five hundred) girls, beeves, asses, and sheep from the half of those that went to war as an offering from the Lord. Therefore, the Lord's portion went to the priest and the rest remained with the men that went to war [the Lord's army] against the Midianites. The half portion: for them that went out to war was:

337,500 – Sheep
36,000 – Beeves
30,500 – Asses
16,000 – Virgin girls

Therefore, the priest received the following portion [1/500]:

675 – Sheep
72 – Beeves
61 – Asses
32 – Virgin girls

The remaining Levites (who were not priest) would take their portion of 1/50 (one out of every fifty) girls, beeves, asses, and sheep from those that did not go to war against the Midianites; for maintaining the tabernacle of the Lord. Now the other half that pertained to those who did not go to war was:

> 337,500 – Sheep
> 36,000 – Beeves
> 30,500 – Asses
> 16,000 – Virgin girls

Therefore, the remaining Levites received the following portion from the children of Israel that did not go to war [1/50]:

> 6750 – Sheep
> 720 – Beeves
> 610 – Asses
> 320 – Virgin girls

In addition, Moses and the priest received additional gifts of gold as an offering to the Lord from the officers in charge of the men of war.

Again, many believe that the Lord in the Bible is their God and the words that were written in the scriptures by men were inspired by God, the creator of heaven and earth, for all people today to believe and live by. Now the questions are: Why slaughter *all* the males including children (little ones)? Why kill mothers and wives, which will result in a child becoming an orphan? What God calls for children to be orphaned or separated from their parents, or loved ones? Moreover, what are priest and men at war going to do with virgin girls (little ones)?

Now, should anyone believe or accept that others who do not share the same race or culture; worship the same god; and live as they do, are worthy to be killed and in every manner, coveted. What happen to the commandments?

If the Lord authored or believed in the Ten Commandments (mainly the last six), then why is it that the Lord told his army and his priest to do the exact opposite of what they say?

20

The Truth about Abraham

Before there was Jacob or the name Israel, there was Abraham, the one consistent and positive character within the entire Bible. Taking a closer look at Abraham's actions in the 'War of the Kings' a clearer picture of who Abraham was and what he represented comes to light.

In the 'War of the Kings,' Abraham (Abram) and 318 men went in pursuit of and subdued the four kings who coveted the five kings; among them was Sodom and Gomorrah. What should have stood out about Abraham is that he returned all the spoils of the war including all the people and took nothing, not even a "thread" or a "shoe latchet" for himself, so that no one would be able to say that Abraham became rich by doing the same thing, seizing, raping, and pillaging other kingdoms and nations (Genesis 14:21–23).

Abraham was living the commandments; the polar opposite of the so-called Lord. Abraham set an example of doing what was right before the Lord who he defined as the most high God, the possessor of heaven and earth: by showing love to his neighbors; and he refused to take any of the spoils of the war even when they were offered to him.

It was this same Abraham to whom the Lord supposedly promised to *give* the land of Canaan. Now the question is: Why would Abraham want the land of Canaan or that of his descendants? When you take an even closer look at the story 'War of the Kings,' the Amorites: Aner, Eshcol, and Mamre communities accompanied Abraham when he went to war against the four kings and took back all that was taken from the five kingdoms, including the people. The Amorites were descendents of Canaan and allies with Abraham (Genesis 14:13). Therefore, Abraham along with the descendants of Canaan saved all five kingdoms, which included Sodom and Gomorrah.

Now, if you think about it, Abraham could have had a total of nine kingdoms under his control. If Abraham did not want nor desire the kingdoms he had taken back that belonged to the five kings; or taken altogether what belonged to the original four kings, which he overpowered, then, why would Abraham take the land of his allies, the descendants of Canaan?

The Scripture say Abraham believed the Lord and it was accounted to him as righteousness, however, the scriptures also tell a different story. The covenant that the Lord made with Abraham and his descendants was to *give* them the land of Canaan as an everlasting possession; and the Lord would be their God. If, Abraham made this covenant with the Lord, then, why did he purchase land in Canaan, even though, the Hittites, descendants of Heth, were willing to give him land at no cost?

Heth: Son of Canaan, great grandson of Noah,
and original ancestor of the Hittites, some of the
original inhabitants of Palestine.
–HBD

It was Abraham who insisted that he pay the going rate of 400 shekels of silver for the land, which he did (Genesis 23:1–16). Now, if Abraham believed the Lord: Why did he not take the land the descendants of Canaan offered him for free?
Abraham said,

Genesis 23:4 – 20 (NIV)
"I am an alien and a stranger among you. Sell me some property for a burial site here so I can bury my dead."

The Hittites replied to Abraham, "Sir, listen to us. You are a mighty prince among us. Bury your dead in the choicest of our tombs. None of us will refuse you his tomb for burying your dead."

Then Abraham rose and bowed down before the people of the land, the Hittites. He said to them, "If you are willing to let me bury my dead, then listen to me and intercede with Ephron... on my behalf so he will sell me the cave... which belongs to him and is at the end of his field. Ask him to sell it to me for the full price as a burial site among you."

Ephron the Hittite was sitting among his people and he replied to Abraham in the hearing of all the Hittites who had come to the gate of his city. "No, my lord," he said. "Listen to me; I give you the field, and I give you the cave that is in it. I give it to you in the presence of my people. Bury your dead."

Again Abraham bowed down before the people of the land and he said to Ephron in their hearing, "Listen to me, if you will. I will pay the price of the field. Accept it from me so I can bury my dead there."

Ephron answered Abraham, "Listen to me, my lord; the land is worth four hundred shekels of silver, but what is that between me and you? Bury your dead." Abraham agreed to Ephron's terms and weighed out for him the price he had named in the hearing of the Hittites: four hundred shekels of silver, according to the weight current among the merchants.

So Ephron's field... and the cave in it, and all the trees within the borders of the field--was deeded to Abraham as his property in the presence of all the Hittites who had come to the gate of the city. Afterward Abraham buried his wife Sarah in the cave... in the land of Canaan. So the field and the cave in it were deeded to Abraham by the Hittites as a burial site.

In addition, Jacob, Abraham's grandson, did not believe the Lord also, because he too purchased land in Canaan for 100 pieces of currency (Genesis 33:18). The same Promised Land that the Lord their god said he would give to Jacob as a descendant of Abraham.

The land Jacob purchased in Canaan was proof that the Lord's assessment of Abraham was accurate when he said, "For I know him, he will command his children and his household after him, and they shall keep the way of the LORD, to do justice and judgment." The LORD who Abraham defined as the "most high God, the possessor of heaven and earth."

Genealogy of Abraham

There is very little written about Abraham, the person, as compared to other characters in the Bible, however, what is clear is that Abraham was the light within the scriptures that could not be hidden. Looking at Abraham's genealogy he is identified in the Scriptures as a Hebrew and had three wives: Sarah, Hagar, and Zipporah. It is through these three women that the descendants of Shem and Ham bonded together under Abraham, making him the father of many nations.

Sarah

The only thing known about Abraham's first wife, Sarah, is that she was his half-sister. They share the same father (Genesis 20:11 – 12), however, nothing is mentioned concerning the identity of either of their mothers. The scriptures reveal a strong relationship between Abraham, a Hebrew, and the Syrian people; a relationship so strong, that Abraham considered a Syrian as his heir.

Genesis 15:2 – 3

> But Abram said, "O Sovereign LORD, what can you give me since I remain childless and the one who will inherit my estate is Eliezer of Damascus?"

Abraham and Sarah's relationship with the Syrian people continued for generations with their son, Isaac, who married his cousin Rebecca, a woman who was part Hebrew and Syrian (Genesis 22:23, 25:19 – 20). Together they had twin sons named Jacob and Esau: Jacob married four women, of which two were not identified and the other two were sisters, Leah and Rachel, who were identified as Syrian (Genesis 28:5–6). Esau married two Hittite women, which were descendant of Ham, namely Canaan and had children (Genesis 36:1 – 5).

Therefore, Abraham (with Sarah) had a Hebrew son, and was the grandfather of heirs possessing Hebrew, Syrian, and Canaanite blood.

Hagar

Abraham's second wife was Hagar, she was identified as an Egyptian. Together they had one son named Ishmael, who would have been part Hebrew and Egyptian.

Genesis 16:3
>   Abram married Hagar in the land of Canaan.

Therefore, Abraham (with Hagar) was the father of an heir possessing Egyptian blood.

---

[1] The Egyptians were descendants of Ham, Psalms 105 and 106.

Keturah

Abraham's third wife was Keturah, together they had six sons, and one of them was named Midian, of which the Midianites descended.

Genesis 25:1

> Abraham took a wife, and her name was Keturah. And she bares him Zimran, Jokshan, Medan, **Midian**, Ishbak, and Shuah.

Moses' wife was a Midianite, a direct descendant from Abraham and identified as an Ethiopian. As a reminder, the Midianites were the same people the Lord ordered his army to kill with the exception of virgin girls that were divided up as spoils along with the animals.

> **Ethiopia:** The region of Nubia just south of Egypt,
> from the first cataract of the Nile into the Sudan.
> *–HBD*

Therefore, Abraham's six sons were part Hebrew and Ethiopian. As a result, Abraham (with Keturah) was the father of Ethiopian blood heirs.

Every nation, kingdom, land, or people that the Lord and 'his' army attacked, coveted, and killed related directly to Abraham by blood or his allies; even the destruction of Sodom and Gomorrah.

About the Lord

Who exactly is the Lord? Analyzing the story of 'Sodom and Gomorrah,' and the 'War of the Kings,' as to how they relate to each other, a whole new understanding about the Lord comes to light. The scriptures reveal something about the Lord that is not commonly taught, just prior to the destruction of Sodom and Gomorrah:

Genesis 18:1–8
> The LORD appeared to Abraham in the plains of Mamre [in the land of Canaan]… three men stood before him: when he saw them, he ran to meet them and bowed and said, my Lord, if now I have found favor in your sight… let me get you some water, so you can wash your feet and rest under the tree, and I will fetch bread to comfort your hearts… then you can go on your way…
>
> Abraham immediately went to Sarah, and said, make quickly three portions of bread. Abraham ran and fetched a calf… and had it prepared. He took butter, milk, and the calf which he had dressed, and set it before them; and they did eat.

It should be clear that the Lord is a man; the same LORD that appears throughout the OT scriptures. Abraham bowed before "three men," one was the Lord and the other two were the witnesses that went to Sodom. Therefore, the Lord appears to be a man of authority; more than likely, a king.

Now notice, Abraham said to the Lord, "my Lord, 'if now' I have found favor in your sight," which implied that Abraham did something to displease the Lord.

Then the Lord said 'shall I hide from Abraham this thing I'm about to do,' meaning the destruction of Sodom, which he did not hide, because the conversation continued.

Genesis 18:23–26

> Abraham said to the Lord, will you destroy the righteous with the wicked? If there are fifty righteous within the city of Sodom: will you not spare the city for the fifty righteous that live there? The LORD replied, if I find in Sodom fifty righteous people within the city, then I will spare all of Sodom for their sakes.... I will not destroy it for ten's sake.

Abraham's plead for mercy was not for the righteous people alone, but for the entire city of Sodom. Why this is important is because Deuteronomy 29:23, says, the Lord destroyed not only Sodom and Gomorrah, but also Admah, and Zeboim a total of 4 out of the 5 kingdoms Abraham and his allies saved, in the war of the kings.

The 4 kings that went to war with the 5 king are as follows (Genesis 14:1–2):

1) King of **Shinar**   1) King of **Sodom**
2) King of Ellasar   2) King of **Gomorrah**
3) King of **Elam**   3) King of **Admah**
4) Tidal king of nations   4) King of **Zeboiim**
                            5) King of Bela

According to Isaiah 11:11, two of the four kings: Shinar and Elam were allies of the Lord or under his control, making the Lord, the King of kings.

Isaiah 11:11

> The Lord shall set his hand again a second time to recover the remnant of his people... **Elam** and Shinar...

From the beginning the Lord was going to destroy Sodom prior to talking with Abraham or sending any witnesses there. The Lord mentioned Sodom to Abraham as a way of rubbing the destruction of what was to come, in his face. Remember, the Lord said to Abraham, "If I find" fifty... "If I find" forty... "If I find" thirty... even ten righteous people in Sodom, I will not destroy it. The Lord found and declared all of Sodom unrighteous except four people; one for every kingdom he destroyed. Now, it would appear that the Lord saved Lot, his wife and two daughters, as a token to Abraham, that he could have saved all four kingdoms: Sodom, Gomorrah, Admah, and Zeboiim, if he wanted to.

Therefore, the sexual immorality (or the attempted rape, of the men/angels) of Sodom appears to be just another lie or pretense the writer(s) used to distract away from the truth. The Lord wanted revenge against his enemies: Abraham; the Amorites (descendants of Canaan): Mamre, Aner, and Eshcol communities; and especially, the five kingdoms they saved from being coveted by the four kings who were allies of the Lord.

The Lord's hatred of Abraham continued to his descendants, with the so-called covenant: a promise of land he never intended to honor, because the scriptures say, that is who the Lord was.

Exodus 34:7
> visiting the iniquity of the fathers upon the children, and upon the children's children, unto the third and to the fourth generation.

Number 14:18
> visiting the iniquity of the fathers upon the children unto the third and fourth generation.

Deuteronomy 5:9
> visiting the iniquity of the fathers upon the children unto the third and fourth generation of them that hate me.

When you compare the actions of the so-called 'Lord' with the actions attributed to Abraham and who he was, the Lord is the polar opposite of Abraham. The scriptures portray Abraham as considerate of others and well respected. Abraham believed in integration, this is why he is known as the father of many nations throughout the Middle East from the continent of Africa to Asia; he made no distinction between himself and his neighbor.

Middle East: 1. region stretching from Egypt to Iran: the region stretching from the eastern Mediterranean to the western side of the Indian subcontinent, including Egypt, the Arabian Peninsula, Israel, Jordan, Lebanon, Syria, Turkey, Iran, and Iraq 2. historical area from Iran to Myanmar: the area extending from Iran to Myanmar, including Afghanistan, South Asia, and Tibet.

–EWED

The same commandments Abraham lived by, he would have given to all his descendants, as the Lord proclaimed (Gen 18:17–19), so they would know how to conduct themselves within their own nation and with other nations throughout the world. Abraham demonstrated his ideology of love in the 'War of the Kings,' by protecting and "not" coveting his neighbor to maintain peace and to have security among all nations. This is the same spirit of cooperation that many nations seek today, via treaties.

The scriptures portray Abraham as a righteous man who believed in and followed the commandments; so, why would Jesus, believed to be the Son of God, say from heaven, that he was of the root of David, a cruel warrior, and not Abraham?

Revelation 22:16

I Jesus have sent my angel to testify to you these things in the churches. I am the root and the offspring of David, and the bright and morning star.

About David

David is seen as a young boy who fought against Goliath, a giant, with a slingshot and won; and was a great warrior for the Lord. David became the king of Judah, then king over Israel (the remaining 12 tribes); however, there is another side to David that is not commonly taught that rivals that of Hitler, in Germany in the early to mid 1900's.

About the Ammonites

The children of Ammon were descendants of Lot (Abraham nephew). The land that they possessed was given to them by the Lord (Deuteronomy 2:19). During the time of David, the Lord had already sewn so much discord among many of the kingdoms and nations of the world that when King David sent mourners into the land of Ammon after the death of their king, they saw them as spies coming to covet their land.

2 Samuel 10:1 – 4

> The king of the children of Ammon died, and his son reigned in his stead. David sent his servants to comfort him. When David's servants came into the land of the children of Ammon; the princes of the children of Ammon said to the dead king's son: Do you think that David sent comforters as an honor to your father or to search the city, and to spy it out, and to overthrow it?
>
> The king's son took David's servants, and shaved off one half of their beards, and cut off their garments, at the waist, and exposed their buttocks, and sent them away to shame them.

In response, King David, a man after the Lord's own heart, sent Joab, the captain of his army, to destroy the children of Ammon and to covet their possessions. Now, what is not taught or preached about David is that he was a sadistic warrior who committed genocide against innocent people by putting the children of Ammon, under earth digging equipment to be crushed and mutilated; in guillotines to be beheaded; and thrown in furnaces to be burned to death, because his servants were shamed by those in authority among the children of Ammon.

2 Samuel 12:29–31

> Joab fought against the children of Ammon and took the royal city. Joab sent messengers to David saying; I have taken the city of waters, gather the rest of the people together, and come and take it: lest I take the city, and it is called after my name. So, David gathered all the people together and took it. He took their king's crown from off his head and it was set on David's head and he brought forth the spoil of the city in great abundance. He also brought forth the people that were there and put them under saws, and under harrows of iron, and under axes of iron, and made them pass through the brick kiln: and this he did in all the cities of the children of Ammon. Then David and all the people with him returned to Jerusalem.

The gospel of Matthew 1:1 says "Jesus Christ, the son of David, the son of Abraham." Now the question is: Why did Jesus declare that he was only of the seed of David, and not Abraham? Even the LORD his God, said David had too much blood on his hands to build a house/church in his name.

1 Chronicles 22:7–8

> David said to Solomon, my son, as for me, it was in my mind to build a house unto the name of the LORD my God: But the word of the LORD came to me, saying, you have shed blood abundantly, and have made great wars: you shall not build a house in my name, because you have shed much blood upon the earth in my sight.

Unlike Abraham, David was a law unto himself: He transgressed many of the commandments, namely, You Shall Not Covet, committed adultery and murder. Now, does David appear to be the kind of person who Jesus, the Son of God, should have aligned himself with?

PART: 3

THE PLAYBOOKS

21

Segregation

The Protestant's OT Bible demonstrates two attributes of King James: segregation and slavery, in Genesis (the first book of the Bible): The story of Babel, which at first glance seems out of place; however, it has significant relevancy for much of the OT. When you include the story of Joseph, they are two of the most powerful stories in the Bible.

The story of Babel is a short yet simple, 'how to segregate' playbook, which is one of the tools the writer(s) devised to cause instability, mistrust, and division among the kingdoms of the world that had come together for a common purpose.

The Story of Babel

Genesis 11:1 – 9

> The whole earth was of one language and of one voice, and it came to pass, as men journeyed east, that they found a plain [a flat dry area] in the land of Shinar [in the Middle East] and they lived there. They had brick for stone and slime for mortar and they began to build a city and a tower, whose top could reach heaven; and they said let us make a name for ourselves, lest we be scattered abroad upon the face of the whole earth.

The LORD came down to see the city and the tower, which the children of men built. The LORD said the people are as one, and they have one language; and this they begin to do: now nothing will be impossible for them, if they imagined doing it.

Let us go down, and confound their language, that they may not understand one another's speech. So the LORD scattered them abroad upon the earth: and they stop building the city. Therefore, the name is called Babel; because the LORD confused the language of all the earth: Then the LORD scatter them upon the earth.

In this fable, men throughout the East (children of men) had come together in the land of Shinar to build a city and a tower, for the future, to prevent the destruction of the Lord and his God upon them and their land. Just prior to the story of Babel was the Great Flood that the Lord and his God had caused.

Genesis 6:7, 11 – 13, 17
> The LORD said I will destroy man whom I have created from the face of the earth; both man, beast, every creeping thing, and fowls of the air; for I regret that I have made them….
>
> The earth also was corrupt before God, and the earth was filled with violence. And God looked upon the earth, and, behold, it was corrupt; for all flesh had corrupted his way upon the earth. And God said to Noah, the end of all flesh is come before me; for the earth is filled with violence through them; and, behold, I will destroy them with the earth….
>
> Behold, I, even I, do bring a flood of waters upon the earth, to destroy all flesh, with the breath of life, from under heaven; and everything that is in the earth shall die.

The story of Babel, metaphorically, was an attempt by men to come together on one accord to ward off the enemy, by building a city with a tower to reach heaven, and to make it waterproof using slime (tar) to protect themselves from a future flood from the Lord; however, the Lord came another way, notice, the Lord said "let us go down," therefore, the Lord was not alone, he sent his allies to help manipulate and stop 'the children of men' from working together in the city of Shinar, so that, he [the Lord] could continue his destructive behavior against 'them.'

Segregation: 3. act of segregating: the separating of one person, group, or thing from others, or the dividing of people or things into separate groups kept apart from each other.
–EWED

Now remember, the King of Shinar was one of the 4 kings that went to war against the 5 king (Genesis 14:1–2) and was listed alongside Elam as an ally of the Lord. Now the question is: Who is Shinar and Elam?

Shinar

The name given, in the earliest Hebrew records, to Babylonia, later called Babel, or the land of Babel…. Shinar is described as the land of the plain where migrants from the East settled, and founded Babel, the city, and its great tower.
–ISBE

The book of Daniel also ties the land of Shinar directly to the king of Babylon; and, Babylon was an ally of the Lord, for a time, against the descendants of Abraham.

Daniel 1:1 – 2

In the third year of the reign of the king of Judah [descendants of Abraham] came Nebuchadnezzar king of Babylon unto Jerusalem, and besieged it. The Lord gave the king of Judah into his hand, along with the vessels of the house of God: which he carried into the land of Shinar to the house of his god; and he brought the vessels into the treasure house of his god.

According to the book of Daniel, the King of Babylon's house of god was in the land of Shinar. Now, the reason the Lord caused division among the 9 allied kingdoms was fear, which was based on what the scripture says he saw: which was the gathering of men; all on one accord having their own language in the city of Shinar; and, worshipping their own god in their own religious temple (or tower).

Biblically, it is more than likely that Babylon would equate to Saudi Arabia today and the land of Shinar with the tower (or mosque) would be Mecca.

Elam

The son of Shem... and the name of the country inhabited by his descendants... lying to the east of Babylonia, and extending to the shore of the Mediterranean, a distance in a direct line of about 1,000 miles.

–PBD

The *Parson's Bible Dictionary* defined Elam by their geographical location. Looking at a current map, east of Saudi Arabia (Babylon) and approximately 1000 miles from the seashore of the Mediterranean moving in land is Iran; biblically, Elam represented Persia (now known as Iran).

According to Jeremiah the prophet, after the Lord had used Elam and Babylon for his own purposes, the Lord would betray his own allies by enslaving Elam and utterly destroying Babylon, as though they were nothing.

Elam

Jeremiah 49:37

> For I will cause Elam to be dismayed before their enemies; and before them that seek their life: and I will bring evil upon them, even my fierce anger, said the LORD. I will send the sword after them, till I have consumed them… It shall come to pass in the latter days, that I will bring again the captivity of Elam, said the LORD.

Babylon[2]

Jeremiah 50:1 – 3

> The words the LORD spoke against Babylon and against the land of the Chaldeans, according to Jeremiah the prophet.

---

[2] Note: The fall of Babylon is also recorded in the book of Prophets, for example: Isaiah 14, Daniel 1 – 5, and Revelations 14:8, 16:19, 17:5, 18:2, 18:10, and 18:21.

Declare among the nations, and publish it, conceal nothing: say, Babylon is fallen... her idols are confounded; her images are broken in pieces.

From the north a nation will come against her and make her land desolate, and none shall dwell there: they shall remove both man and beast.

Therefore, biblically, it would appear that the Lord had devised a plan to segregate the people by any means necessary to cause dissention among the 9 allied kingdoms, so much so, that 4 kingdoms, including the Kings of Mecca and Persia, became allies of the Lord, knowingly or unknowingly, and went to war against the other 5 kingdoms, which included Sodom and Gomorrah, and ultimately stopped them all from continuing to build and worship together in the house of their god; making the stories of Babel, the War of the Kings, and Sodom and Gomorrah about religion.

22

Slavery

Many church leaders use the story of Joseph as an inspiration to the masses that they too can overcome a variety of problems like Joseph, if they just trust in the Lord their God. The problem is, the story of Joseph is not uplifting; it's a fable about how he embodied segregation and instituted slavery.

Slavery: 3. hard work: very hard work, especially for low
pay and under bad conditions 4. state of being dominated: a
state of being completely dominated by another.
–EWED

Looking at the story of Joseph (a young man who was sold into slavery in Egypt, by his brothers) from the standpoint of what Joseph did; his story reads as a manual on 'how to destroy a democracy and enslave a nation, within 2 years.'

The real story of Joseph begins with Joseph, a popular and well known prisoner, who distinguished himself from the rest by interpreting the Pharaoh's reoccurring dream; and making him believe his interpretation was from God.

About Joseph

Genesis 41:14 – 56

Pharaoh sent for Joseph, and they brought him quickly out of the dungeon: shaved and with clean clothes. Pharaoh said to Joseph, I had a dream, and no one can interpret it: I have heard that you can. Joseph said: it is not me who will interpret it; God shall give Pharaoh an answer of peace.

Pharaoh's Dream

Pharaoh said to Joseph, in my dream, I stood upon the bank of the river: and, there came up out of the river seven cows, fat and strong; and they grazed in a meadow. Then, seven other cows came up after them, poor, very ill, and lean; and the lean cows ate the fat cows: After they had eaten up all the fat cows, no one could tell because they were still lean and very ill. Then I woke up. Also, I saw in my dream, seven ears of corn come up in one stalk, full and good: then I saw seven ears of corn withered and thin, come up after them: And the withered corn devoured the good corn: and I told this to the magicians; but they could not explain it to me.

Joseph's Interpretation

Joseph said to Pharaoh, both dreams are the same: God has shown you what he is about to do. The seven good cows are seven years; the same as the seven good ears of corn, which will be seven years of plenty. The seven thin cows are the same as the seven withered ears of corn, which is seven years of famine.

What God is about to do he has shown it to Pharaoh. Behold, there will be seven years of great prosperity throughout all the land of Egypt: followed by seven years of famine which will consume the land; and all the food that was store up shall be forgotten because of the famine, which will be very grievous.

The reason the dream reoccurred was because God will shortly make it happen. Now, let Pharaoh look for a man discreet and wise, and set him over the land of Egypt, and let him appoint officers to take up and store one fifth of the food supply throughout the land for the seven good years. They will store food in the cities; and that food will be for sell to the people of the land during the seven years of famine, so that, the people do not die.

Joseph the Chosen Man

Joseph's interpretation seemed good in the eyes of Pharaoh and all his servants… Then Pharaoh said to Joseph, God has shown you what is to come, there is none as discreet and wise as you, therefore, you shall be over my house, and according to your word shall all my people be ruled: only I will be greater than you. Now, I have set you over all the land of Egypt; then Pharaoh took off his ring and put it upon Joseph's hand, and dressed him in fine linen, and put a gold chain about his neck and said, without your say so shall no man lift up his hand or foot in all the land of Egypt….

What Joseph Did

Joseph was thirty years old when he stood before Pharaoh-King of Egypt…. In the seven plenteous years Joseph gathered up all the food in the land of Egypt, and stored the food in the cities…. When the seven years of famine began the land of Egypt had more than enough food. The people cried to Pharaoh for bread and he said to them: Go to Joseph and do whatever he tells you to do. As the famine spread throughout the earth, Joseph opened all the storehouses, and sold bread to the Egyptians….

Jacob and his Descendants (Treated Well)

Genesis 45:4 – 11

Joseph said unto his brothers [who came to Egypt for food], I am Joseph your brother, whom ye sold into Egypt. Now be not grieved, nor angry with yourselves, that ye sold me: for God did send me before you to preserve life. For two years famine has been in the land: and there are five years left. God sent me before you to preserve you and all your descendants. So now it was not you that sent me here, but God. God has made me a father to Pharaoh and lord over his house, and a ruler throughout all the land of Egypt. Now, go tell my father, that God has made me lord over Egypt and to come down to me: And you shall live in the land of Goshen, and be near me, you, and your children, and your children's children, flocks, herds, and all that you have. Here will I nourish you, for there are five years of famine which remain; lest you, and your household, and all that you have, come to poverty….

Genesis 47:11, 27

Joseph gave Jacob (his father) and brothers the best land in Egypt as a possession, as Pharaoh commanded him; and he nourished his father, brothers, and all his father's descendants with bread…. Jacob and his descendants [the children of Israel] lived in the land of Egypt; and they had many possessions and were fruitful, and multiplied in numbers.

The Egyptians (Treated Poorly)

Genesis 47:14 – 26

Joseph collected all the money within the lands of Egypt and Canaan, for the corn the people purchased: and Joseph brought the money into Pharaoh's house.

Having no money, all the Egyptians came to Joseph and said, Give us bread or we will die in your presence. Joseph replied: Give us your cattle and I will give you bread. The Egyptians brought their cattle to Joseph and he gave them bread in exchange for their horses, flocks, cattle, and donkeys for that year.

When that year was ended, they came to Joseph the second year, and said: our money is gone and you have all of our herds of cattle; there is nothing left, but our bodies and land. Shall we die before your eyes, both we and our land? Buy us and our land for bread, and we will be servants of Pharaoh. Also, give us seed to plant, that we may live, and not die, that the land be not desolate.

Joseph bought all the land of Egypt for Pharaoh; for the Egyptians sold every field, because the famine prevailed over them: so the land became Pharaoh's. As for the people, he removed them from their land to cities throughout Egypt. Only the land belonging to the priests was saved, because the priests had food allotted to them by Pharaoh.

Then Joseph said to the people, Behold, I have bought you this day and your land for Pharaoh: here is seed for you, and you shall sow the land; and you shall give one fifth to Pharaoh, and the rest shall be yours, for your households, and for food for your little ones. Then the Egyptians said to Joseph, 'you have saved our lives,' let us find grace in your sight, my lord, and we will be Pharaoh's servants. Joseph made it a law over the land of Egypt to this day that Pharaoh should have one fifth of the yield; and nothing from the land belonging to the priests.

Pharaoh's reoccurring dream represented fear, notice, Joseph said to him, "God shall give Pharaoh an *answer of peace;*" and Pharaoh, in essence, turned over the keys to his kingdom to Joseph because he trusted him and believed in his God; and a good outcome for his people. However, Joseph used 'God' to manipulate the Pharaoh of Egypt who he believed to be child-like, saying "God has made me a father to Pharaoh;" therefore, Joseph took advantage of Pharaoh's fear and manufactured a crisis: a food shortage, for his own purpose, against the Egyptians people.

Famine: 1. a severe shortage of food
resulting in widespread hunger.
–*EWED*

Now it is true that Joseph did not lie to Pharaoh, but, he did not tell him everything. For seven years Joseph collected and stored the food in the cities all over Egypt. During the first year of the famine, Joseph opened up the storehouses so the Egyptians could buy food, as he said, "so that, the people would not die," of starvation. In the process, he took everything they owned "for Pharaoh" (which Joseph used to enrich his own people); then Joseph gave the Egyptians bread to live and seed to plant.

Therefore, the Egyptians could have been given or purchased seed all along, except, for Joseph scheme which prevented them. In retrospect, Joseph manufactured a crisis by withholding the seed which the Egyptian people needed to grow food to live; then he bankrupted them of everything they owned, including their own bodies. At the same time, Joseph protected and supported himself and his family who came into Egypt as strangers, saying in essence, to his brothers that God sent him to Egypt to preserve them and all their descendants.

Preserve: 6. to protect somebody or something from danger,
especially the danger of being killed or damaged.
–EWED

To be clear, there was never a famine in Egypt; yet, Joseph depleted the Egyptian people of their wealth and turned them all into sharecroppers, in essence slaves, in less than 2 years.

Sharecropper: a tenant farmer who farms land for the owner
and is paid a share of the value of the yielded crop.
–EWED

Furthermore, to keep the Egyptian people under his control, Joseph levied a tax of 1/5 on everything they would produced in the future, saying, I have bought you and your land for Pharaoh, "here is seed for you, and you shall sow the land; and you shall give one fifth to Pharaoh, and the rest shall be yours."

The moral to the story of Joseph is this: Joseph turned the Pharaoh of Egypt into a very wealthy 'Pharaoh King, of Egypt' who did not care enough about his own people. As a playbook, it demonstrates how to take a democracy of the people, by the people, and for the people and turned it into an autocracy; by creating a crisis that would affect the economy and/or the financial stability of the masses, as a distraction, so that the people would focus only on themselves, and not what their government was doing against them and for the benefit of others, until it was too late.

23

About Jesus

It was Jesus who said "keep the commandments," but, did he mean all of them? The commandments are the pillars the Church preach and teach to the masses to live by. When looking at the original last six of the Ten Commandments in the OT, the last commandment mentioned is 'You shall not covet.'

The OT Commandments
Exodus, chapter 20:12 – 17
5 Honor your mother and father
6 You shall not kill
7 You shall not commit adultery
8 You shall not steal
9 You shall not bear false witness
10 You shall not covet

When you compare the last 6 of the original Ten Commandments, in the OT, to those spoken by Jesus in the NT (NT), a clear picture of who Jesus really was and what he represented comes to light.

The four gospels: Matthew, Mark, Luke, and John, in the NT, are suppose to be a record of what Jesus did and said while on the earth; however, they cause confusion when they say different things on the same topic. The one thing known about Jesus and his view concerning the commandments is the story of a man seeking eternal life, which appears in three out of the four gospels: Matthew, Mark, and Luke.

The Gospel of Matthew

Matthew 19:16 – 22

A man came to Jesus saying, Good Master, what good thing shall I do, that I may have eternal life? And Jesus said to him: **Why do you call me, good? There is none good but one, that is, God: but if you want to enter into life, keep the commandments.** The man replied, which ones? Jesus said,

6 You shall not murder
7 You shall not commit adultery
8 You shall not steal
9 You shall not bear false witness
5 Honor your father and your mother
* You shall love your neighbor as thyself?

The young man replied, all these things have I kept from my youth: What do I lack? Jesus said to him, **if you want to be perfect, go and sell everything you have, and give it to the poor, and you shall have treasure in heaven: and come and follow me.** When the young man heard that saying, he went away sorrowful: for he had great possessions.

The writer(s) of Matthew intentionally omitted the commandment, You Shall Not Covet and added in its place, 'you shall love your neighbor as thyself,' which is not a part of the original ten; however, it is a part of the law, in the OT.

Leviticus 19:18

You shall not avenge, nor bear any grudge against the children of your people, but you shall love your neighbor as thyself: I am the LORD.

This scripture in Leviticus 19:18 refers to infighting among the children of Israel, hence the phrase "against the children of your people," it has nothing to do with coveting. Now, one would think that obeying commandments 5 through 9, would equate to loving thy neighbor, so why not include, You Shall Not Covet?

Now notice, Jesus answered the man's first question when he told him to "keep the commandments' he listed, however, he never answered the man's second question: What do I lack? Instead, Jesus changed the subject; he used the word "if" in the statement, "if you want to be perfect," as though it was a choice in comparison to something the man may have lacked. One thing is clear from the man's questions, he was not seeking perfection.

The Gospel of Mark

Mark 10:17 – 21

...There came one running, and kneeled before Jesus, saying, Good Master, what shall I do that I may inherit eternal life? And Jesus said to him: **Why do you call me good? There is none good but one, that is, God. You know the commandments,**

7 Do not commit adultery,
6 Do not kill,
8 Do not steal,
9 Do not bear false witness,
*** Defraud not,**
5 Honor your father and mother.

The man replied Master, all these have I observed from my youth. Then Jesus beholding him loved him, and said to him, **one thing you lack: go your way, sell whatever you have, and give to the poor, and you shall have treasure in heaven: and come, take up the cross, and follow me.** And he was sad at that saying, and went away grieved: for he had great possessions.

The writer(s) in the gospel of Mark also omitted the commandment: Do Not Covet; but, added defraud not, which is a part of the OT law, but has nothing to do with the commandment: Do Not Covet.

Leviticus 19:13
> You shall not defraud your neighbor; neither rob him of his wages.

Notice, Jesus says to the man there is 'one thing you lack,' yet never mentioned what the one thing was; however, based on the OT commandments, it is more than likely it was, Do Not Covet. Why mention that the man had great possessions when he is seeking eternal life?

The Gospel of Luke

Luke 18:18 – 23
> A certain ruler asked him, saying, Good Master, what shall I do to inherit eternal life? And Jesus said to him: **Why do you call me good? None is good, save one, that is, God. You know the commandments,**
>
> **7 Do not commit adultery,**
> **6 Do not kill,**
> **8 Do not steal,**
> **9 Do not bear false witness,**
> **5 Honor your father and your mother.**

The ruler replied, all these have I kept from my youth up. Now when heard these things, Jesus said to him, **yet you lack one thing: sell all thayou have, and distribute it to the poor, and you shall have treasure in heaven: and come, follow me.** And when he heard this, he was very sorrowful: for he was very rich.

The writer(s) of the gospel of Luke made it plain omitting the commandment, Do Not Covet without adding something else in its place. Now, notice the original question was: What good thing shall I do, that I may have or inherit eternal life? Jesus saying, you shall love your neighbor as thyself, or defraud not, would have answered the question; or simply saying "keep the commandments" which would have included all of them. However, omitting the commandment, Do Not Covet, which means to take by force what belongs to someone else, would more than likely negated or nullified some of the other commandments Jesus listed.

The man's question implied that he was seeking something greater than what or who he was as an individual, but not perfection. Taking all three gospels into account, the statement, in Matthew, "if you want to be perfect," appears to be an indirect choice; either the man could continue to covet (the one commandment not mentioned and more than likely the one commandment he lacked) or give everything he had coveted to the poor and have treasure in heaven. Moreover, Jesus answers seemed to imply that a rich man with great possessions could still covet other people, nations, or kingdoms, and have eternal life, if he so chooses.

It was Jesus who said, "out of the abundance of the heart the mouth speaks" (Matthew 12:34), then, he could have said: You Shall Not Covet, if it was in his heart to do so. Now the question is: Why didn't Jesus say, You Shall Not Covet?

King of Kings

Jesus is believe to be the 'Son of God' born of a virgin who was impregnated by a Holy Ghost, to take the throne of David and reign as king over all 13 tribes, in the land of Israel, with the blessing of the Lord God.

The Virgin Mary

Luke 1:26 – 35

> The angel Gabriel was sent from God to the city of Galilee, named Nazareth, to a virgin espoused to a man whose name was Joseph, of the house of David; and the virgin's name was Mary…. The angel said to her, fear not, Mary: for you have found favor with God.
>
> You shall conceive and have a son, and you shall call his name JESUS. He shall be great, and shall be called the Son of the Highest: and the Lord God shall give to him the throne of his father David: and he shall reign over the house of Jacob forever; and of his kingdom there shall be no end.
>
> Mary said to the angel: I am a virgin, how shall this be? The angel replied, the Holy Ghost shall come upon you, and the power of the Highest shall overshadow you: that holy thing which shall be born of you shall be called the Son of God.

Many today await their Lord and Savior, Jesus Christ, and his great return, because many believe that the Bible is prophecy. Here is the prophecy according to Paul:

Thessalonians 4:16 – 17

> For the Lord himself shall descend from heaven with a shout, with the voice of the archangel, and with the trump of God: and the dead in Christ shall rise first: Then we which are alive and remain shall be caught up together with them in the clouds, to meet the Lord in the air: and so shall we forever be with the Lord.

Paul was describing what many believe to be the resurrection, when Jesus returns to the earth and gathers his saints or followers, including the dead ones.

According to the writer(s) of Matthew, it appears as though the resurrection already happened following Jesus' crucifixion and death on the cross.

Matthew 27:50 – 53

> Jesus, cried again with a loud voice, then, yielded up the ghost. Behold, the veil of the temple was torn in half from top to bottom; and the earth did quake, and the rocks tore apart; and the graves were opened; and many bodies of the saints which slept arose and came out of the graves after his resurrection, and went into the holy city, and appeared unto many.

Nonetheless, if Jesus is the Lord and Savior, what is he the Lord of, and who did he save?

The story of Jesus

Matthew 2:1 – 8, 12 – 14, 19 – 22

> Jesus was born in Bethlehem of Judaea in the days of Herod the king and there came wise men to Jerusalem, saying: Where is he, that is born King of the Jews? When the king heard these things, he was troubled, and all of Jerusalem with him.
>
> The king gathered all the chief priests and scribes together and demanded to know where Christ would be born and they told him, in Bethlehem of Judaea: for it is written by the prophet: Bethlehem, in the land of Judah: for out of you shall come a Governor that shall rule my people Israel.
>
> The king sent the wise men to Bethlehem to search for the young child… Joseph being warned of God in a dream that they should not return to Herod, they departed into their own country another way. The angel of the Lord appeared to Joseph in a dream, saying, take the young child and his mother, and flee into Egypt, and stay there until I bring you word: for the king will seek and destroy the young child. Joseph took the young child and his mother and went into Egypt….

When the king died, an angel of the Lord appeared in a dream to Joseph in Egypt, saying, take the young child and his mother, and go into the land of Israel: for they are dead which sought the young child's life, therefore, Joseph took the young child and his mother and went into the land of Israel, but, when he heard that Herod's son reigned in Judaea he was afraid to go there: notwithstanding, being warned of God in a dream, he went into Galilee.

Biblically, the land of Israel was the country and birthplace of Jesus and why he is referred to as a Jew, and at times mocked as the "King of the Jews." Jesus was born to be the King: Lord and ruler, of the tribe/land/nation of Judah, which included Jerusalem; but also, like David he was to be the King over all thirteen tribes of Israel: the land of Israel. Now notice, when baby Jesus sought refuge from King Herod he was taken to Egypt (the land of the descendants of Ham) and Galilee, to be among the Gentiles.

Gentile: 2. somebody Christian: a Christian, as distinguished from somebody who is Jewish.
–EWED

When Jesus left Galilee (at the approximate age of 30 years old), he went to Jordon to be baptized, not for the remission of sin, because the scriptures say Jesus knew no sin, but as an outward conversion to Christianity, being born a Jew in the land of Israel. After his baptism he returned to Galilee, a state with over 20 cities. Biblically, Galilee was a very undesirable place and referred to as Cabul, in the OT (1 Kings 9:10 – 13).

Cabul: Place name meaning, "fettered" or "braided."
Region of cities in Galilee Solomon gave Hiram, king of Tyre, as payment for materials and services in building the Temple and the palace. Hiram did not like them and called them Cabul, a Hebrew word play meaning, "as nothing."
–HBD

Matthew 4:13 – 17

> Jesus came and lived in the borders of Zebulun and Naphtali: That it might be fulfilled which was spoken by Isaiah the prophet, saying, the land of Zebulun, and Naphtali, by the way of the sea, beyond Jordan, Galilee of the Gentiles; The people which lived in darkness saw great light… From that time Jesus began to preach, saying: **Repent, for the kingdom of heaven is at hand.**

The use of the word "repent" implied wrong doing, even though it does not say what they should repent for. (Based on the OT and mentioning two of the 13 tribes, Zebulun and Naphtali, which coveted the land of the Canaanites and enslaving its people, were more than likely the wrong they needed to repent for.)

Numbers 13:29

> … The Canaanites lived by the sea, and by the coast of Jordan.

Jesus began his ministry in Galilee (land that belonged to the Canaanites; also known as Nazareth), where his mother Mary was said to be impregnated by the Holy Ghost. Many of the descendants of Canaan lived in Galilee or among the thirteen tribes as their servants; therefore, the land of Israel consisted of Jews and Gentiles. It was in Galilee among the Gentiles that Jesus selected his first four apostles.

Matthew 4:18 – 25

> Jesus, walking by the Sea of Galilee, saw two brothers, Peter and Andrew and he said to them, **follow me and I will make you fishers of men.** Going on from there, he saw James and John his brother, and called them also.

> Jesus went about all of Galilee, teaching in their synagogues, and preaching the gospel of the kingdom and his fame went throughout all of Syria; and great multitudes followed him from Galilee, Decapolis, Jerusalem, Judaea, and beyond Jordan.

After Jesus had gathered all 12 apostles (Matthew 10, Mark 3:16 – 19) from among the Gentiles he sent them out to preach to the lost sheep of the house of Israel.

Matthew 10:5 – 7, 16 – 23

> These twelve apostles Jesus sent forth, and commanded them, saying, **do not go to the Gentiles or any city of the Samaritans: go rather to the lost sheep of the house of Israel. As you go, preach, saying, the kingdom of heaven is at hand….**
>
> **I send you forth as sheep in the midst of wolves: be wise as serpents and harmless as doves. Beware of men: for they will deliver you up to the councils, and they will scourge you in their synagogues; you shall be brought before governors and kings for my sake, for a testimony against them and the Gentiles… you shall be hated of all men for my name's sake: but he that endures to the end shall be saved.**
>
> **When they persecute you in this city, flee into another: I say, you will not finish going through all the cities of Israel, before the Son of man comes.**

As a continuation of the OT, Jesus was in essence fighting and preaching against the thirteen tribes of Israel, and teaching and preparing his apostles and like followers to do the same. Taking a closer look at the apostles selected by Jesus in Matthew, six of them were identified by their profession, four were fishermen: Simon Peter, Andrew, James, and John, whom Jesus said he would make fishers of men (Matthew 4:19, Mark 1:17, and Luke 5:10); a collector (a publican), named Matthew (Matthew 9:9, 10:3); and a Canaanite, named Simon (Matthew 10:4, Mark 3:18). Now the question is: Why would Jesus select fishermen; a collector; and a Canaanite to send among the remaining 12 tribes of Israel? Was it symbolic?

By profession a fishermen lays bait or traps for fish, to capture them, so that they or others may kill and devour them. A collector, according the Black's Law Dictionary is defined as the following:

A Canaanite is a descendant of Ham, namely Canaan, who was handpicked by Jesus, to sit in judgment of the remaining twelve tribes of Israel.

Luke 22:28 – 30

> **You [apostles] have continued with me in my temptations. I appoint to you a kingdom, as my Father has appointed unto me; that you may eat and drink at my table in my kingdom, and sit on thrones judging the twelve tribes of Israel.**

It would appear with the use of the word "kingdom," Jesus implied territory/land and people, to be ruled and judged by him as the king of Israel and the Lord and Savior of the Gentiles and converts, in Judah; and for his chosen twelve apostles he would assign a kingdom, from among the remaining twelve tribes of Israel to rule and judge as well.

In the NT, the covenant between the Lord Jesus and his chosen apostles was: the promise of property and land; and eternal life through faith, in the world to come.

Now, remember in the gospel of Mark, Peter said to Jesus, we have left all and followed you, and Jesus replied:

Mark 10:28–30

There is no man that has left his house, brothers, sisters, father, mother, wife, children, or lands, for my sake, and the gospel's; he shall receive an hundredfold now in this time, houses, brothers, sisters, mothers, children, and lands, with persecutions; and in the world to come eternal life.

This was the covenant Jesus made with his twelve apostles, because they have followed and obeyed him. The words "with persecutions," means more than one persecution of a person or group. So, who are they going to persecute in order to have a hundred houses, lands, and people who they can declare as their own other than all twelve tribes of Israel, the same tribes they are going to judge?

Persecution: 1. the persecuting of somebody: the subjecting of a race or group of people to cruel or unfair treatment, e.g. because of their ethnic origin or religious beliefs.
–EWED

Jesus was preparing to covet and make regime changes throughout the land of Israel with his 12 Gentile apostles and many followers, this is how Jesus was going to fulfill the covenant he made with his apostles to give them one hundred houses and parcels of land, by giving them established kingdoms within the land of Israel, which his army would covet; and each apostle would become king; and Jesus the king of Judah; and the thirteenth tribe would rule over the 12 tribes; making Jesus the King of kings over all the land of Israel.

Therefore, Jesus was, in essence, taking back from the children of Israel (the Lord's army) in the OT, the land they coveted from the descendants of Canaan and giving it to his chosen Gentiles.

Now, it makes sense that Jesus would omit the commandment, You Shall Not Covet and align himself with David, the warrior, and not Abraham the peace keeper.

Now, the question is: Many believe that Jesus is coming in the future, to wage war based on the scriptures, who is he coming against, the current State of Israel, in the Middle East?

24

About Japheth

Taking another look into the story of Noah and again setting aside the fantastical portions of the story of building an Ark and the Great Flood, what is revealed is a world view with a focus on the Middle East, which begins with Noah's three sons: Shem, Ham, and Japheth. Each son represents an identity of people, based mainly on language; racial makeup; and/or geographical location.

The descendants of Shem were originally identified as Hebrew (Genesis 14:13).

Shem
Noah's oldest son and original ancestor of
Semitic peoples including Israel.
–HBD

The descendants of Ham were divided up by their geographical location, such as, Syria, Egypt, Ethiopia, etc., and at times, identified by their religious gods.

Ham
Ham became the original ancestor of the Cushites,
the Egyptians, and the Canaanites.
–HBD

The descendants of Shem and Ham are both mentioned throughout the scriptures, in the Old and NTs, in one form or another, however, it is not clear, based on the scriptures what language, ethnicity, race, religion, or geographical location, that can be identified as belonging to Japheth and his descendants.

Genesis 10:2 – 5

> The sons of Japheth; Gomer, Magog, Madai, Javan, Tubal, Meshech, and Tiras. The sons of Gomer; Ashkenaz, Riphath, and Togarmah. The sons of Javan; Elishah, Tarshish, Kittim, and Dodanim. By these were the isles of the **Gentiles** divided in their lands; every one after his tongue, after their families, in their nations.

The name Japheth appears multiple times as part of the genealogy of Noah; however, in Genesis 10:5, the descendants of Japheth are referred to as the Gentiles. Looking again to the blessing Noah bestowed upon Japheth above his brothers: Shem and Ham reveal the mystery of the Bible.

Genesis 9:25 – 27

> Noah said, Cursed be Canaan; a servant of servants shall he be to his brothers, and blessed be the LORD God of Shem; and Canaan shall be his servant. God shall enlarge Japheth, and he shall live in the tents of Shem; and Canaan shall be his servant….

Now notice, Noah blessed the "Lord God" of Shem, not Shem, but the Lord God "of" Shem; and Canaan would be the servants of the Lord God of Shem. Then he continued saying that "God" shall increase Japheth and he shall live in the "tents," of Shem. In other words, under the authority or protection of the Lord God of Shem, Japheth will live in the tents or houses of Shem; and The Lord God of Shem would give to Japheth, Canaan, to be his servant. Now, also notice, the scriptures does not say that Japheth will live with Shem, it says "he," meaning Japheth shall live in the tents of Shem, and Canaan, shall be *his* servant," not their servant. The NIV Bible says it this way:

Genesis 9:25 – 27 (NIV)

> He said, "Cursed be Canaan! The lowest of slaves will he be to his brothers." He also said, "Blessed be the LORD, the God of Shem! May Canaan be the slave of Shem. May God extend the territory of Japheth; may Japheth live in the tents of Shem, and may Canaan be his slave."

Japheth was to supplant Shem, in what was the land of Canaan: the Promised Land; now known as the land of Israel. Therefore, the story of Japheth in the OT is exactly the same in theme as the story of Jesus in the NT; that the Gentiles would covet the land of Israel.

A Closer Look
at the
Descendants of Japheth

Besides what is already mentioned, you learn very little about Japheth, other than being Gentiles. Searching the scripture for Japheth descendants, namely, Gomer and Magog there is some information from the book of the prophet Ezekiel, in chapters 38 and 39. Ezekiel gave three progressive prophesies concerning the Lord God of Shem, which outlined how Noah's blessing upon Japheth was to come to past.

Prophet: 1. somebody who claims to interpret or transmit the commands of a deity.
–EWED

Prophesy: 1. To predict what is going to happen 2. to supposedly reveal the will of a deity in predicting a future event.
–EWED

The first prediction suggested in the book of the prophet Ezekiel is that the descendants of Japheth: Magog; and Gomer with his son Togarmah, would be allied with the descendants of Ham: Persia (Iran), Ethiopia, and Libya.

[Note: The word "against" has different meanings throughout Ezekiel 38 and 39, for example, in Ezekiel 38:2, it is not being used in opposition to Gog, but in proximity to, meaning: before, next to, alongside, over, above or among. Also, in other places it may mean in opposition to.]

Ezekiel 38:1 – 7

> The word of the LORD came to me [Ezekiel], saying, Son of man, set your face against Gog, of the land of Magog, the overseer of Meshech and Tubal, and prophesy against him, say, the Lord GOD [of Shem] says; I will turn you back, and put hooks into your jaws, and I will bring you forth and all your army, horses and horsemen,

all of them clothed with all sorts of armor, even a great company with bucklers and shields, all of them handling swords:
Persia, Ethiopia, and Libya with them; all of them with shield and helmet:

Gomer, and all his bands; the house of Togarmah of the north quarters, and all his bands: and those who are with you.

Be ready and prepare yourself [Gog: Magog, Meshech and Tubal], and all your company that are assembled with you [Gomer and his son Togarmah with their bands, along with the armies of Iran, Ethiopia, and Libya], and watch over them.

The second prediction, which is a continuation of the first with more details, suggested that the descendants of Japheth: Gomer and Togarmah, along with the armies of Iran, Ethiopia, and Libya would surround the land of Israel, and assist the 'army of Gog' in supplanting the descendants of Shem in the Promised Land.

Ezekiel 38:14 – 16, 18
Therefore, son of man [Ezekiel], prophesy and say to Gog, the Lord GOD says; In that day when my people of Israel live safely… you shall come from your place out of the north parts, you [Gomer and Togarmah], and those with you [Iran, Ethiopia, and Libya], all of them riding upon horses, a great company, and a mighty army: You [Gog] shall come up against my people of Israel, as a cloud to cover the land; it shall be in the latter days, and I will bring you against my land, that the heathen may know me, when I shall be sanctified in you, O Gog, before their eyes….

The third prediction suggested appears to be a more in-depth continuation of the first and the second. What you now learn is that the army of Gog would betray and destroy Gomer and Togarmah and all their bands (a small private army or mercenaries), along with the armies of Iran, Ethiopia, and Libya in the mountains of Israel, who assisted them in supplanting the descendants of Shem in the Promised Land.

Ezekiel 39:1 – 5, 9, 11 – 13, 23

Therefore, son of man, prophesy against Gog, and say, the Lord GOD [of Shem] says; Behold, I am against you, O Gog, the chief prince of Meshech and Tubal: I will turn you [Gog] back and leave 1/6 of you [Gomer and Togarmah] and will cause you to come up from the north parts, and will bring you upon the mountains of Israel: I will smite your bow out of your left hand, and will cause your arrows to fall out of your right hand and you shall fall upon the mountains of Israel: You [Gomer and Togarmah], and all your ands, and the people that are with you [Iran, Ethiopia, and Libya]: I will give you to the ravenous birds of every sort and to the beasts of the field to be devoured. You shall fall upon the open field: for I have spoken it, said the Lord GOD....

Peace Time

They [the army of Gog] that live in the cities of Israel shall go forth, and shall set on fire and burn the weapons: shields, bucklers, bows, arrows, hand staves, and spears; and they shall burn them seven years:

Change of Ownership

It shall come to pass, that I will give to Gog a burial place in Israel... and there shall [Gog] bury a massive amount of his soldiers and they shall call it, the valley of Hamongog. Seven months shall **the house of Israel bury their dead**, that they may cleanse the land; and it shall be a day of celebration when I shall be glorified, said the Lord GOD [of Shem].

The [Old] house of Israel [descendants of Shem] went into captivity for their iniquity: because they trespassed against me, therefore I hid my face from them, and gave them into the hand of their enemies: so they all fell by the sword. According to their uncleanness and according to their transgressions have I done unto them, and hid my face from them.

Notice, Gog, now being referred to as "the house of Israel" (the same as the descendants of Shem were once referred) would bury their dead in the land of Israel. Biblically, the burial place represented ownership of the land. Remember, Abraham purchased a burial place and land in Canaan where he lived, died, and was buried; Jacob's body was taken out of Egypt and buried in the land of Canaan (Genesis 50:12 – 13), which he believed the Lord gave to him and his descendants; also, Joseph, the governor of Egypt, had his bones moved to the land of Canaan, the Promised Land (Exodus 13:18 – 19) when the children of Israel left Egypt, under the guide of Moses. Likewise, the Lord God of Shem giving Gog a burial place in the land of Israel would signify a change of ownership.

The Search for Japheth's Identity

Noah's blessing along with Ezekiel's predictions demonstrated a segregated world view of mankind as fitting into three families: Shem, Ham, and Japheth; however, the scriptures do not identify who Japheth or his descendants are as it relates to race, religion, or geological location. Searching biblical reference materials for additional information about "Japheth," here are three examples of what you will find.

Japheth (1)

- The root of *yapht* is *ya❖❖pha❖❖h*, "to make wide." This etymology, however, is not universally accepted, as the word-play is so obvious, and the association of Japheth with Shem ("dark") and Ham ("black") suggests a name on similar lines—either gentilic, or descriptive of race. Japheth has therefore been explained as meaning "fair," from *ya❖❖pha❖❖h*, the non-Sem and non-Hamitic races known to the Jews being all more or less whiteskinned.

  –ISBE

Japheth (2)

- The third son of Noah... father of some 14 nations forming the Indo-Germanic family, originally inhabiting the Caucasus... spreading E and W.

  –WBE

Japheth (3)

- The progenitor of many tribes inhabiting the east of Europe and the north of Asia.

- The three great races thus distinguished are called the Semitic, Aryan, and Turanian (Allophylian). "Setting aside the cases where the ethnic names employed are of doubtful application, it cannot reasonably be questioned that the author [of Gen. 10] has in his account of the sons of Japheth classed together the Cymry or Celts (Gomer), the **Medes** (Madai), and the Ionians or Greeks (Javan), thereby anticipating what has become known in modern times as the 'Indo-European Theory,' or the essential unity of the Aryan (Asiatic) race with the principal races of Europe, indicated by the Celts and the Ionians…"

  –PBD

Searching non-biblical reference material such as the *Encarta ® World English Dictionary* for an in-depth description of who the "three great races" are, this is what you will find.

- **Semitic:** languages spoken by Semites: a group of languages belonging to the Afro-Asiatic family and spoken in North Africa and Southwest Asia, including Hebrew, Arabic, Aramaic, Maltese, and Amharic

- **Aryan:** 1. Nazi ideal: in Nazi ideology, a white person of non-Semitic descent regarded as racially superior.

- **Turanian:** 1. Ural-Altaic speaker: a member of any of the peoples who speak a Ural-Altaic language; adj: relating to ancient Turkistan, or to its people or culture. Turkistan: mountainous region of central Asia that stretches from the Caspian Sea to the Gobi Desert.

  It is divided into three sections, Russian or Western Turkistan, which includes Kazakhstan, Kyrgyzstan, and Uzbekistan, Chinese or Eastern Turkistan, made up of the Xinjiang Uygor Autonomous Region of China, and Afghan Turkistan, consisting of the northeastern part of Afghanistan.

When you search biblical reference materials for additional information on the first two descendants of Japheth: Gomer and Magog, here is what you will find.

Gomer

- He is apparently seen as representing the Cimmerians, an Indo-European people from southern Russia who settled in Cappadocia in Asia Minor.
  –HBD

Magog

- Region of Gog, the second of the "sons" of Japheth. In Ezekiel **38:2**; **39:6**, it is the name of a nation, probably some Scythian or Tartar tribe descended from Japheth.
  –PBD

  - **Scythia:** ancient region in what is now Moldova, Ukraine, and eastern Russia.
    –EWED

Therefore, according to reference materials the racial identity of Japheth and his descendants are white: Aryan or Nazis sympathizers, and referred to as Indo-Europeans, and were more than likely, Russian. There geographical location, as noted prior, would be Russia or areas belonging to the former Soviet Union.

Now, it would appear that Noah's blessing upon Japheth and Ezekiel's predictions for the future indicated that the descendants of Japheth: the Russian army, would deceive their own people: Gomer and Togarmah and all their bands (a small private army or mercenaries), along with the armies of Iran, Ethiopia, and Libya into helping them: the 'Russian army' supplant the descendants of Shem in the land of Israel, the Promised Land. Thereafter, the Russian army would destroy Gomer and Togarmah and all their bands along with the armies of Iran, Ethiopia, and Libya in the mountain region of the land of Israel to be devoured by the birds of the air and the beast of the field. Then, the Lord God would transfer ownership over to Gog: the Russian army and they would begin burying their dead in the land of Israel.

The *Parsons Bible Dictionary* also listed the Medes as descendants of Japheth, under the heading Japheth (3). In the books of Isaiah and Jeremiah (the prophets) the destruction of Babylon (Saudi Arabia), at the hands of the Medes is foretold.

Isaiah 13:1 – 4, 13 – 21 (NIV)

An oracle concerning Babylon that Isaiah saw: Raise a banner on a bare hilltop, shout to them; beckon to them to enter the gates of the nobles. I have commanded my holy ones; I have summoned my warriors to carry out my wrath-- those who rejoice in my triumph. Listen, a noise on the mountains, like that of a great multitude! Listen, an uproar among the kingdoms, like nations massing together! The LORD Almighty is mustering an army for war....

Therefore I will make the heavens tremble; and the earth will shake from its place at the wrath of the LORD Almighty, in the day of his burning anger. Like a hunted gazelle, like sheep without a shepherd, each will return to his own people, each will flee to his native land. Whoever is captured will be thrust through; all who are caught will fall by the sword. Their infants will be dashed to pieces before their eyes; their houses will be looted and their wives ravished.

See, I will stir up against them the Medes, who do not care for silver and have no delight in gold. Their bows will strike down the young men; they will have no mercy on infants nor will they look with compassion on children. Babylon, the jewel of kingdoms, the glory of the Babylonians' pride, will be overthrown by God like Sodom and Gomorrah. She will never be inhabited or lived in through all generations; no Arab will pitch his tent there, no shepherd will rest his flocks there. But desert creatures will lie there, jackals will fill her houses; there the owls will dwell, and there the wild goats will leap about.

And,

Jeremiah 51:11 (NIV)

Sharpen the arrows, take up the shields! The LORD has stirred up the kings of the **Medes,** because his purpose is to destroy Babylon. The LORD will take vengeance, vengeance for his temple.

The Three Great Races
Semite, Aryan, and Turanian

The Bible (believed to be written in the 1600's) does not identify Japheth or his descendants in any way, especially as being German, Russian, Aryan, or Nazi sympathizers. So, how is it that biblical reference books, such as: the *Holman Bible Dictionary*, *Wycliffe Bible Encyclopedia*, *Parsons Bible Dictionary*, and many others written in the late 1900's (20th Century), seem to know? Are their missing books and chapters that only they have? Or, Did they write the Bible and/or modify it?

Semite

Taking a closer look at the words "Semite" or "Semitic" they are not limited to those of Jewish decent or those who speak Hebrew; it includes many different groups of people and languages throughout the Middle East. Looking up the word "Semite" in the *Holman Bible Dictionary* (below) it is similar to the non-biblical dictionary listed prior.

Three major divisions exist in the Semitic family of languages.
- East Semitic would include Akkadian used in ancient Babylon and Assyria.
- Northwest Semitic involves Hebrew, Aramaic, Syria, Phoenician, Samaritan, Palmyrene, Nabatean, Canaanite, Moabite.
- South Semitic includes Arabic, Sabean, Minean, and Ethiopic.
- Approximately 70 distinct forms of Semitic languages are known.

The word "Semite" or "Semitic" means strength, because it represents Abraham, the father of many nations, which included both descendants of Shem and Ham. By definition anyone living in the Middle East would be considered a "Semite or Semitic," including Iran, Ethiopia, Libya, Egypt, and Saudi Arabia.

Now, it would appear that the descendants of Japheth would not only try, in the future, to supplant the land of Israel, but the entire Middle East. Therefore, based on the scriptures and the definitions of a "Semite," the Bible appears to be anti-Semitic.

Aryan and Turanian

Both *Wycliffe*, written in 1975; and *Holman*, written in 1994, identify Japheth's descendants as being German or from the vicinity of Germany (based on a current map).

- The third son of Noah... father of some 14 nations forming the Indo-Germanic family, originally inhabiting the Caucasus... spreading E and W.

  –WBE

- The progenitor of the Indo-European peoples who lived to the north and west of Israel, farthest from Israel.

  –HBD

The *Parsons Bible Dictionary* stands out more than any other because it, outright, injected Nazi ideology into the Bible, when they identified Japheth's race as being Aryan, and the Turanian race by their location as east of Europe and North of Asia, which is Russia.

Now, it would appear that the *Parsons Bible Dictionary*, written in 1999, have chosen Russia as the newly defined 'Aryan race,' and according to the scriptures, it would also appear as though they were predicting another holocaust!

Holocaust: 1. destruction of human life: wholesale
or mass destruction, especially of human life.
–EWED

PART: 4

RELIGION AND POLITICS

25

Makings Sense of History

Protestant Christianity is believed to have begun in 1491 with King Henry VIII and the creation of the Church of England, as a slap in the face to the Roman Catholic Church for the King of England not getting his way; and, many believe that King James brought both the Old and NTs together in 1611, in his version of the Holy Bible. Now the question is: How did the KJV Bible survive over 400 years?

Looking through history there appears to be no meeting of the minds between the Protestants (P) and the Roman Catholics (RC) rulers in England, according to a *Historical Timeline*[3]. For example:

1549   Edward VI (P): "The First Act of Uniformity is passed, making the Roman Catholic mass illegal."

1554   Mary I (RC): "Mary marries Philip of Spain… Parliament meets to re-establish Catholicism in England. The persecution of Protestants begins, and heresy laws are revived, and England is reconciled to Papal authority. 1555 - Protestant bishops are burned at the stake for heresy."

1559   Elizabeth I (P): "Act of Supremacy and Uniformity restored the Protestant Church in England and made Elizabeth Supreme Governor of the Church of England."

1611   [James I (P): the authorized KJV Bible completed, which supports segregation and slavery]

---

[3] English Kings and Queens Timeline_Britroyals.pdf

1639   King Charles I (married a Roman Catholic): "Act
        Toleration in England established religious toleration"

1646   *The Cartwright Case*[4] – "It was resolved that a
        slave brought from Russia by an English
        merchant was instantly a free-man, coming
        upon English ground, and breathing our pure
        air."

1673   Charles II (P): "Test Act keeps Roman Catholics out of political
        office."

1677   *Butts v Penny*[5] – The King's Bench ruled in
        England that slaves were, in fact, property.

1685   James II (RC): "Issues the Declaration of Indulgence to suspend all
        laws against Catholics and Non-Conformists and repealed the 1673
        Test Act."

1689   William III and Mary II (P): "Bill of Rights is passed by Parliament. It
        stipulates that no Catholic can succeed to the throne.

It was not until 1760 that George III ascended to the throne in England, in
all appearance, he was neutral when it came to religious matters. George
reigned over Great Britain and the British Empire, which included the 13
colonies (now known as the U.S.). Politically, England was already
trending away from slavery on its shore, with every Roman Catholic or
Non-Conformist that ascended to the throne. Under the authority of King
George III, slavery in England moved much further toward complete
abolishment.

---

[4] LHM legalhistorymiscellany, Krista Kesselring, February 1, 2019
[5] Cited in: Encyclopedia of Black in European History and Culture [2 Volumes],
   English Common Law; and Somerset v Stewart

1765	Grandville Sharp: British Abolitionist - *The Case of Jonathan Strong*: A slave who was badly beaten by his owner was set free [in England] when his owner attempted to sell him back into slavery in the Caribbean. He also played a huge role in the *Somerset v Stewart* case and supported the Slave Trade Act *(Wiki)*.

1772	*Somerset v Stewart:* secured a ruling by the King's Court that slavery no longer existed in England in any form, and could not for the future exist on English soil, and that any person brought into England as a slave could not be removed except by legal means applicable in the case of any free-born person" *(BLD. Somersett's Case)*.

Four years after the *Somerset v Stewart* case, the 13 colonies declared their independence in 1776, from England based on variety of issues, including taxation, but mainly England's abolishment of slavery on it shore. The crown recognized the United States as independent in 1783, after an eight year war; and, ratified their Constitution in 1788. In 1794 the slave Trade Act of 1794 was passed by the United States Congress to outlaw the importation of slave; although slavery in the States continued. It took nearly a century for the United States to end slavery.

Just as every King or Queen ascended to the throne in England had their own religious and/or political beliefs, the same can be said for every Pope that ascended to throne in Rome; for some it was all about covetous behavior, riches, material possessions, segregation, slavery, and keeping the masses under their control. On the other hand, some Popes were all about the masses, building schools, hospitals, shelters, soup kitchens, food banks; and protecting and fighting for the poor, downtrodden, and the broken-hearted. A power play over religious dogma and politics between the Protestants and the Roman Catholics existed with many of the Kings and Queens that ascended to the throne in England, before and after King James I, so again, how did the Bible survive to this very day. For all intensive purposes the Holy Bible is a Protestant Bible, because it supports segregation and slavery in the Old and NTs; also, both testaments are very similar in many other aspects. For example:

3 Deities
-   **In the Old:** God; LORD; and LORD God.
-   **In the New:** Father; Son; and the Holy Spirit/Ghost.

Raised from the Dead
-   **In the Old**, Elisha, the prophet, brought back to life a woman's dead son (2 Kings 8:1 – 5).
-   **In the New**, Jesus raised a woman's brother: Lazarus, from the dead after being buried 3 days (John 11:1 – 44).

Virgin Birth
-   **In the Old**, the virgin son to be born was to be called Immanuel (Isaiah 7:14).
-   **In the New**, the virgin son to be born was to be called Jesus.

The Covenant
-   **In the Old,** was about land
-   **In the New**, was about property and land
-

The Human Hierarchy
-   **In the Old**, The Lord was the head of man; the man was the head of the woman; and the husband was the head of his wife. The priesthood was subject to the Lord their God.
-   **In the New**, the head of every man is Christ, the Lord; and the head of the woman is the man; and the head of Christ is God (I Corinthians 11:3). The husband is the head of the wife, and the church is subject to Christ (Ephesians 5:22 – 24).

Church and State:
-   **In the Old**, Moses sent by the Lord, his God (to lead the children of Israel from slavery to battle) became the Lord's mouthpiece; and Aaron, the high priest, was the head over the tabernacle and the priesthood.
-

- **In the New**, Jesus Christ (sent by his Father, God – John 5:23) was his father's mouthpiece; and Paul established the church.

Law and Order:
- **In the Old**, the Law of Moses (in Deuteronomy) dictated how the children of Israel were to live before the Lord, their God, in order to please him.
- **In the New**, Paul dictated through his gospel how the Gentiles were to live in order to please God and the Lord Jesus Christ.

The Ten Commandments:
- **In the Old**, the Ten Commandments were ignored, by the Lord and the Priesthood.
- **In the New**, the commandments were made useless in the gospels by Jesus omitting the commandment, Do Not Covet; and Paul, the head of the Church, abolished them all together.

The Lord's Army:
- **In the Old**, the Lord built his army from among the enslaved descendants of Abraham, Isaac, and Jacob in Egypt: the children of Israel, also known as, the thirteen tribes of Israel.
- **In the New**, Jesus is Lord, building an army among the enslaved Gentiles living in Galilee and converts from among the thirteen tribes of Israel.

Now, the question is: How did the Greeks come to write nearly the same Bible as the Hebrew people, hundreds if not a thousand years later? More importantly, when did the Roman Catholic's, NT Bible about social issues to indoctrinate and control the masses, become the same as the Protestant's OT bible about segregation and slavery, the Middle East, namely, Israel, and covetous behavior?

How it all Began

Authors Thompson and Scofield both wrote reference Bible in the early 1900s; and both of their Bibles are still in circulation today and may be found in other forms, such as NKJV, NIV, NASB and ESV. Now the question is: What inspired American born 'authors' to write and publish reference bibles (to explain or understand what is believed to be biblical scriptures compiled over two hundred years earlier), one year apart?

- *Thompson Chain-Reference Bible,* Dr. Frank Charles Thompson, D.D., PH.D. (1858-1940) – Copyright 1908, **1917**, 1929, 1934, 1957, 1964, and 1982

- *Scofield Reference Bible,* Rev. C. I. Scofield, D. D. (1843-1921) – Copyright 1909, **1917**, 1937, and 1945

Thompson

Thompson was born in New York, he became an ordain minister at the age of 21, in 1879. Most of his life is unremarkable, until he began working on his 'Chain-Reference' system because he was dissatisfied with the reference Bibles that were available to preachers at that time.

In the Thompson Chain-Reference Bible (TCRB) Preface, it states that "the new Chain-Reference Bible is the product of over thirty-one years of intense Bible study…" What the TCRB does is link the reader or researcher to other scriptures within the same topic. For example, at Genesis 1:1 the topic is noted in the margin – Creator:

Genesis 1:1 - In the beginning GOD created the heaven and the earth.

The chain links you to Ex.20.11

Exodus 20:11 - For in six days the LORD made heaven and earth…

Therefore, the TCRB steers the reader to believe or accept that God, the Creator of heaven and earth, is the same as the Lord who made a so-called covenant (land deal) with Abraham and his descendants (the children of Israel) to become their God. Biblically, they are not the same!

Scofield

Scofield is a much more interesting character, according to *Scofield: The Man Behind The Myth,* he was believed to have left his first wife (a Catholic) and two daughters, and the same year his wife divorced him because of abandonment, Scofield remarried; he committed fraud and was jailed for it; he was a liar, thief, and a forger; a preacher; a state congressman in the state of Kansas; and the US District Attorney for Kansas, but resigned soon after, due to alleged illegal actions, all the while, he was a born-again Christian.[6]

The *Scofield Reference Bible* (SRB) is similar to TCRB, it also links scriptures; however, the SRB for the most part provides summaries and "explanations of seeming discrepancies" for many of the scriptures. The introduction of the SRB, states the following:

> "this edition of the Bible had its origin in the increasing conviction of the Editor through thirty years' study and use of the scriptures as pastor, teacher, writer, and lecturer upon biblical themes, that all of the many excellent and useful editions of the Word of God left much to be desired…. **The last fifty years have witnessed an intensity and breadth of interest in Bible study unprecedented in the history of the Christian Church.**"

Now the question is: What was happening during the last fifty years prior to Scofield's published work in 1909 that caused such an 'intense interest' in the Bible?

Looking back at the last fifty years from 1909, places one in 1859, two years before the United States Civil War: between the pro-slavery Confederate South and the anti-slavery pro-Union North. Abraham Lincoln was elected

---

[6] Information about Scofield's personal life gathered from
http://poweredbychrist.homestead.com/files/cyrus/scofield.htm, and *Wiki*: C.I. Scofield

and sworn in as the president of the United States in 1861, shortly after, the civil war began. At that time, Scofield, 18 years old, was already a soldier in the Confederate army fighting to maintain slavery in the southern states.

On January 1, 1863, Lincoln issued the Emancipation Proclamation which declared that all persons held as slaves "within the rebellious states" were free. In less than two years the Civil War ended on April 9, 1865 when Confederate General, Robert E. Lee surrendered. Six days later President Abraham Lincoln was assassinated on April 15; on December 6 of the same year, the Thirteenth Amendment was ratified to abolish slavery in the United States; It was followed by the Fourteenth Amendment in 1868, which states all persons born or naturalized in the U.S are citizens…; and the Fifteenth Amendment in 1870, states that citizens have the right to vote regardless of race, color, or previous condition of servitude.

After the Civil War and well into the early 1900s, nearly 9 to12 million people migrated into the United States in large groups, from around the world, looking for work and a better life, which caused resentment among settled European Protestant Americans.

The Chinese:
> "A relatively large group of Chinese immigrated to the United States between the start of the California gold rush in 1849 and 1882, when federal law stopped their immigration…. With economic competition came dislike and even racial suspicion and hatred. Such feelings were accompanied by anti-Chinese riots and pressure, especially in California, for the exclusion of Chinese immigrants from the United States. The result of this pressure was the Chinese Exclusion Act, passed by Congress in 1882. This Act virtually ended Chinese immigration for nearly a century."

> *Chinese Immigration to the United States - For Teachers (Library of Congress)*

The Arabs:

"While Arabs have been immigrating individually to North America since before the United States became a nation, the first significant period of Arab immigration began in the 1870s and lasted until 1924, when the Johnson-Reed Quota Act was passed, nearly ending immigration from this region for the time being. During this period, an estimated 110,000 immigrants entered the United States predominantly from the Ottoman province of Syria, which currently encompasses the countries of Syria, Lebanon, Jordan, and Palestine."

Arab Immigration to the United States | Wikipedia

The Jews and Catholics:

"By the 1880s, new arrivals from southern and eastern Europe began to form a distinctive "second wave" of immigration to America. In addition to Protestant Scandinavians were Italian Catholics and Eastern European Jews. This period was distinctive for the sheer numbers of immigrants arriving, the diversity of their languages and cultures, and the extent to which their religious practices were unfamiliar not only to the American-born residents, but also to the immigrants who had arrived mid-century. In the feverish years between 1892 and 1924, more than 12 million immigrants passed through Ellis Island, and a new American cultural milieu emerged.

While there had been small communities of Catholics and Jews since the Colonial period, the massive immigration of the nineteenth and early twentieth century's brought a new influx of Catholics and Jews to America. For the first time, Anglo- Protestant Americans were presented with a new level of ethnic and religious diversity and with it came the challenge to assess the true meaning of America's commitment to religious freedom."

Catholic and Jewish Immigrants | The Pluralism Project, pluralism.org

Newly freed slaves who more than likely could not read or write would not have had an intense interest in Bible study. Many of those who migrated to the United States were fleeing political and religious persecution, famine, and disease and were more than likely not Protestant. The Catholic Church within the United States did not allow its members to read or study the Bible and delivered Mass in Latin to English speaking people, until the late 1970s. What was new and could account for the "intensity and breadth of interest in Bible study" was the birth of the Ku Klux Klan (KKK), made up of young former Confederate soldiers and what would become their ties to the Protestant Church.

The First Klan (1865-1870's):

> "In December 1865, eight months after the South's surrender, a group of six young men... All were veterans of the Confederate Army and some had attended college where fraternities with three-letter, Greek-based names were popular. In mock-imitation, they came up with the alliterative title Ku Klux Klan for their group.... Soon terrorizing blacks became a prime sport and the transition of the KKK from an innocuous social club to a ruthless vigilance committee began.
>
> The rapid expansion of the Klan was fuel by a wide-spread fear among many Southern Whites of an insurrection by former slaves and seething resentment against Northern "carpet-baggers" who had invaded the South since the end of the war.
>
> The KKK's reign was short-lived, its decline hastened by the revulsion of many southerners to its extreme methods and suppression by local governments. By 1868, its power was beginning to wane. In 1871 Congress passed the Ku Klux Klan Act that authorized the use of federal troops in the Klan's suppression and for the trial of its members in federal court. The Klan melted away, or at least did not make any further public appearances until its revival in 1915."

"The Ku Klux Klan, 1868", Eyewitness to History,
www.eyewitnesstohistory.com (2006).

The Second Klan (1915-1944):

> "In 1915, the second incarnation of the Ku Klux Klan was born. The second Klan, a memorial to the Reconstruction Klan and its work in the postbellum South, was to act as a restructured fraternity that supported white supremacy, the purity of white womanhood, nationalism and Protestant Christianity. William J. Simmons, a fraternalist and a former minister, organized the charter for the new

order and consecrated its beginning by setting afire a cross on the top of Stone Mountain, Georgia….

The second Klan required its members to be not only white and male but also Christian. Religion became the centerpiece of the second Klan's platform, and Klansmen showed their allegiance to their faith through church attendance, speeches and writings, and the recruitment of ministers as members."

Readex Report: Religion and the Rise of the Second Ku Klux Klan,
1915-1922, Kelly J. Baker, University of New Mexico

Is it a coincidence:
- The KKK originally made up of young former Confederate soldiers shared the same history as Scofield, a well established Confederate soldier at the age of 18, who actually fought in the Civil War?
- Six years after Scofield published *The Holy Bible* in 1909, the KKK was 'born again;' and their 1915 introduction came with cinematic theater, the movie, *The Birth of a Nation*, a medley of the earlier Klan in the late 1800's?
- Two year after Scofield's death in 1921 the Klan was divided and eventually, diminished in membership?
- Four years after the death of Thompson in 1940, the once organized Klan was no more?

"At its peak in the mid 1920s, the organization claimed to include about 15% of the nation's eligible population, approximately 4-5 million men. From 1923 there were two Ku Klux Klan organizations: that founded by Simmons, and a splinter group founded by D.C. Stephenson. The main group's membership had dropped to about 30,000 by 1930. It finally faded away in the 1940s."

Ku Klux Klan - A History of Racism and Violence, 6th Edition,
The Southern Poverty Law Center, Montgomery, AL

Looking at the copyright dates of the TCRB and the SRB, one thing stands out, 1917. Is it another coincidence that Thompson and Scofield who both have a copyright date a year apart, then a second copyright date in the same year, 1917? According to the 1909 Copyright Law a copyright needed to be renewed every 28 years. After Scofield's death his Reference Bible copyright appears to have been renewed in 1937 exactly 28 years after its initial 1909 copyright. Now the question is: What was so important about 1917 that both Thompson and Scofield marked that year?

1917

Many believe that the Bible was written hundreds or even thousands of years ago, and therefore, it is prophetic, but, what if it was not, and the Protestant's OT Bible was based mainly on the 20th Century.

In 1917, the First World War (WWI) was underway and had been for three years with Germany, Austria-Hungary, and the Ottoman Empire (the Middle East) fighting against the British Empire, France, Russia, Italy, the United States, and others. The Ottoman Empire consisted of 10 nations and/or kingdoms: Turkey, Egypt, Iraq, Iran (Persia), Jordan, Palestine, Lebanon, Syria, Arabia, and parts of North Africa, until, the British government intervened.

When you compare the stories of Babel, which ties directly to the War of the Kings; and the Promised Land, they are all reminiscing of WWI in many aspects. Here's why.

Background

Prior to WWI, the British government had the largest and the most powerful army in the world. Egypt, a part of the Ottoman Empire, was attracted to Britain and the western world because of its modernization, technology, and military; by the early to mid 1800s Britain's footprint in Egypt grew expeditiously, for the most part, Egypt was in debt to, and dependent upon Britain (and Western banks) financially. Over time, Egypt began to be dominated by the West, mainly Britain; they took vital positions within the Egyptian government: military, police, finance, health, engineering, etc. By the 1880s Egypt was a part of the British Empire. Nonetheless, Egypt was still predominately Arab and Muslim: followers of

Islam. They maintained their religious tradition of a pilgrimage to the Holy cities of Medina and Mecca, in Arabia; however, non-Muslims were not allowed within the city of Mecca, which clearly was of concern to the West, namely Britain, because they were in control of a Muslim country, which religiously they knew very little to nothing about.

According to the BritishMuseum.org, Muhammad Sadiq Bey (1832-1902), was an Egyptian army engineer and surveyor who was the first person to actually take detailed photographs of the Hajj (pilgrimage to Mecca), Medina and Mecca including the holy mosque. Bey's photographs were said to be published in 1881, during the same time Egypt was under Britain's authority.

> The Ottoman Empire was one of the mightiest and longest-lasting dynasties in world history. This Islamic-run superpower ruled large areas of the Middle East, Eastern Europe and North Africa for more than 600 years. The chief leader, known as the Sultan, was given absolute religious and political authority over his people. While Western Europeans generally viewed them as a threat, many historians regard the Ottoman Empire as a source of great regional stability and security, as well as important achievements in the arts, science, religion and culture.
>
> *- HIST:OttomanEmpire*

WWI and the 'War of the Kings'

On July 28, 1914, WWI began with Egypt now a part of the British Empire, which meant that the Ottoman Empire was already divided against itself militarily. Nonetheless, the British government needed more Arab support to win the war, so in 1915 the British government made false promises of an independent Arab state to manipulate Husayn ibn Ali, Sharif (ruler) of Mecca (whom they were at war with at the time), into leading a pan-Arab revolt within the Ottoman Empire against their own leader, namely, Turkey (also known as the Turks) and other non-Arab states. It was Husayn's actions that further segregated the Ottoman Empire and ultimately tore it apart; even though, one year later, Britain and France had secretly made plans of their own to keep Arabs states segregated for their own purposes.

1916 Sykes–Picot Agreement

Plans for a post-war division of the Ottoman Empire, which had joined the war on Germany's side, were secretly drawn up by Britain and France under the 1916 Sykes–Picot Agreement. This agreement was not divulged to the Sharif of Mecca, who the British had been encouraging to launch an Arab revolt against their Ottoman rulers, giving the impression that Britain was supporting the creation of an independent Arab state.

–WIKI: BritishEmpire

The Arabs, however, who had learned of the Sykes-Picot Agreement through the publication of it... were scandalized by it. This secret arrangement conflicted in the first place with pledges already given by the British to the Hashemite dynast Ḥusayn ibn ʿAlī, sharif of Mecca, during the Ḥusayn-McMahon Correspondence (1915–16)[7]. Based on the understanding that the Arabs would eventually receive

---

[7] JewishVirtualLibrary.org: for more information on all correspondence between Britain and King Ḥusayn.

independence, Ḥusayn had brought the Arabs of the Hejaz into revolt against the Turks in June 1916.

On April 1920 – the Allied powers agreed to divide governance of the region into separate Class "A" mandates... along lines similar to those agreed upon under the Sykes-Picot Agreement. The borders of these mandates split up Arab lands and ultimately led to the modern borders of Iraq, Israel and the Palestinian territories, Jordan, Lebanon, and Syria.

–Brit: Sykes-Picot-Agreement

Therefore, under the Sykes-Picot Agreement the Arab nations/kingdoms were not united as a one; and after the First World War had ended in 1918,

Egypt gained its independence from the British Empire 4 years later, in 1922.

Biblically, the British government (the Lord) used the ruler of Mecca (King of Shinar) with other Arab states, one being Persia (Elam) to segregate and ultimately tear apart the Ottoman Empire, pitting Arab states (identified as the four kingdoms) against the non-Arab states (identified as the five kingdoms).

The Promised Land

Biblically the Lord's so-called covenant to give to Abraham, a Hebrew, and his descendants: the children of Israel, the land of Canaan (which included Jerusalem based on Joshua 12:7-10) also appear to be taken from actual events in the 20th century, during WWI.

Canaan: in the Bible, the part of ancient
Palestine west of the Jordan River
–EWED

During the war in 1917, the British government coveted the Holy City of Jerusalem in Palestine (proof, that Jerusalem was a British territory, they buried their dead there; to this day the Jerusalem British War Cemetery is located on Mount Scopus and contains more than 2,500 graves). On November 2, 1917 the British government wrote to their allies and stated their support for a Jewish nation, in Palestine.

Balfour Declaration of 1917[8]

Foreign Office
November 2nd, 1917

Dear Lord Rothschild,

I have much pleasure in conveying to you, on behalf of His Majesty's government, the following declaration of sympathy with Jewish Zionist aspirations which has been submitted to, and approved by, the Cabinet

"His Majesty's Government view with favour the establishment in Palestine of a national home for the Jewish people, and will use their best endeavours to facilitate the achievement of this object, it being clearly understood that nothing shall be done which may prejudice the civil and religious rights of existing non-Jewish communities in Palestine, or the rights and political status enjoyed by Jews in any other country."

I should be grateful if you would bring this declaration to the knowledge of the Zionist Federation.

Yours,

Arthur James Balfour

The British government cemented their promise to the Jewish people on May 14, 1948, after 30 years of uprising on both sides, between the Arabs and Jews; in the end the Jews received Palestinian land and Statehood, and today it is known as the State of Israel.

---

[8] From the Jewishvirtuallibrary.org

The State of Israel

The name Israel or Israeli did not appear to exist prior to WWI; meaning, the British government only referred to them as Jews or Jewish and not Israel or Israeli. Many believe that the name Israel given to the Jews came from the OT scriptures. The biblically story that is commonly preached to the masses, was that Jacob's name was changed to Israel after he wrestled with a stranger (believed to an angel) who injured him; and, Jacob insisted that the man who injured him bless him before he would let the man go; then, the man said to Jacob "your name shall no longer be called Jacob, but Israel." Now the question is: Where did the name Israel really come from, that makes sense?

It is more than likely that the State of Israel was named after Benjamin Disraeli[9] (December 21, 1804 – April 19, 1881) who was the first elected prime minister of Great Britain, of Jewish decent; he was elected in 1868 and also in 1874, two consecutive 6 year terms. Disraeli was born and initially raised Jewish, for the most part, however, it is believed that his father converted him to Christianity at an early age, which allowed him to ascend to the highest office within the British government. Now, could it just simply be a coincidence that the State was named Israel and the people Israeli, and it had absolutely nothing to do with Benjamin Disraeli?

Benjamin Disraeli Policies

Social reforms passed by the Disraeli government included: the Artisans Dwellings Act (1875), the Public Health Act (1875), the Pure Food and Drugs Act (1875), the Climbing Boys Act (1875), the Education Act (1876).

Disraeli also kept his promise to improve the legal position of trade unions. The Conspiracy and Protection of Property Act

---

[9] All Information from the Jewishvirtuallibrary.org

(1875) allowed peaceful picketing and the Employers and Work men Act (1878) enabled workers to sue employers in the civil courts if they broke legally agreed contracts.

JVL

Is it another coincidence that Author Balfour was a private secretary for his uncle who was appointed Foreign Secretary by Prime Minister Disraeli? In 1902, Balfour became Prime Minister and then later appointed Foreign Minister, where he wrote the 1917 Balfour Declaration in support of the Jewish people on behalf of the British government.

The Bible is history rewritten with a twist and packaged as the Word of God. It would appear that the writer(s) of the Bible used the history of WWI and remastered it to get the outcome they wanted in the future (using the prophets) which is, in the OT, the total destruction of the Middle East; and in the NT, the rebuilding of a New Jerusalem (religious order) for true believers to follow and obey.

Now, what sense does it make for King James to have commissioned scholars and clergy from the Church of England or elsewhere in the early 1600's to write about an imaginary land called Israel, and future events, in such detail, even if it was his playbook; while at the same time, entangled in real world endeavors? Therefore, it would appear that the Bible was named after King James I of England for two reasons: his promotion of segregation; and slavery, in his quest for world domination through colonization.

26

The Holy Bible

What the churches are teaching today is incompatible with the Bible itself. They are not actually teaching the truth, but, lies and deception, to make the masses believe that the Bible is about God's love and protection for them as true believers; and hellfire for sinners and non-believers, because it is profitable financially for them to do so. Lying about what the bible says should cause concern. What the Bible predicts for the future: perpetual war, the enslavement of nations, and the destruction of the Middle East which includes Israel, Iran, Syria, Libya, Ethiopia, and Saudi Arabia, just to name a few, should also cause concern. However, the Bible, a privately owned book, which discriminates against the masses, being used within any government as the Word of God, should be of greater concern for everyone.

Unfortunately, throughout the world, especially in the United States, it would appear, we are all still living under the King James' Rule. Segregation and slavery was built into the fabric of the United States since it was founded and well before. Many believe that slavery in the United States was abolished when the thirteenth amendment was ratified on July 9, 1868, it was not. In fact, the thirteenth amendment within the Constitution guaranteed that slavery would never end, with one word, 'except,' and because of it, slavery continues on to this very day, through the criminal justice system.

The Thirteenth Amendment

Section 1.
Neither slavery nor involuntary servitude, *except* as a punishment for crime whereof the party shall have been duly convicted, shall exist within the United States, or any place subject to their jurisdiction.

Section 2.
Congress shall have power to enforce this article by appropriate legislation.

Segregation and slavery are the playbooks for wealth for some authoritarians, dictators, or want-to-be kings. It works best, when they can divide the people against one another (us and them), by any means necessary; take away the peoples wealth and/or health through manufactured crisis; and ultimately, separate the people from their own government: by placing the people's government into private hands; and convincing them that their government does not work, saying, it's too big; it doesn't create jobs; it destroys businesses, etc.

Fascism: dictatorial movement: any movement, ideology, or attitude that favors dictatorial government, centralized control of private enterprise, repression of all opposition, and extreme nationalism
–*EWED*

The one true thing they will never tell, and that is: The people are the Government; and a government of the people, by the people, and for the people, that works for everyone, is good for everyone.

EVIL is inevitable if given the opportunity to do evil without consequences

Anita L Nottuh

www.ingramcontent.com/pod-product-compliance
Lightning Source LLC
Chambersburg PA
CBHW081204170626
46813CB00010B/3321